J. Robinson

The Present State of the Empire of Morocco

Vol. 2.

J. Robinson

The Present State of the Empire of Morocco
Vol. 2.

ISBN/EAN: 9783741194252

Manufactured in Europe, USA, Canada, Australia, Japa

Cover: Foto ©Andreas Hilbeck / pixelio.de

Manufactured and distributed by brebook publishing software
(www.brebook.com)

J. Robinson

The Present State of the Empire of Morocco

THE

PRESENT STATE

OF THE

EMPIRE of MOROCCO.

ITS

ANIMALS, PRODUCTS, CLIMATE, SOIL,
CITIES, PORTS, PROVINCES, COINS,
WEIGHTS, AND MEASURES. WITH THE
LANGUAGE, RELIGION, LAWS, MAN-
NERS, CUSTOMS, AND CHARACTER,

OF THE

MOORS;

THE HISTORY OF THE
DYNASTIES SINCE EDRIS;

THE NAVAL FORCE AND COMMERCE OF MO-
ROCCO; AND THE CHARACTER, CONDUCT, AND
VIEWS, POLITICAL AND COMMERCIAL,

OF THE

REIGNING EMPEROR.

TRANSLATED FROM THE FRENCH OF
M. CHENIER.

VOL. II.

LONDON:
Printed for G. G. J. and J. ROBINSON,
Paternoster-Row.
M.DCC.LXXXVIII.

THE
PRESENT STATE
OF THE
EMPIRE OF MOROCCO.

BOOK III.

History of the Sovereigns of Fez, Morocco, Suz, and other States—Different Dynasties from the foundation of the kingdom of Fez, to the succession of the Sharifs of the reigning family.

CHAP. I.

Decline of the Empire of the Caliphs. Accession, and reign of Edris. Expulsion and destruction of his family. Various usurpers.

AFTER the Arabs had possessed themselves of Mauritania, and had introduced their religion there, it was for some time

governed

governed by the lieutenants of the Caliphs. The diftance of the feat of government of thefe Caliphs, who, extending
their conquefts, had fucceffively removed
their throne from Medina to Damafcus,
from Damafcus to Cufa, and from Cufa to
Bagdad, foon changed the order of things,
and infenfibly enfeebled their authority.
The Arab generals in Africa profited by
thefe circumftances in favour of their ambitious projects, excited commotions toward the end of the eighth century, and
afpired themfelves at fovereignty. The
defcendants of Mahomet, called, as it
were, to the throne by the veneration in
which they were held by the vulgar, raifed
new factions; the Edriffites, who took
their name from Edris, fon of Abdallah,
defcendant of Ali, hufband to the daughter
of Mahomet, were the firft. From Herbelot it appears that their dynafty was exterminated by the Fatimites, who pretended they were the defcendants of Ali
and Fatima, the daughter of Mahomet;
this latter dynafty, the founder of which
took the name of Mohadi, director of the
faithful, had fome fuccefs in Egypt; but

its

its duration in Mauritania, which was expofed to numerous revolutions, was only
momentary. This part of Africa was afterward governed by four principal dynafties, the Morabethoon, the Moahedins,
the Benimerins, and the Sharifs of two
different branches.

Africa, remaining in the power of the
Arabs from the beginning of the eighth
century, was governed by the lieutenants
of the Caliph Walid, and his fucceffors,
till the year 739, of the Chriftian æra.
Yezid, lieutenant of the Caliph Omar II.,
who then governed, being deceafed at Cayroan, Abul-Hages, who had been lieutenant
of the Caliph Abdelmelek, took advantage
of his death to raife an infurrection, and,
at the head of the infurgents, reduced the
country, proceeded as far as the north of
Mauritania, and, defying every effort of
Gualid, eftablifhed himfelf as the commander of the faithful. It is probable
Gualid was the chief of the principal tribe
that then inhabited the province of Rif in
the leffer Atlas, where ftill is found the
Cafile of Beni-Gualid. This Shaik, whom

his

his tribe confidered as King, oppofed with all his power the invafion of foreigners, in a country which has ever been ftrongly de-fended by nature:

We learn; from the Spanifh authors, that the oppreffions of the Arabs in the north of Mauritania, and the contributions they exacted from the Moors; gave birth to many revolts, in which the negroes, who inhabited the deferts to the fouth of Morocco, took part. The Caliph, in-formed of thefe commotions, fent a con-fiderable reinforcement of cavalry, which produced not the leaft effect; the Arabs and their horfes having been terrified by that multitude of black men, who, riding almoft naked, had an appearance of great ferocity, and infpired dread.

The example of thefe feditions had a bad effect in Spain, where the Arabs and Moors were equally divided and agitated. Abul-Hages having been flain in the in-furrections of Africa, his fon put himfelf at the head of the weftern Africans; nor was the revolt appeafed till the fon alfo

fell

fell in battle, combating the army of the governor of Egypt.

At the same period the Caliph Abdallah, competitor of the Caliph Abdelmelek, who had rendered himself master of the Hegias, desirous of ascertaining the Caliphet to his son Mahomet Mahadi, put to death all the kinsmen of Ali at Medina, forgetting only one old man, the descendant of Hassan, son of Ali, son in law of Mahomet, whose posterity a special providence seemed to protect. One of the sons of this old man was beheaded; the other, named Edris, had the good fortune to escape, and fled in 768 into Mauritania, there to avoid the persecuting sword. Edris settled at Tiulit, in the mountain of Zaaron, between Fez and Mequinez, where he behaved with so much prudence that he gained the confidence of the people, who, highly respecting his virtues, were desirous to live under his government, and embrace his religion. The arrival of this Edris, his exemplary conduct, and the lessons he gave, first scattered the seeds of Mahometanism in these countries, where that reli-

gion,

gion, having great analogy with the manners of the Moors, was well calculated to
make a rapid progrefs.

Edris, profiting by his afcendant over
the minds of men, fent troops into Spain
to fuccour the Mahometans ; and this zeal
for the propagation of his religion ftill increafed the affection of the Moors. Edris
dying left a pofthumous fon, who was
alfo named Edris, and whom, out of refpect for the father's memory, the people
acknowledged as Sovereign : it even appears that, during the minority of this
prince, the Moorifh armies gained fome
victories.

In 793 Edris II. founded the city of
Fez, capital of the kingdom fo called.
This was the firft monarchy eftablifhed in
Africa after Mahomet ; and the Mahometans long called it the court, or kingdom
of the weft. Edris interefted himfelf
much in favour of the Arab Moors in
Spain ; and having profited by the war,
and by the œconomy he had eftablifhed,
he continued building the city of Fez in
840,

840, and erected the mofque called after his name, in which his memory and his tomb are still held in reverence.

The ardour with which this prince infpired the Mahometan Africans induced them to build in the fame city the famous mofque called Carubin, for which the city was indebted, perhaps, to the devotion and liberalities of the people of Cayroan, who, having retired to Fez that they might not be expofed to the commotions which then difturbed the eaftern part of Africa, may have contributed to the foundation of that magnificent mofque.

We are not acquainted with the race of the kings of Mauritania, the defcendants of Sidi-Edris, but we know that family continued to reign, and that Edris beftowed the government of cities on ten of his fons. From Marmol we learn that the houfe of Edris and the houfe of Mequineci reigned in Mauritania in 914, and that Mahomet Motaras, Lord of Ceuta, paffed over into Spain, with troops, at the folicitation of Abdelrahaman, king of Cordova.

It

He afterwards fent new reinforcements from Mauritania into Spain in 920 and 925.

The divifions which were in the kingdom of Fez, during the tenth century, were but the prefage of thofe by which that empire has fo long been convulfed; and the family of Edris, that had reigned about a hundred and fifty years, was difturbed by a croud of ufurpers. The tribe of Zenetes, called Mequineci, feized about that time on feveral provinces, and founded the city of Mequinez, nearly ten leagues from Fez. A Marabout of that tribe, profiting about the fame time by the fluctuating ftate and credulity of the people, feduced their minds by fanatic predictions, and brought much difcredit on the fucceffors of Edris. Having formed a confiderable party in the province of Temfena, he marched againft the king of Fez, declared war againft him; and the latter, wearied of that he fuftained againft the Zenetes, rather chofe to conclude a peace, and yield him the crown, than to behold

an

an increase of enemies, or expose himself to the fickleness of his subjects.

The progress these missionaries made in Mauritania, among an ignorant people flocking after innovators, raised up one who proclaimed himself El-Mohadi, the director, or pontif, of the Mussulmen, a descendant of Ali and Fatima, and whose origin, according to Herbelot, was doubtful: this man declaimed against the house of Edris, which he accused of heresy, and of following the sect of Ali, a sectary unknown to the Moors. Having made himself master of various cities, he deposed the sons of Edris from their governments before the succours they had intreated from the king of Cordova were arrived. El-Mohadi cut off the descendants of Edris, after having seized on their governments *, declared himself Caliph, and marched toward Mount Atlas to extend his domains.

---

* One of these princes, named Sharif El-Edrissi, author of the work, entitled *Geographia Nubiensis*, fled at this time into Sicily to the court of King Roger, to whom he dedicated his book.

Arrived

Arrived at Sugulmessa, the governor had him seized as an impostor ; but, fearing to irritate the people, and respecting his origin, he calling himself the descendant of Fatima, the daughter of Mahomet, the governor gave him his liberty.

El-Mohadi was in the south, when one of the generals of the king of Cordova arrived with an army to aid the house of Edris : this general, named Al-Habid El-Monsor, conquered a part of the kingdom of Fez, fortified Arzilla near Tangiers, left a garrison there, and that city for some time remained under the government of the kings of Cordova.

By this revolution El-Mohadi could not preserve the kingdom of Fez to himself. This prince going to visit the governor of Sugulmessa, that he might gratify the resentment he had conceived against him, assassinated him, excited new troubles, and thus became odious to the people who had followed his standard. The usurper, whose reign was momentary in Mauritania, was obliged to pass into the eastern part

part of Africa, where he met with new
obstacles from another bigot, who, in turn,
had brought him into discredit, in the opinion of the people whom he had deceived
by an affectation of humility. This latter
chief was, in derision, called the Knight of
the Ass, because one part of his pretended
humbleness consisted in always riding on
an ass, with his face covered like the Molathemins. Molathemins is a name given
in Africa to a tribe who, going to battle
with another more powerful, obliged the
women to take arms; and, that they might
not be distinguished, the men, like them,
artfully veiled their faces,

All Africa at this time was torn by divisions, on a tradition that, three hundred
years after Mahomet, another director of
the faithful, or Mohadi, should come from
the west; and various impostors profiting
by this tradition imposed on the vulgar
credulity, that they might seize the government. Obeidallah, founder of the
dynasty of the Fatimites, left Sugulmessa,
and, penetrating as far as Egypt, he there
vanquished the troops of the Caliph. The
wars

wars he sustained in Egypt, Syria, and the
eastern parts of Africa, changed the situation of affairs in the west, where a succession of innovators, profiting by these divisions to the furtherance of their projects,
reciprocally snatched the sceptre from the
power of their predecessors.

CHAP.

CHAP. II.

Of the Dynasty of Morabethoon.

ABU-Teffifin Marabout, nephew of
Abu-Beker Ben-Omar, of the tribe of
Lumthunes *, and chief of the Morabethoon, profited by the commotions which
had drawn the arms of the Arabs toward
Egypt to produce an infurrection; he fent
Marabouts to preach, and excite the people
to revolt, under the pretext of defending
their liberties. The Moors, weary of the
arbitrary government of thefe Arab foreigners, willingly followed the ftandard of

---

* The country which the Marabouts inhabited, lying
between Mount Atlas and the defert, was called Lamtha;
whence the tribe had the name of Lamthoonah, or Lumthunes.

Herbelot, Bib. Orien.

Teffifin,

Teffifin, who prefently found himfelf at the head of a numerous army.

The tribe of this chief was furnamed Morabethoon, becaufe of the rigidity with which religion was by them obferved ; the word Marabout fignifying a monk, or a man engaged to the performance of his vow. This tribe firft took birth in the neighbourhood of Tunis, but was obliged to leave that country for the weftern part of Africa, that it might efcape the perfecution of fects more voluptuous, whofe intereft it was to extirpate this rifing tribe.

Abu-Teffifin, at the head of his followers, traverfed Mount Atlas in 1051, and conquered the city of Agmet and its environs : here he fixed his refidence, at the foot of Mount Atlas, extended thence his conquefts northward, and proclaimed himfelf Emir El-Mumenin, or chief of the faithful. He is one of the firft fovereigns known of the race of Morabethoon, or more commonly called Morabites ; his armies were conftantly victorious, and, after various

battles,

battles, he remained sovereign of Mauritania.

Abu-Teffifin died in 1086, and was succeeded by his son Joseph, whose subjects proclaimed him King *. This prince not being pleased with the situation of the city of Agmet, at the foot of the mountains, built or finished that of Marakesch, or Morocco, which had been begun by his father, and there established his seat of empire.

During his reign the province of Temfena afforded an asylum to a multitude of Zenetes, who preached new errors. Joseph was very industrious to prevent these innovations among his subjects, and sent them Morabite preachers to reconvert them to their former religion; but the people, fond of novelty, were so far from listening to the remonstrances of the reformers,

---

* The Arab authors of Spain call this prince Abul-Isa Ibrahim-Ben-Joseph-Ben-Teffifin. It was the custom of these people to call their children by the names of their ancestors.

whom

whom Jofeph had fent them, that they put them to death at Anafai, where they were affembled.

Irritated by a conduct fo infolent, Jofeph paffed the Morbeya with a powerful army. At the news of his march the Zenetes, with their chief, thought proper to retreat, and proceeded toward Fez, where they demanded aid of the king; but this prince, inftead of granting fuccour to thefe public difturbers, went in fearch of them with his forces, and, having come up with them on the banks of the Buregreb, where they were harraffed with famine and fatigue, he fell upon them, and cut them in pieces.

Jofeph, after having ravaged the lands of Temfena, and deftroyed all its habitations, returned victorious to Morocco. Ambitious and defirous of extending his power, he fome time after marched with his army and made war on the king of Fez, whom he vanquifhed; taking advantage of the inconftancy of the people, he feized on his kingdom, which was thus, for the firft time, united to that of Morocco.

Encou-

Encouraged by the fuccefs of his arms, Jofeph advanced as far as Tremecen, thence he proceeded to Bugia, and having obliged the Moors of that part of Africa, and even thofe of Tunis, to become his vaffals, he once more returned triumphant to Morocco, where he was again proclaimed, with this increafe of power, commander of the faithful. He afterward made war upon the Brebes, who had retired among the mountains, and over whom he gained feveral advantages.

The victories of Jofeph Ben-Tefifin had acquired him reputation fo great that, in 1097, the Mahometan kings of Spain fought his alliance, and even offered him the fupreme fovereignty, hoping, by his affiftance, they fhould be enabled once more to eftablifh and extend their empire. On this invitation Jofeph paffed over into Andalufia, and, joining his forces to thofe of the Mahometans of Spain, conquered the city of Seville and its environs ; whence, after projecting further victories, he returned into Africa to make the neceffary preparations.

In Africa, Joseph proclaimed the Gazia, or war, of religion. Having assembled numerous troops, drawn together by fanaticism, and the hope of plunder, he marched, embarked at Ceuta, and proceeded to Malaga. This campaign, and those which followed, were highly glorious to the king of Morocco, since, in 1102, he was master of all Andalusia, Grenada, and Murcia, and in the same year returned into Africa loaded with laurels.

The following years this prince again passed over into Spain to continue his conquests, penetrated as far as Cordova, and gained several battles, particularly that fought on the twenty-ninth of May, 1107, against the army of Don Alphonso VI. whose son, Don Sancho, the commander, with six other of the first nobility, lost their lives. This is the battle which the Spaniards have called the battle of the seven Counts. After this victory Joseph returned to Morocco, where he died, in 1110, and was succeeded by his son Ali,

Ali, the fon of Jofeph, third king of Morocco, of the race of Morabethoon, built the grand mofque at Morocco, continued to fuccour the Mahometans of Spain, and made his power refpected there by the armies which he perfonally headed, between the years 1112 and 1115. Some authors fay he was killed at the battle of Moriella, where his army was attacked by that of king Alphonfo; that his fon, Teffifin-Ben-Ali, continued in Spain with fome troops, and that the remainder were tranfported into Africa.

Brahem, the fon of Ali, and the laft king of Morocco, of the fame dynafty, who was proclaimed after the death of his father, confirmed the princes who governed the oriental provinces dependent on him in their poffeffions, and was declared commander of the faithful. Africa, under the reign of this prince, was torn by inteftine divifions, which were fatal to the dynafty of the Morabites, and which did not permit Brahem to go himfelf into Spain, nor to maintain that fovereignty there which the Arab Moors had offered to his ancef-

tors,

tors, and which they had fo well deferved
by their valour.

The governors of the principal places
of Andalufia profited by this momentary
weaknefs to erect the cities and provinces,
over which they prefided, into fmall principalities : the king of Morocco was at this
time too much employed in oppofing the
infurgents of his own ftates to prevent
thefe their ufurpations. Brahem was befide
an indolent prince, and addicted to pleafure ; to the gratification of which he facrificed affairs the moft important. His
fubjects, at length, loaded with taxes, and
oppreffed, refufed to acknowledge him as
their mafter.

The relaxed ftate of the government,
and the difcontent of the people, favoured
a revolt, which was at this time incited toward Mount Atlas by another innovator,
who, affuming the impofing title of Mohadi, director of the faithful, entered Mauritania, and drew the people to his party,
who were eafy to feduce, by projects of
reformation.

This

This preacher, whose name was Mahomet Abdallah, calling himself a descendant of Ali, met, according to Herbelot, near Melilla, another doctor, named Abdulmomen, who said he was the Mohadi, or prophet, expected at the end of ages. These two men, united, approaching Morocco, preached there publicly, drew over proselytes to their belief, and Abdallah was acknowledged king.

Brahem, absorbed in pleasure, had despised this revolution, but was at length obliged to head his army, and give the Reformer battle, who was now become strong in consequence of discontent and enthusiasm. Brahem was defeated, and forced to fly. Pursued from one place of refuge to another, he at length came to Oran, where the Moors, not daring to expose themselves to the resentment of Abdulmomen, who was following to take Brahem, refused him an asylum. Brahem, seeing himself thus hunted, unable to survive his grief, threw himself, according to some historians, headlong from a rock; others affirm he perished in a castle, which

was

was fired by Abdulmomen, and the death of this prince ended the dynasty of Morabethoon.

Abdulmomen, general of Abdallah, having subjected all the provinces of Mauritania to the power of his master, during this expedition, and bearing with him hostages to insure their submission, returned to Morocco. Here he found Mahomet Abdallah dead in his camp. The chiefs, being assembled, acknowledged Abdulmomen, who also affirmed himself one of the descendants of Mahomet and Ali, their sovereign, and commander of the faithful.

CHAP,

CHAP. III.

Dynasty of the Moahedins.

ABDULMOMEN * was the first king of the race of the Moahedins, whom the Spaniards have called Almohades; he was chosen king of Morocco in 1148: after his election he destroyed the city of Morocco, into which the inhabitants refused him entrance, and which they would have preserved for Isac son of Brahem. Abdulmomen was so enraged at this that he made a vow the city should pass through a sieve,

After carrying Morocco by assault, he, with his own hands, strangled the young

---

* Herbelot calls him Mohamet Abdulmomen Ben-Tomrut; according to Marmol, his name was Abulmomen Ben-Abdallah Ben-Ali.

Isac,

Ifac, fon of Brahem, who had there been acknowledged king, and who was the laft of the houfe of Teffiün, the founders of Morocco, as well as of the empire. Abdulmomen, that he might perform his vow, reduced a part of that capital to duft, and paffed its afhes through a fieve; and that he might leave no veftige of the grandeur of its kings, and bury their name in oblivion, he deftroyed their palaces and mofques.

This prince afterward rebuilt the city, and gave orders that all the Morabethoon found throughout his empire fhould be put to death, that he might have nothing to fear from their vengeance. The animofity that was maintained, between thefe two fects, occafioned a fucceffion of revolutions in Africa, while they mutually enfeebled each other, and gave the eaftern provinces the power of fhaking off the yoke of the kings of Morocco, and electing independent chiefs for themfelves.

Abdulmomen, however, remained mafter of all Mauritania, and preferved the

two

two kingdoms of Fez and Morocco, which
had been united under Joseph Teffifin.
He was also able, in 1149, to send aid to
the Mahometans of Spain, and to permit
them to recruit among the mountains of
Gomera, between Tetuan and Tremecen.
In 1151, the power of this prince being
still more firmly established, the Mahometans of Grenada and of Jaen, who stood
in need of his support, offered him homage
and submission; he accordingly sent thirty
thousand men to their succour.

This army having been vanquished, Abdulmomen sent more considerable reinforcements, by which the Mahometans of
Spain were empowered to prolong the
war with some success. This prince had
an intention of going himself into Spain
with a mighty army, but he died in
1155 during these his preparations. The
castle of Bulahuan, in the province of
Duquella, is said to have been built by Abdulmomen; it has since been augmented
and embellished by a Sharif of the reigning
family.

After

After the death of Abdulmomen, his son Joseph was unanimously acknowledged king of Morocco. Joseph, out of deference to the memory of his father, and also to merit the love of his subjects, testified his aversion to the Christians, and passed over into Spain, in 1158, with a powerful army. On his arrival, the Mahometan kings of Andalusia, as well from respect to his power, as to acknowledge the services they received, swore fidelity to him, and proclaimed him sovereign. The kings of Murcia and Valencia, who were more distant, were the sole who did not think proper to submit. Having united his army with that of the Arab Moors in Spain, Joseph seized on some places in despite of the efforts of Don Sancho III. The nobility who commanded the army of the latter, consulting their valour only, followed Joseph to Seville, and gained a victory over him under the walls of that city. Profiting by the divisions of the Spaniards, Joseph, the next campaign, obliged the kings of Valencia and Murcia to become his vassals.

Joseph

Joseph remained at Seville till the year 1168 employed in making incursions upon the territories of the Christians, or in repelling those which the Christians made on his domains. Receiving information at this time that some tribes of the Zenetes had taken advantage of his absence to raise commotions in his African states, he returned thither; and, after having quelled the insurgents, again came to Spain in 1171 with a powerful army.

Joseph now obliged all the Mahometan kings to acknowledge him sovereign, nor was there one who did not pay him homage: he continued to keep up his armies in Spain, where his son long commanded during his absence; he once more returned thither in 1184, and took the city of Santaren by assault. He was attacked before this place by the armies of the kings of Portugal and Leon, and, falling from his horse, was killed by the accident; this occasioned the loss of the battle, and most of the Moors who composed his army returned into Africa.

No

No fooner was the death of Jofeph known in Africa than feveral divifions arofe among the Moors; but Abu-Jacob, his fon, furnamed Almonfor, the invincible, and who had already diftinguifhed himfelf at the head of armies, having taken upon him the government of the empire, fubdued thefe commotions, and was proclaimed Emperor.

The kings of Tunis and Tremecen, who had been feudatory dependents on his anceftors, and who were defirous to fhake off this dependency, endeavoured to incite rebellion among the diftant tribes that they might embarrafs Jacob. This prince marched with his forces, and, after having reftored tranquillity, he tranfported thofe tribes, among whom commotions had been incited, to the centre of his empire, and difperfed them, through the different provinces of his ftates, fo diftant from each other that they might be unable to reunite. This is a political fyftem which all the kings of Morocco have obferved with refpect to powerful tribes; and, thus divided, by the prudence or caprice of the fovereigns,

reigns, thefe tribes have infenfibly loft all memory of their origin.

The conduct, courage, and activity, of Jacob, foon eftablifhed his fupremacy over the African coafts as far as Tunis, and at the fame time preferved that which had been acquired over the Arab Moors of Spain. Of all the fovereigns who have reigned in Africa after the Caliphs, he was, beyond difpute, the moft powerful ; thence happened it that he acquired the furname of Almonfor, the invincible, to which might likewife be added the magnificent.

Almonfor built the caftle of Manfooria, at the entrance of the province of Tem-fena, eight leagues from Sallee, of which fome ruins ftill remain ; the city of Al-caffar-Quiber, three leagues from Laracha ; that of Alcaffar-Seguar, fituated on the ftraits of Gibraltar, between Tangiers and Ceuta ; and the city of Rabat, facing Sallee. After erecting a caftle toward the fea for the defence of this laft place, he built in a vaft enclofure, ruins of which ftill exift, magnificent palaces, that

2   time,

time, infurrections, and the caprices of men, have laid wafte. During fummer this prince refided in that beautiful cincture called Guadel, where tafte and fplendor were alike difplayed. He alfo employed Rabat as a place of arms, whence he might with facility invade Spain with his forces.

After adding the furname of invincible to that of commander of the faithful, Jacob Almonfor paffed over into Spain with a powerful army; but the ficklenefs of the Moors being incited by his abfence throughout the vaft ftates he poffeffed in Africa, he was obliged to return without performing any memorable act. Marmol fays, he left a part of his army under the command of Don Ferdinand Ruis de Caftro, lieutenant general, who, although a Chriftian, had entered into his fervice from motives of difcontent.

No fooner had Jacob Almonfor again reduced his fubjects to fubordination than he publifhed the Gazia, or war againft the infidels, fimilar to the crufades

of

of the Chriftians; the Moors flocked in
multitudes to his ftandard, and he embarked for Spain with a powerful army,
where, being landed, he marched toward
Toledo. Alphonfo III. coming to oppofe
him was not terrified by the numbers of the
Moors, but moft valoroufly attacked the
army of Jacob, which defended itfelf with
intrepidity, and which gained a complete
victory over the Chriftians, in fight of the
town of Alarcos, July the eighteenth,
1195. This victorious army had a continuation of fuccefs till the year 1197, when
Almonfor, having figned a truce with the
king of Caftile, returned into Africa,
where new commotions rendered his prefence neceffary.

The governor of Morocco, profiting by
the abfence of Jacob Almonfor to incite
the neighbouring people to revolt, the latter, on his return, found them all in arms.
The intimidated rebels, not daring to wait
this valiant prince in the open field, fhut
themfelves up in that capital, which he
was obliged to befiege. Almonfor, having
paffed a tedious year under the walls of the
place,

place, determined to scale the city; and, animatedly addressing his soldiers, shewed them t at, independent of the glory they would acquire in taking Morocco, there was still a more legitimate and more honourable motive, that of recovering their wives and children, who were then in the power of the usurpers.

Enflamed by his discourse, the besiegers assaulted the city, which was unable to resist their impetuosity; and, falling furiously upon the inhabitants, put all to death they met. Almonfor, that he might chastise the rebels, even after their death, refused them the rites of burial *; and, when he was reminded of the effects which might result from putrefaction, said, " Nothing smells so well as the body " of a dead enemy, and especially of a " traitor."

* The Moors believe that the souls of bodies, deprived of the rites of burial, are driven from the abodes of the blessed. In fabulous ages it was further believed that the souls of such bodies wandered on the banks of Cocytus, and were refused admittance into the Elisian fields

, After

After Almonfor had taken Morocco, the governor, having ſhut himſelf up in the caſtle with ſome ſoldiers, mediated his peace by the good offices of a Marabout, whoſe ſanctity was held in veneration; but Almonfor, although he had granted this man pardon, put him to death the moment he had him in his power, and, by the violation of his promiſe, tarniſhed his glory. The Marabout reproached him with his ill faith. I am not, anſwered the prince, obliged to keep my word with thoſe who have forfeited theirs.

According to the Arab hiſtorians, the ſovereign, full of regret for not having obſerved his promiſe, diſappeared, and wandered over the world. The probability is that this prince performed the pilgrimage to Mecca, as a private perſon, in expiation of his crime. His brother, Brahem, governed during his abſence; but, he not returning in the ſpace of a year, his ſon, Mahomet Ben-Naſſer, called alſo Naſfer-Al-Melek Ben-Manſoor, was proclaimed king by the people.

Mahomet

Mahomet Ben-Nasser, having succeeded his father in 1210, confirmed the princes of Africa in the possession of their states, and broke the truce which Almonsor had concluded with Alphonso of Castile. This prince being desirous of extending his conquests in Spain, went thither with a powerful army, conquered some towns, ravaged their territories, and returned to repose under the walls of Cordova. Thither Alphonso, having received considerable reinforcements from the Christian princes, marched to give the king of Morocco battle. The two armies met on the sixteenth of July, 1212, in the plains of Tolofo, and the Moors suffered a total rout. This defeat, beside humbling the Mahometans, infinitely decreased that consideration in which Mahomet Ben-Nasser had been held.

After this action Mahomet returned to Africa, and left the command of his army to his brother Aben Saad, living himself in a kind of retirement; and, despised by his subjects, who, prejudiced as they were, attributed

tributed the lofs of the battle to his ill conduct and cowardice.

Preyed upon by chagrin, Mahomet Ben-Naffer died a fhort time after, and left his empire to Said Barrax, one of his grand-fons, againft whom the governors of the eaftern provinces of Tremecen and Tunis revolted. Said raifed an army in fupport of his authority, but, having been affaffinated by a traitor, the fpirit of difcord renewed its progrefs.

After the death of Said, the principal perfons of the Moahedins elected his uncle, Abdel Cader, in his ftead ; but, this prince not having gained the confidence of the people, and finding that, in thefe times of trouble, his party was not fufficiently powerful, he fled toward Morocco, and the governors of the principal places profited by this momentary weaknefs to divide the empire.

D 2 CHAP.

C H A P. IV.

Dynasty of the Benimerins.

ABDALLAH, governor of Fez, of the race of the Benimerins, was the first of that dynasty who possessed himself of the sovereign authority. Jacob, his brother, having assembled troops, took the cities of Rabat and Anafa, and defeated an army of Moahedins between Fez and Mequinez; his successes awed the people, and supported the authority of his family in that part of Africa.

After the death of Abdallah, who, from governor of Fez, had become the sovereign, his son, still young, was his successor, under the regency of Ben-Joseph, his uncle; who also, in his turn, was sovereign, his nephew being first dead.

Similar

Similar r.volutions took place at the same time in the provinces of Morocco: that of Tedla, with those of the mountains in its neighbourhood, headed by Mahomet-Budobus, joined with the king of Fez, to aid him against Abdel Cader, of the race of the Moahedins. Abdel Cader, informed of this treaty, escaped from Morocco at the approach of the rebels; but, having been overtaken in his flight, he was murdered at Sugulmessa.

Budobus, now become master of those provinces that lay near the capital, thought proper to renounce the alliance he had made with Ben-Joseph, and further declared war against him, in expectation of conquering the kingdom of Fez. A quick termination was put to this war by the death of Budobus, and the defeat of his army. Ben-Joseph not only preserved the kingdom of Fez but also conquered that of Morocco; and, by this revolution, the Moahedins were wholly deprived of sovereign power.

The

The kingdom of Morocco, by this change of its monarchs, which long held the minds of the people in fufpence, loft the fovereignty of Spain. Thofe who governed the provinces of Seville, Cordova, Jaen, and others, in the abfence of the king of Morocco, erected themfelves into fovereign princes; and, feconded by the African troops, that had remained in Andalufia, were thus enabled to maintain thofe divifions, and that diverfity of opinions and interefts, which were inceffantly renewed.

Ben-Jofeph, now mafter of Mauritania, eftablifhed his authority there the more folidly by not occupying himfelf with foreign conquefts, or government. The affairs of Spain felt fome relaxation by the truces which were renewed between Caftile and the Mahometan kings, till the acceffion of Don Ferdinand, to the throne of Caftile. War again broke out in 1240, with an obftinate zeal, and the Mahometans loft, almoft in an inftant, the kingdoms of Cordova and Seville, and the greateft part of Andalufia.

The

The kings of Grenada and Murcia then called loudly for affiftance of Ben-Jofeph, fovereign of Fez and Morocco. Alphonfo X., the fucceffor of Ferdinand, fent a fleet, by way of diverfion, to befiege Sallee in 1261, and the place was taken, but was afterward abandoned on the approach of the king of Fez.

Don Alphonfo being folely occupied by his political interefts in Europe, the king of Grenada took advantage of the truce to make a new alliance with the king of Morocco, to whom he even offered the fovereignty of his ftates with the towns of Tariffa and Algefira, as a fecurity that he would perform his promife, and alfo as places for the debarkment of the troops.

Thus invited, Ben-Jofeph took fhipping for Spain in 1275, with his army, poffeffed himfelf of the two above-named places, committed ravages in the territories of Andalufia, and then returned into Africa. He fent his brother, Ottman, the next year with troops, who again brought new havoc. Ben-Jofeph returned himfelf

the

the following campaign, and his army, united to that of Grenada, gained very decided advantages over that of the Chriftians. After vanquishing the Caftilian fleet, Ben-Jofeph raifed the fiege of Algefira in 1278, and rebuilt that town in the place where it at prefent ftands. This prince afterward made a truce with Don Alphonfo, and generoufly granted him aid againft his fon, Don Sancho, who, with the confent of the people, had feized on the fovereign authority.

After the death of Ben-Jofeph he was fucceeded by his fon Abu-Said, who, like his father, made feveral expeditions into Spain; all of which were unfuccefsful. Having loft Tariffa, which had been taken by Don Sancho III., he made fruitlefs efforts to recover that place; but, perceiving that his attempts to regain the fovereignty of Spain exhaufted his revenues, he renounced them in future, and in 1294 reftored the town of Algefira to the king of Grenada. The empire of Morocco was, during a time, delivered from wars and revolutions. Abu-Said, occupied folely by
the

the adminiftration of his African ftates, reigned in tranquillity to the year, 1303. At his death he was fucceeded by Abu-Artab-Ben-Said; but neither did he take any part whatever in the Mahometan wars of Spain: his fucceffor, indeed, Jofeph-Ben-Jacob, in 1318, appears to have fent fuccours to the king of Grenada, who ceded fome places to him, of which his troops took poffeffion.

After the death of Jofeph-Ben-Jacob, king of Fez and Morocco, his two fons, Abul-Haffen and Said, made war on each other for the fucceffion. Said, having been vanquifhed, withdrew to the king of Grenada, and his brother, Abul-Haffen, was proclaimed. The latter took offence at the afylum given by the king of Grenada to Said, and fhewed tokens of his refentment; on which the king of Grenada determined to pafs over into Barbary, in 1330, that he might come to an explanation with this prince.

This voyage had the moft fortunate fuc-cefs, for the king of Grenada, after having
removed

removed all the fuspicions of Abul-Haffen, obtained from him a confiderable body of troops, commanded by his fon Abdelmelek, who went in 1333, landed at Algefira, took poffeffion of that place, and was there acknowledged fovereign. This army, protected by a fleet, afterward feized on Gibraltar, which the Spaniards, in vain, attempted to retake.

The war, which fome years after broke out between the king of Tremecen and Abul-Haffen, obliged the latter to recall his his fon Abdelmelek, with his troops. To thefe were likewife added a detachment, fent by the king of Grenada, who had made a truce with Caftile. This war was unfortunate to the king of Tremecen, who, with his kingdom, loft all he poffeffed toward Sugulmeffa. The king of Fez, profiting by his victory, purfued his conquefts as far as Algiers and Tunis, which he again brought under the fubjection of the kings of Fez and Morocco.

Inflated with fuccefs, Abul-Haffen refolved to recommence the Moorifh expeditions

ditions into Spain, hoping there to recover the dominion his predecessors had enjoyed; for this purpose he sent troops, stores, arms, and ammunition, under the conduct of his son Abdelmelek. Abdelmelek committed many ravages on the territories of Andalusia, but the Christians were able to repulse his attacks; and, after several campaigns, in which the advantages were nearly equal, his army was attacked and routed by the Castilians. Abdelmelek, having found an opportunity to fly on foot, perceiving the approach of Christians, counterfeited death, and the latter coming up gave him two wounds with their lances, of which he died in reality. The body of this prince was transported into Barbary, and inhumed at Shella, near Rabat, where his tomb is still to be seen.

The death of Abdelmelek afflicted the king of Fez so deeply that he determined to go and take personal vengeance on the Spaniards. For this purpose he fitted out more than two hundred vessels at Ceuta, in 1340, which, in despite of the efforts of the king of Castile, being favoured by

circum-

circumſtances, met no obſtacle in the ſhort paſſage from the coaſt of Africa to the coaſt of Spain. Beſide his troops, he took with him many Mooriſh families, who were to people ſome towns round Malaga. The Mo riſh fleet, being in the bay of Gibraltar, was attacked by the fleet of Caſtile, but which, being by no means ſo powerful, was totally defeated.

The kings of Fez and Grenada, at the head of a mighty army, firſt laid ſiege to Tariffa; but the kings of Caſtile and Protugal, with their combined forces, marched to the relief of that place, and attacked and defeated the Mahometan army near Rio-Salado; which afterward retreated to Algeſira. The king of Fez, fearing he ſhould be there beſieged, immediately embarked for Ceuta.

That he might revenge the Mohometan defeat at the battle of Rio-Salado, Abul-Haſſen again made great preparations of troops ánd ſtores to return into Spain. His fleet, united with that of his allies, was attacked in port, and he loſt about

twelve

twelve veffels; but this check did not prevent the remainder of the fleet from fetting fail : this, however, being once more
attacked in the Strait by the combined fleet
of the Chriftians, was entirely defeated ;
the invafion of the Mahometans was thus
prevented, and, notwithftanding every effort of the king of Fez and Morocco,
Algefira was taken, in March 1344, and a
ten years truce concluded.

The expences which had been incurred by
Abul-Haffen to fupport thefe his attempts
in Spain, and the ill fuccefs that followed,
occafioned his fubjects to murmur, as is the
cuftom of nations, that judge only from
appearances.   Abdalharaman, one of the
king's fons, feized this moment of difcontent to revolt, and drew over feveral tribes
to his fide.   Don Alphonfo, in the mean
time, broke the truce in Spain, where he
attacked the Mahometans.   Abul-Haffen,
although he had ftifled the rebellion, found
his own ftates in too critical a fituation to
admit of his going in perfon to affift the
Mahometans of Spain.   He fent his fon,
Abu-Ali, thither, with a body of troops, to
aid

aid Gibraltar, which the king of Caftile befieged in 1349; the troops of Morocco, however, could effect nothing, but were obliged to repafs the ftrait, a rebellion having been once more raifed by Abu-Hennon, another of the fons of Abul-Haffen. The king was unfortunate in this civil war, and was obliged to retire into the province of Sugulmeffa, his fon having feized on his kingdom.

Abu-Hennon was an ambitious prince, and defirous of eftablifhing his fame with his fubjects; for which purpofe he prepared formidable armaments for the invading of Spain. His father took advantage of thefe preparations to attempt recovering his domains, and, affembling fome troops round Sugulmeffa, affaulted and fubjected various cities of the kingdom of Fez. The projects of Abu-Hennon were fufpended by this diverfion; but, having overcome his father in 1354, near the mountains of Fez, he remained in peaceable poffeffion of his ftates, and preferved his fupremacy over the fmall kingdoms of the coaft from Tremecen to Tunis. This

prince

prince entered into a negotiation with Peter the cruel, who had afcended the throne of Caftile, and who, from political motives, was difpofed to favour the rebellion of Abu-Hennon. The latter, at length, in full enjoyment of peace, embellifhed the city of Fez with fome edifices, and built a college there, which ftill bears his name.

Abu-Hennon died in 1409, and his fon, Abu-Said, was his fucceffor. Addicted to pleafure and debauchery, this prince occupied himfelf too little with the care of his own eftates to think of fuccouring the Mahometans of Spain; he even neglected to fortify, or fend aid, to Ceuta, which was befieged and taken in 1415 by Don John, king of Portugal; the neighbouring Moors united to recover the place, but their attempts were unfuccefsful, as well from their ignorance, in the art of befieging towns, as from the fkill with which they were repulfed by Don Henry, fon to the king of Portugal.

The cities of Spain, which had been under the government of Abu-Said, feeing they

they were to expect no affiftance whatever from him, were reunited to the Mahometan kingdom of Grenada, Gibraltar alone remaining in the poffeffion of the king of Fez. Hither Abu-Said fent his brother Said with fome troops, as well to preferve that place, and to recover others that had been loft, as to remove Said, whofe valour and eminent qualities made him remarked by the people, and who foon or late might become a dangerous rival.

This expedition was unfuccefsful, the king of Grenada having befieged Gibraltar, Said, in vain, demanded fuccours from his brother, who faw, with fecret pleafure, the difficulties in which he was involved. Said notwithftanding defended himfelf with the utmoft fortitude; but, having been conquered, he was taken prifoner to Grenada, where his brother wifhed he might be put to death. The king of Grenada, more politic, preferved the life of this prince, as well out of refpect to his birth as in the hope of being able to make him a party in thofe infurrections which fo often divided the Moors of Africa.

Future

Future events juftified the forefight of the king of Grenada: the Moors of Fez, offended at the conduct of their fovereign, rebelled againft him, and he was ftabbed by his Vizier, who, at the fame time, affaffinated his children. The kingdom of Fez fell into the greateft diforder in confequence of the death of this prince; the people lived fome time totally independant, each province and each tribe governing itfelf according to its will. The king of Grenada profited by this ftate of anarchy to fend over Said into Barbary with troops, and thus to infure his friendfhip and alliance; but this Prince had many difficulties to encounter, having a competitor in Jacob, one of his brothers, whofe ftandard had been followed by the principal tribes, which occafioned open war between thefe two princes.

The kingdom of Fez, troubled by thefe civil broils, remained eight years without a fovereign, when, in 1423, a fon of Abu-Said appeared, named Abdallah, with whom his mother had fled to Tunis. Abdallah was received with the greater joy

VOL. II. E because

because that the people, divided in their choice of a prince, thought it their duty to reunite in favour of one whom Providence seemed miraculously to have preserved, that their calamities might find a period. The uncles of Abdallah Said and Jacob approved the nation's choice, and relinquished the throne.

Abdallah reigned with justice for some years; but, at length, he imposed so many vexatious and tyrannical oppressions, on his people, that they were incited to revolt. In the midst of the civil commotions which ensued, an inhabitant of Fez, who was a Sharif, and who bore the name, slew the king Abdallah, who was the last of the family of the Benimerins, and was proclaimed in his stead.

All the grandees attached to the Dynasty of the Benimerins rose against the usurper, and an obstinate war ensued. Muley Shaik, one of the generals who was at the head of this party, and who commanded toward Arzilla, presented himself before Fez to besiege the city; but, hav-

ing been vanquished by the Sharif, he retired into his government. The Sharif
then sent an army into Temsena to subject
that province; and Muley Shaik, while
the Sharif was thus weakened, made a second attempt upon Fez, in which he besieged the Sharif.

Don Alphonso, of Portugal, desirous of
profiting by the intestine distractions of
the empire, appeared before Arailla with
his fleet, and took it in 1471. Muley
Shaik, being informed of this, departed
from the blockade of Fez to go and succour Arzilla, which, as well as Tangiers, he found taken on his arrival. The
Moorish prince then determined to make a
truce with the king of Portugal, that he
might once more undertake the siege of
Fez; and he accordingly obliged the Sharif to abandon that city.

Muley Shaik, now become master of the
capital and the appending monarchy, was
the first of the kings of the race called
Merini, the descendants of a branch of the
Benimerins. The dominion of the Me-

rini

rini only extended over the kingdom of Fez, becaufe, in thefe difcordant times, the provinces of Morocco, Suz, Sugulmeffa, and others, were fubjeƈted to other fovereigns, who found themfelves capable of maintaining their independence.

CHAP.

C H A P. V.

Sharifs of the Merini — Troubles that hap-
pened under their reign.

T H E family of Merini, which is also
called Beni-Aotas, was so lightly esteemed
that it was not able to render its authority
respectable in the kingdom of Fez.   Independent of those provinces which had
shaken off obedience, there were cities that
were governed within themselves, or by
the authority of chiefs which they had
elected. The Portuguese, who already had
got footing on the coast, profiting by the
weakness of these small governments and
their internal divisions, possessed themselves of various places, and insensibly extended their conquests. Several tribes of
Moors, from animosity, or provoked by the
ambition of their chiefs, rather chose to

become

become the allies of the Portuguese, than to remain dependant on numerous masters, who reciprocally deposed each other.

The kingdoms of Fez and Morocco continued in this kind of anarchy till the beginning of the sixteenth century; and the race of Merini, whose power was feeble, reigned only over the city of Fez and the neighbouring provinces. At this time a Moor, of the province of Dara, whose name was Mahomet-Ben-Achmet, calling himself a Sharif and descendant of the Prophet, perceiving that the contentions which existed in the provinces might favour a revolution; and knowing, also, the ascendant which religion has over the minds of the vulgar, thought proper to employ these means to accomplish his projects of ambition.

· This Sharif sent his three sons, Abdel-Quiber, Achmet, and Mohamet, in 1508, on pilgrimage to Mecca, that they might thereby acquire the greater consideration. These young men, on their return, affecting all the exterior of religion, were most
respectfully

respectfully received by the Moors, who flocked after them in crouds, contested who first should touch their garments, and venerated them as faints, who were come to console them amid their afflictions.

The superstition and enthusiasm of the people raised their fame so high that, when they returned into their province, the father, without hesitation, sent the two youngest to Fez to make themselves known in that metropolis, famous for its science and religion. The eldest of these two became the head of the first college, and the king confided the education of his children to the younger.

When the reputation of these Sharifs was well established, their father, who slowly pursued projects which had been deeply laid, engaged them to represent to the king of Fez the calamities which resulted from the divisions among the Moors, and those which were in future to be dreaded in consequence of their alliance with the Portuguese, who, soon or late,

E 4 would

would feize on their wealth, and reduce their perfons to flavery.

They artfully infinuated to this prince how glorious it would be to himfelf, and how conducive to the profperity of religion, could he unite all the Mahometans to repel, and drive thefe foreigners from the ftates. This enterprize might be crowned with fuccefs, according to their flattering reprefentations, would he permit them to traverfe the provinces with a drum and a ftandard, awaken the fpirit of religion among the people, inftruct them in their true interefts, and incite them to rife in arms againft the Chriftians. Acknowledging this prince as their legitimate fovereign, they requefted he would beftow on them fome mark of authority which might give credit to, and make their miffion refpectable in the fouthern provinces, where the Portuguefe were fo powerful.

The king of Fez, who had no authority in thefe fouthern provinces, and who had no fufpicion that the intentions of the Sharifs were inimical to himfelf, granted their

their requeſt, in contradiction to the repre-
ſentations made to him by his brother,
Muley Naſſer, who, better informed than
he was concerning former revolutions,
affected by the Morabethoon and the Mo-
ahedius, under the veil of religion, pro-
pheſied evil from this project of the Sharifs,
and foreſaw in it more of ambition than of
zeal. Neglecting this advice, the king of
Fez granted them a drum, ſome ſoldiers
to protect them, and royal mandates diſ-
playing the object of their miſſion. The
two Sharifs entered the province of Duquella, and paſſed through the others till
they came to that of Suz, in every place
exciting the enthuſiaſm of the people
againſt the Portugueſe, whoſe ambition
they failed not to exaggerate.

Politically conſidered, this miſſion was
neceſſary, ſince, on one ſide of the coaſt, the
Portugueſe, in 1508, were maſters of Saffi,
and had made alliance with the moſt powerful of the neighbouring tribes, while,
on the other, the Duke of Braganza, in
1513, had lately taken Azamora, inſo-
much that, from thence to Santa Cruz, the
coaſt

coaft for more than a hundred leagues was in their power toward the fouth, independent of the towns of Arzilla, Tangiers, and Ceuta, which they poffeffed to the north. In this critical fituation, the empire being enfeebled and divided as it then was, they might moft eafily have conquered the whole coaft; all which perfectly juftified thofe alarms which the Sharifs fpread, although their perfonal motives had a very different tendency.

The miffion of the Sharifs had every effect which might reafonably be expected, and, under the pretence of the defence of religion, a number of tribes, that were then governed by themfelves, eagerly joined their ftandard. Money being neceffary to the Sharifs for the maintenance of thefe armies, the tribes granted them the tenth, as ordained by the Koran, which gave them a femblance of fovereign power.

The city of Tarudant, which had been ravaged by the wandering tribes, acknowledged the old Sharif for its chief, and enabled

bled

bled him also to maintain some troops,
Thus aided, Mahomet-Ben-Achmet fortified himself in Tarudant, pretending thereby to free himself from the dominion of
the Portuguese, and impede their incursions. Succoured by the Moors of Suz and
Dara, he was presently able to make war
on the tribes near Cape Aguer, or Santa-
Cruz, and also to enter the provinces of
Hea, Duquella, and Temsena, where the
people, as much moved by his sermons as
terrified by his arms, acknowledged him
their sovereign, under the modest title of
Prince of Hea.

The Portuguese, and Moors of the environs of Saffi, their allies, made incursions
at the same time into the province of Duquella, and spread terror to the very walls
of Morocco : the old Sharif alone opposed
their progress ; but, dying during the time
he was warring with them, he left the ac-
complishment of his projects to the care of
his sons.

These princes, having by their arts obtained the people's veneration, and who
were

were as exact in paying their tenths as
they were prompt at obedience, gradually
extended their power. They remained
with their forces between Saffi and Morocco to oppose the incursions of the Portuguese, whom, in various actions, they repulsed; but their advantages were, in some
sort, balanced by the death of Abdel-
Quiber, the eldest of the three brothers,
who fell in battle.

The Sharifs, having formed the design
of seizing on Morocco, made an alliance
with Nasser Bushentuf, who commanded
in that city, and held the neighbouring
tribes in dependence. This governor,
having made himself sovereign, received
the Sharifs in Morocco, respecting their
piety, and in the hope that he himself
might find his advantage in their alliance.
This confidence became fatal to Nasser
Bushentuf, for his death quickly followed,
which happened on returning from a hunting party with one of the Sharifs, who
has been accused of having given him a
poisoned biscuit. Achmet, the eldest of
these princes, who had remained in Mo-

-rocco, profited so well by his death, that, aided by the principal men of the city, whose friendship he had gained, he was proclaimed king.

Muley Achmet, now king of Morocco, sent information of his election to the king of Fez, and, in gratitude for the services he had received from the latter, affirmed, he only intended to govern under his authority, and paying him feudal homage. This quieted the fears of the king, and gave Muley Achmet time to establish his power.

Morocco and its environs being thus subjected to the Sharifs, they, by artifices, endeavoured to possess themselves of other provinces, and with such adroitness did they foment factions that, when the different parties made war on each other, each of them depended on the assistance of the Sharifs, should either need their aid. These princes, however, who had only raised dissentions that they might enfeeble the tribes, put their troops in motion, fell upon them, totally defeated them, plun-

dered

dered their Douhars, and returned to Morocco victorious, and enriched with fpoils.
Their victories fpread terror among the
people, and the province of Duquella and
its environs were thus fubjected.

Become more powerful, the Sharifs now
freed themfelves from that acknowledgement of fuperiority which they had voluntarily paid to the king of Fez, only
fending him fome fmall prefents as they
pleafed, which were lefs to be confidered
as tributes than as tokens of friendfhip.
The king of Fez complained of their in-
attention, but his death foon after happened, and his fon, who had been the
difciple of the Sharif Mohamet, diffembled, and confirmed the ufurpers in their
principalities, on condition of fome fmall
acknowledgement.

After the death of the king of Fez the
ambition of the Sharifs increafed with
their power; they artfully allied themfelves with the chiefs of tribes in the environs of that city, that they might fow di-
vifion; and, not only refufed to fubmit to
the

the leaſt homage, but, ſent to inform the new king, their benefactor and ſovereign, that, being deſcendants of Mahomet, they had a more inconteſtible right than any perſon whatever to the Mahometan throne.

The two brothers at the ſame time divided their conqueſts; the eldeſt, Muley Achmet, retained Morocco; Muley Mohamet took up his reſidence at Tarudant, by which they could mutually ſuccour each other againſt the Portugueſe and their allies, who were maſters of moſt of the weſtern coaſt, from the cape of Aguer to the province of Duquella incluſive.

The king of Fez, who had too long connived at the perfidious conduct of the Sharifs, reſolved, though ſomewhat late, to make them repent of their ingratitude, and, with two pieces of cannon, went in perſon to beſiege Morocco. His army, not being ſufficiently numerous to inveſt the city, could not prevent Muley Mohamet from throwing in ſuccours, which he brought from Tarudant. This ſame Sharif

rif made a fally, a few days after, with his troops, and fell on the camp of the king of Fez with fo much intrepidity that he forced his army to retreat, leaving the field of battle covered with the flain.

After this check the king of Fez was obliged to raife the fiege, as much for want of fufficient force as to go and re-eftablifh order in his own kingdom, where his brother, Muley Meffaoot, profiting by his abfence and ill fortune, had raifed an infurrection. He was followed in his retreat by the Sharifs, who attacked his rear-guard, which they came up with in the province of Efcura; after which, paffing into that of Tedla, and coafting the mountains, they obliged the people, fubjects to the king of Fez, to pay them contributions.

Having appeafed the revolt, incited by Muley Meffaoot, the king of Fez, more than ever enraged againft the Sharifs, marched once again to befiege Morocco. The Sharifs likewife marched to meet him, though with an inferior army, and waited for him on the banks of the river of negroes.

to difpute his paffage. The king of Fez, arriving at the oppofite fhore, encamped likewife, and the two armies obferved each other for fome days; at length, the king determined to attempt the paffage; he divided his army into three corps, gave the command of the firft to Abu-Abdallah, king of Grenada, who, having loft his own kingdom, had taken refuge with the king of Fez, the fecond to his brother-in-law, and headed the third himfelf.

The king of Grenada, having with him the fon of the king of Fez, paffed firft; and, as he proceeded to the middle of the ford, and his van-guard began to afcend the banks of the river, where the land was high, the king of Suz attacked this van-guard with fo much valour that it was defeated: the fon of the king of Fez was killed, as alfo was the king of Grenada. This prince, who never had expofed his life in defence of his own kingdom, loft it on this occafion in defence of another; the confufion among the foldiers was so great that the van-guard of the king of Fez, forced back in the river, overwhelmed those who were coming to their assistance, and they thus mutually drowned each other. The king of Fez, not having yet begun the passage with his detachment, seeing the disorder irretrievable, retired with so much haste that he abandoned his wives, baggage and artillery, took the road to Tedla, and returned to Fez.

This victory, which highly influenced the vulgar opinion, was so favourable to the Sharifs, that they were emboldened to greater undertakings, and determined the following year to pass mount Atlas with numerous forces, where they seized on the kingdom of Tafilet. On their return they raised contributions on the provinces of Fez, left troops in them, and forced those of the king of Fez to retire. After this success, Muley Mohamet left his brother at Morocco, and returned to Tarudant. In 1556, this prince came before Aguadier, or Santa Cruz, then in the power of the Portuguese; the siege of this place was somewhat

somewhat long, but it was obliged at laſt to capitulate. The power of the Sharifs was ſtill farther extended after this conqueſt, becauſe that the Moors, who had been allies of the Portugueſe, unable longer to receive aid from them, determined to pay homage to theſe princes.

This increaſe of dominion, which every where embroils nations, became at length a ſubject of diſcord between the Sharifs. Muley Achmet the eldeſt, who poſſeſſed the kingdom of Morocco, had ceded that of Suz to his brother Muley Mohamet, on condition of ſome tribute being paid; but the latter, whoſe valour, and other qualities, had rendered him the moſt popular, felt how eaſy it would be for him to rid himſelf of this dependence; and, inſtead of remitting his brother the fifth of the ſpoils he had made during the laſt campaign, thought proper to ſend a ſmaller part. This offended the king of Morocco, who imagined he had a right to preſcribe ſuch homage as he pleaſed. Muley Mohamet refuſed compliance, and explana-

tions

tions enfued between the brothers, which did but incite new aggravation, and each of them began to commit hoftilities on the domains of the other till war became almoft inevitable.

To prevent the confequent calamities, a Moor, who was held in veneration, perfuaded the two brothers to an interview, which gave occafion to an irreconcileable hatred. Muley Achmet treacheroufly endeavoured to ftrangle his brother as they embraced, but the latter, more adroit, efcaped the danger ; and, now become open enemies, they prepared for war.

Muley Achmet immediately fent his fon, Muley Sidan, with troops into the province of Dara, which appertained to the kingdom of Suz, there to levy contributions. Muley Mohamet, on his part, oppofed thefe hoftilities, and different actions enfued between the armies of the two princes, in which fortune generally was in favour of the king of Morocco. The loffes of Muley Mohamet did not, however, difhearten him; but rather ferved farther
ther

ther to raise his courage. Having affembled the governors of provinces, and the chiefs of tribes, he rehearsed to them his brother's acts of injuftice, and fo effectually infpired them with a dread of his tyranny that they all fwore eternal fidelity to Muley Mohamet. After receiving their proteftations, the fovereign gave them affurance, holding by his beard in token of a vow *, that, if they would be as faithful as they promifed, he would vanquifh his brother, and lead him prifoner to Tarudant.

The two armies foon took the field, each endeavouring to profit by every kind of ftratagem to furprize the other. Having, at length, met at the entrance of a valley, that of the king of Suz, which was upon the height, affaulted the army of the king of Morocco with fuch impetuofity that it was obliged to give ground, and the

---

* When the Moors hold by their beards, while they fwear, it gives ftrength to the oath, which, after this formality, they rarely violate.

cavalry,

cavalry, being so confined as to be unable either to form itself or act, the soldiers were obliged to alight from their horses, that they might escape with greater facility.

During the rout the king of Morocco, and his son Muley Bezza, were made prisoners, and conducted to Tarudant; but his eldest son, Muley Sidan, after collecting the remains of the army, retreated to Morocco. In this extremity the inhabitants of this city thought the best means were to negociate, and, after council held, Muley Sidan sent his wife to the king of Suz, his uncle, to effect an accommodation, and implore his clemency. The princess pleaded so effectually that Muley Mohamet granted his brother freedom, on condition that they should divide their conquests. There were many other clauses in their treaty, but, it was so little observed, that, to recite them, would be superfluous.

The king of Morocco, once again returned to his states, protested against the validity of the treaty, affirmed that, it having

having been made while he was a prisoner, it could neither injure his rights nor those of his descendants, who, by their birth, had a legitimate claim over his domains, which it was not in his power, by any renunciation, to take from them. After such a protestation the two brothers, equally irritated, again made dispositions for war, and the king of Suz passed Mount Atlas, by hasty marches, to invade the territories of Morocco.

The two armies met, seven leagues from that capital, on the nineteenth of August, 1544; and Muley Mohamet attacked his brother with so much valour that he totally defeated his army, and pursued it to the very gates of Morocco.

Here he summoned the inhabitants to deliver up the city, if they would not expose themselves to all the rigours of war; and the governor, having received no tidings of his master, supposing he might have been taken or slain, and not daring to defend the place, represented to the inhabitants

F 4

habitants that, Suz and Morocco being governed by princes of the fame blood, it was but juft that he fhould open the gates. Muley Mohamet, on his entrance, was faluted by the people as their fovereign.

After having vifited the fortrefs, and placed guards in every part, the prince entered the palace of his brother, where all was in confufion; the treafury was pillaging; the wives and daughters of Muley Achmet were folely occupied, during the tumult, to conceal what they poffeffed moft precious; but the prince foon quieted their fears, and took care at the fame time to fecure the treafury.

Muley Achmet, who had loft himfelf during the night, arrived while thefe things paffed, with few followers, at the private gate of the palace, where he knocked aloud. He was anfwered from the top of the walls, and advifed to fly, for that his brother was mafter of the city. Accordingly this prince retired immediately to the fanctuary of Sidi-Abdallah-Ben-Cefii, as to an inviolable afylum.

From

from this place Muley Sidan and Muley
Bocza went to Fez, to intreat assistance
from the king, who beheld, with secret
satisfaction, the divisions of those Sharifs,
whose perfidy he himself had proved, and
therefore promised aid to the most feeble,
hoping by this means he should be enabled
to destroy the most mighty.

The consecrated persons appertaining to
the sanctuary where Muley Achmet had
fled for refuge, were busied in their endeavours to procure an interview between the
two brothers, which accordingly, in a few
days, took place. Muley Mohamet, who,
on similar occasions, had made proof of the
ill faith of his brother, took his precautions, and received him in his tent, as well
as his children, with his sabre in his hand;
these saluted their uncle, and prostrated
themselves before him to embrace his
knees. Muley Achmet approached the
last, and his brother went to receive him
at the entrance of his tent, where they
embraced, wept, and remained for sometime silent.

Muley

Muley Mohamet, at length, reproached his brother concerning the little faith with which he had obferved the treaty concluded at Tarudant, adding that, to this his breach of faith, more criminal in kings than even in other men, he muft attribute his misfortunes; that Providence had defpoiled him of his ftates but to revenge his having broken a promife, pledged; that, being his elder brother, he had ever treated him as his fuperior and fovereign, and that, ungrateful as his conduct had been, he fhould ftill continue fo to do; but that, having given his word to the inhabitants of Morocco not to fuffer him any more to enter the city, he could not break it, left he fhould thereby incur fimilar reproaches; it therefore appeared moft proper that he fhould, for a time, retire to Tafilet with his fons, and there await a better deftiny; that they ought to regard the conquefts they had already made, with the aid of the Almighty, as harbingers of ftill greater fuccefs. Muley Achmet made fome reply, in his own juftification, and, confiding in the generofity of his brother, took the way to Tafilet.

Muley

Muley Mohamet, thus become mafter of the fouth of the empire, put himfelf in a condition to make Muley Oatas Merini, king of Fez, repent the kind reception he had granted his nephews. Seeking a quarrel with him, he demanded the province of Tedla as appertaining to the kingdom of Morocco, and at the fame time fent his fecond fon, Muley Abdel Cader, with troops to levy contributions, and befiege a caftle, which was in that province. This caftle, which was well defended, was vigoroufly attacked by the young prince, who yet was unable to take it, the king of Fez having come to its relief.

Hearing this, Muley Mohamet affembled all the cavalry of Suz and Morocco, marched in perfon toward Tedla, and joined the troops that were under his fon's command. The army of the king of Fez was fuperior to that of the king of Morocco; but, being compofed, in part, of the inhabitants of Fez, who were fickle of temper, not inured to war, but rather accuftomed to effeminacy and pleafures, this army was daily weakened by defertion.

Muley

Muley Mohamet, well acquainted with the levity of the people of Fez, eluded action as long as he thought convenient, till, at length, determined to give battle, he harangued his troops, and declared, that, desiring only to fight with men who were determined on victory, he gave liberty to all those to retire who felt they wanted this resolution; that, persuaded as he was, men, bred in the city of Fez, though superior in numbers, were unable to stand before soldiers so courageous as those he commanded, he intended to give battle, confiding in their valour, and not doubting but that the victory would render him the greatest sovereign of Africa.

Animated by this discourse, the soldiers called aloud to be led to the enemy, and, on the next morning, the army advanced in order of battle. This order was in the form of a crescent, according to the custom of the Moors; the two extremities of which were commanded, the one by Muley Meflaoot, the king's son, and the other by the Alcade Mumen, son of a Genoese renegado; the king was in the centre with

his

his other children, having the Arquebu-
fiers in his front, and the artillery drawn
by peafants, or carried by mules.

The two armies remained facing each
other without beginning the attack; the
Sharif had commanded that no motion
fhould be made till the fignal had been
given; the heat of the day was exceffive,
and the prince artfully waited till the fun
was on the decline; and at the moment
when, being behind his army, it fhone in
the face of his enemies, the firing of a
cannon was the fignal of attack, aud this
was made with fuch impetuofity, and fuccefs, that the army of the king of Fez
was immediately put to rout. As this
prince was riding to pafs the river of
Derna, and rally his flying forces, his horfe
felt, and he and his fon, Muley Buker, were
made prifoners. All the troops of Fez,
that compofed the main body of the
army, retired in diforder. Muley Buhafon, Prince and Lord of Gomera, in the
province of Rif, who commanded a detachment, was the only Moor who fought
courageoufly, and retired in good order.

A de-

A detachment of Turks, commanded by a resolute Persian, intrenched behind a battery, likewise prevented the victorious Moors from surrounding them. The Sharif, astonished at the valour of these foreigners, offered to take them into his service on the same conditions they had enjoyed under the king of Fez. The Persian general accepted the proposal for himself, and such of his detachment as thought proper to follow him, provided the king of Morocco would pledge his word for their safety. Muley Mohamet sent his ring by one of his sons, and the Persian general entered into his service with those of his soldiers who were not married at Fez; the rest laid down their arms and retreated.

After he had restored order in the camp, Muley Mohamet sent for Muley Oatas, king of Fez, and consoled him in his misfortunes, which, he said, must be attributed to the sins that were openly committed at Fez without reprehension. The king of Fez, enfeebled as he was by his wounds, assumed strength enough to reply, that it

was

was not always in the power of the sovereign to extirpate habitual and rooted
vices, and that, be the irregularity in his
administration what it might, it did not
thence result that he had a right to make
war upon him, and seize upon his states,
more especially when the benefits were remembered which he had received from his
father. An agreement was afterward made
between the Sharif and the king of Fez,
that the latter and his son should be restored to liberty, for which he should yield
up the city of Mequinez.

The Sharif took the road to Fez to enforce this agreement, but Muley Buhafon,
who had entered Fez with the remains of
the army, beholding the confusion there
was in the city, while it remained without
a monarch, had Muley Caffari, a young son
of the king, proclaimed, on condition that
he should restore the crown to his father fo
foon as he should recover his liberty.
The king of Morocco mean while came
and encamped, with his army, four leagues
from Fez, whence he dispatched letters from
the king, his prisoner, to his mother and
the

the principal men of the city, that they should put Mequinez into his power; but Buhafon, who directed in Fez, occafioned the anfwer to be delayed, that he might fhut up the Sharif, between the army of Fez and another which was raifing at Mequinez. Being informed of this, the the king of Morocco decamped before the paffes were feized, taking with him his prifoners.

Muley Mohamet, having gained intelligence of the diffenfions among the Moors in the environs of Fez, profited by thefe, in 1548, to fend troops thither, the command of which he beftowed on his two eldeft fons, Muley Haram and Muley Abdel Cader, who committed fome ravages round Alcaffar and Mequinez. This diverfion, and the want of concord throughout the government of the north, further fhook the wavering faith of the towns, and tribes of the kingdom of Fez, who were half in commotion, and who were with difficulty reftrained from rebellion. In this conjuncture the Moors, who were by profeffion faints, interfered, as ufual, to pacify the people:

people; and it was at length agreed that the city of Mequinez should be given to Muley Mohamet, on condition that the king of Fez should be restored to liberty, which was accordingly performed; but the Sharif exacted a promise from the king, before his departure, that, whenever he should make the demand, he would also yield him the city of Fez.

The king being come to Fez, his son restored him the government; but Muley Mohamet, who would not give him time to re-establish his authority, appeared before the metropolis about two months afterward, of which he demanded the possession. The king of Fez answered that his son, and the inhabitants, would not suffer this, and therefore it was not in his power to comply. The Sharif was so enraged, by this message, that he caused the ambassador who brought it to be beheaded, and sent a detachment of cavalry to the very gates of the city to commit hostilities; but this detachment was beaten, and forced to retreat.

Muley Mohamet then repaired to Mequinez, whence he sent for two of his sons to join him with what troops they could affemble in Morocco, and the fouthern provinces; after which he marched to meet this reinforcement, and encamped near the river Seboo. The different actions that happened between the troops of the king of Fez, and thofe of the king of Morocco, were to the advantage of the latter, who marched toward Fez and blockaded the city. Some fallies were made by the king of Fez, which made but little impreffion, while the inhabitants, in want of provifions, went by hundreds to the Sharif; who received them with open arms, and further ftraitened his lines to cut off all communication. After a long fiege, the inhabitants gave up the place to the Sharif, who, for form fake, beat down a part of the walls, and entered the city unknown to the king, who was then in New Fez

The news being brought him, this prince flew to recover his capital; the two parties fought from ftreet to ftreet with equal rage, and he would even have reco-

vered

vered Fez, had not the people, according to their ufual inconftancy, declared them-felves for the Sharif, and forced his troops to retire. Without fubjects, and without foldiers, the king rather chofe to fubmit to the clemency of the conqueror than to abandon his crown, his wives, and children. The king of Morocco, however, took pof-feffion of the city and caftle of Fez, mar-ried one of the king's daughters, and fent him and his children to Morocco and Ta-rudant, where he caufed them to be affaffi-nated. Such was the tragical end of the houfe of Merini, and fuch the ingratitude and perfidy it received from thofe Sharifs which itfelf had raifed, and who, having ftripped it of its poffeffions, and extermi-nated its race, foon themfelves felt the vi-ciffitudes of fortune.

CHAP.

C H A P.   VI.

The Revolutions of the Sharifs.

AFTER having feized on the kingdom
of Fez, Muley Mohamet fent his brother,
Muley Achmet, into the defert, with a part
of his family, that he might have nothing
to fear from his ambition. The change of
government in Fez, however, foon raifed
troubles in the northern provinces, which
obeyed with repugnance a prince who had
depofed their rightful fovereign. Muley
Mohamet therefore determined to fend
troops into the provinces, as well to make
his authority refpected as to keep the foldiers occupied, and prevent the effects of
their inconftancy. He fent his three fons,
Muley Haram, Muley Abdel Cader, and
Muley Abdallah, againft the city of Tremecen, of which they poffeffed themfelves

I   without

without the least resistance. Haram advanced toward Oràn, but could not conquer it; and, having returned to Fez, he there fell sick and died. The Algerine Turks, having heard of the reduction of Tremecen, marched with an army to effect its recovery. The king of Morocco sent three of his sons, with various detachments, to its relief; but the want of concord between these brothers, who, born of different mothers, had little affection for each other, and acted as if they had opposite interests, occasioned the loss of the place, and of a battle, in which one of them was killed, and another wounded.

At the same time, Salah Reis, governor of Algiers, who had acquired the reputation of valour, informed by Muley Buhafon, prince of Gomera, of the perfidious conduct of the Sharifs, to the king of Fez, offered his alliance to dethrone Muley Mohamet. Buhafon accepted the proposal, and also assured him he would allow a thousand pistoles, daily, for the maintenance of his troops, and abandon to him

G 3

all

all the filver, gold, and jewels, which
might be taken from the Sharif. Salah
Reis accordingly departed, in 1553, with
his artillery, and 4000 men, who were
joined during their progrefs by a multitude of volunteers, that continually increafed.

The Sharif, then engaged in fubjecting
the mountaineers of the environs of Morocco, having heard of this march, went to
the relief of Fez, and fent all the cavalry
he could collect to encamp in its neighbourhood. Salah Reis, as he advanced toward this city, had an engagement with
Muley Abdallah, fon of the king of Morocco, who commanded the rear-guard of
his army, in which the young prince loft
the baggage and ftores, which obliged the
Sharif to haften his march and enter Fez.
Salah Reis, a few days after, having encamped near the city, the king of Morocco
determined to fally out, becaufe the inhabitants enjoy the privilege of capitulating,
if the enemy approach the city within
half a league.

The

The king of Morocco, after having held council, marched to difpute the paffage of the Seboo with the enemy. His pofition was nearly the fame as it had formerly been when oppofed to the king of Fez, with this difference, that Salah Reis was a more able general, had a more formidable artillery, and better gunners. Salah Reis, intending to pafs the river, cannonaded the army of the Sharif to prevent its acting, while his cavalry effected a paffage; each horfeman carried an Arquebufier behind him, who, as faft as they gained the fhore, entrenched themfelves behind palifadoes, which they brought with them, while protected by their cavalry, whom the Moors were unable to drive from their pofts. By this fkilful conduct Salah Reis gained the oppofite fhore, encamped, and lay all night under arms.

The next morning the Sharif difpofed his army in order of battle. Salah Reis did the fame; and, notwithftanding the fuperiority of the Moors, whofe numbers

were

were more than five to one, by his good ge-
neralſhip, taking advantage of his enemy's
miſtakes, and oppoſing art to ſtrength, Sà-
lah Reis obliged Muley Mohamet, whoſe
troops began to give ground, to ſound a
retreat, and retire into New Fez. Salah
Reis and Buhaſon then advanced toward
Old Fez, where they found ſome reſiſtance
from one of the ſons of the Sharif; but
Buhaſon, having advanced with five hundred reſolute Turks, burſt the gates and
entered the city, which was eaſily taken,
Muley Abdallah, while he attacked the
one gate, retiring through the other to
join his father in New Fez. Muley Mohamet, perceiving the enemy maſter of Old
Fez, thought only of flight, bade his wives
carry every thing they had muſt precious
with them, and follow him; but he, being
in haſte to ſecure himſelf, could not wait
for them, and ſeveral of them fell into the
conqueror's power. Before he left the
city he opened his treaſury, and ſuffered it
to be pillaged by his own people, to prevent its falling into the hands of his enemies, whoſe booty conſequently was
ſmall.

After

After Salah Reis had taken Fez, there was some altercation concerning the election of a king; he consented, however, at length, that Muly Buhason should be proclaimed, according to stipulation; and, having been paid, agreeable to treaty, he returned to Algiers with his troops, loaded with plunder. Yet was not Salah Reis contented with Buhason; he therefore informed the king of Morocco of his departure, and assured him he would grant his enemy no farther assistance, should he undertake the recovery of Fez. Muley Mohamet, however, who had hastily marched for Morocco, did not confide in this intelligence, but even wrote to Muley Abdallah, his son, to abandon Mequinez, which thus fell likewise into the power of the conqueror.

Muley Achmet, who had abandoned Tafilet by the order of his brother Muley Mohamet, and retired to the desert, learning that he had lost Fez, profited by this momentary weakness to seize upon Tafilet, in which there were no troops. He sent informa-

information of his intentions to Muley Buhafon, and intreated his aid:

Muley Mohamet diffembled his knowledge
of thefe proceedings, till he was well certified
of the return of Salah Reis, and his forces,
to Algiers ; he then affembled two armies,
at Morocco, the one of which he led toward
Tafilet, and gave the command of the
other to his fon, Muley Abdallah, for the
recovery of Fez. The latter approaching
this city, Muley Buhafon fent his two
fons, Nacer and Mohamet, to oppofe him
with an army ; but the two princes, dif-
united in opinion, did not concert their
operations together. The latter, defirous
of obtaining all the honour of victory, advanced with his detachment, attacked the
army of Muley Abdallah, was totally defeated, and obliged to fly.

Irritated at this defeat, Buhafon affembled his forces, and marched himfelf to
attack Muley Abdallah, who now, being
himfelf routed, was obliged to return to
Morocco.

Muley

Muley Mohamet, who had blockaded Tafilet, being informed of the defeat of his fon, carefully fpread a contrary report, by which the courage of Muley Achmet was fo funken that he imagined there was no refource, except in his brother's clemency; to intreat which he fent his fons. By this artifice Muley Mohamet retook Tafilet, fent his brother to a fanctuary near Morocco, and detained his two fons, whom he fhortly after caufed to be maffacred.

He then departed from Tafilet toward Fez, to make another attempt on that city, and revenge the defeat of his fon Abdallah. Muley Buhafon marched to meet and give him battle; victory was difputed by both with the greateft obftinacy; but Muley Buhafon, having been killed by a lance, his troops took to flight; the Sharif remained mafter of the field, and victorioufly re-entered Fez.

In his wrath againft the inhabitants, whofe ficklenefs and cowardice he had proved, he treated them with the utmoft
[feverity,

feverity, exacted the repayment of his loft
treafury, and an indemnification of his ex-·
pences, for the defence and recovery of the
city. In vain did the people remonftrate
on the impoffibility of paying a fum fo ex-
orbitant, efpecially after the loffes to which
they had been expofed. They agreed,
however, to pay him the amount of three
millions of livres, or one hundred and twenty-five thoufand pounds, to relieve themfelves from perfecution. The king afterward feized on the poffeffions of wealthy
individuals, and cut off many that he might
obtain their riches. To avoid witneffing
the hatred of the inhabitants, he made
Morocco his place of refidence, and left
his fon Abdallah at Fez, in quality of Viceroy.

Returned to Morocco, Muley Mohamet
brought his brother thither, and put him
under a guard. In 1556, he made difpofitions to fubject the Brebes of the mountains, who had given figns of commotion,
and left his fon, Muley Abdulmomen, at
Morocco, with Ali-Ben-Buker, as governor. He paffed Mount Atlas with his
army,

army, but nothing remarkable happened during the campaign, except the death of this king, who was killed by a Turk, that had entered into his service with that express intention. Thus, as he rose to empire by treachery, he himself perished by the hand of a traitor.

After the death of this prince, while waiting for the arrival of Muley Abdallah, who was at Fez, Ali-Ben-Buker, governor of Morocco, fearing the people might elect Muley Achmet, had him murdered in his prison; and thus both these Sharifs, who had perfidiously made religion and good faith a pretext to despoil their masters and benefactors of sovereignty, whom, between them, they caused to perish, fell themselves, as did most of their posterity, by the hands of murderers, the merited reward of their crimes.

Muley Abdallah, hearing at Fez of the death of his father, left the government of this city to his brother, Muley Abdulmomen, and departed, in 1557, for Morocco, where

where he was joyfully received. Having assembled the chiefs of the army, and the principal men of the city, he was proclaimed king of Fez, Morocco, and other towns and provinces, under the dominion of the Sharif. In the beginning of his reign this prince gave tokens of generous sentiments, by which he acquired the affection of his people; but it was not long before he began to act the tyrant. Uneasy at perceiving the popularity of his brothers, on whom he had bestowed governments, he determined to recal them, intending to rid himself of them and his fears.

Muley Ottman, who was at Tarudant, repaired to court, as did his two nephews, who were governors, the one of Dara, and the other of Mequinez; but his brother, Muley Abdulmomen, excufed himfelf on a pretext of bufinefs. Muley Abdallah put the three others to death, and, that he might varnish his tyranny, accufed them of not having fulfilled the duties of their office, and of failure in their adminiftration of juftice. This cruel act rendered Abdal-

Abdallah odious to his fubjects, and infupportable to himfelf, which occafioned a fit of ficknefs that almoft brought him to the grave.

After his recovery, Muley Abdallah once more fent to his brother, Abdulmomen, to concert with him a meditated enterprize againft Mazagan ; but the latter, knowing what had happened to Ottman and his nephews, replied, he would be at Morocco as foon as poffible, and, under the pretext of departing for this city, having collected his riches, he took the road to Tremecen, in 1559, that he might pafs thence to Algiers. He was received with diftinction at Algiers by Haffen, fon of Barbaroffa, Dey of that city ; and, after acquiring reputation by his good conduct and bravery, Haffen beftowed one of his daughters on him, and confided to him the government of Tremecen.

Muley Abdallah heard, with difpleafure, of the reception his brother had met from the Dey of Algiers, dreading left their union fhould affect the good intelligence

telligence he had held with that regency, the power of which he had proved; he confoled himfelf, however, with reflecting that, being rid thus of his brothers and ne+ phews, he had no competitors now to dread. The principal governments in his kingdoms he beftowed on his fons, and, in t562, determined to lay fiege to Mazagan, which he had for fome time meditated; but his enterprize was unfuccefsful, and he was conftrained to retreat, after fuffering great loffes.

Muley Abdulmomen remained in peace+ able enjoyment of his government of Tremecen, when the fon of Muley Abdallah, then governor of Fez, refolved to have him affaffinated. He concerted the means with one of his faithful fervants, who, pretending he had quarrelled with his mafter, fled from him, and took refuge at Tremecen. This Moor acted his part fo well that Abdulmomen gave him a moft gracious reception, and granted him unlimited confidence. The favourable moment being come, the traitor, having made every preparation for flight, killed the

prince

prince, while at prayers, with his crofs-
bow, and had time to mount his horfe
and return to Fez, where he was generoufly rewarded by his mafter. Another
kind of reward, however, followed, and
fuch as his crime deferved ; for the inhabitants of Morocco, who loved Abdulmomen, their former governor, having accufed the king, Muley Abdallah, of the
murder of this prince, he, to juftify himfelf, fent to Fez for the guilty Moor,
whom he dragged through the ftreets
without hearing him, that he might neither betray himfelf nor his fon.

The conduct of Muley Abdallah toward his brothers and nephews difgraced
him the more with his fubjects, becaufe he
had alienated their affections by his mode
of life. He wanted courage, and addicted
himfelf to drunkennefs and pleafures, regardlefs of all decorum ; he had, neverthelefs, fome good qualities, employed his
revenues to ufeful purpofes, built palaces,
added colleges to the mofques, and, in
1572, erected the caftle of Cape Aguer,

VOL. II.　　　　H　　　　having

having received information that Don Sebastian, king of Portugal, was equipping a fleet at Lisbon, that he might again possess himself of Santa Cruz and its road. Notwithstanding the dislike of his subjects, this prince, who had removed his brothers that he might indulge himself more licentiously in his pleasures, reigned seventeen years without suffering any revolution, and, dying in 1574, left his eldest son, Muley Mohamet, his successor.

Muley Mohamet, surnamed the negro, because he was the son of a negroess, had scarcely ascended the throne before, imitating the inhuman policy of his father, he dispatched two of his brothers, and imprisoned the third, that he might enjoy his power in tranquillity. This cruelty rendered him also odious to his subjects, and Muley Abdelmeleck, or Moluc, one of his uncles, profiting by this disposition, incited them to revolt, and dethroned him without difficulty.

I

Muley

Muley Mohamet, availing himself of the intelligence there was at that time between the Moors and the Portuguese, repaired to Lisbon to supplicate assistance from Don Sebastian, who was then assembling an army to invade Africa. In this army Muley Mohamet served, and convinced the king of Portugal that his presence was of great utility to his projects. The expedition of Don Sebastian, however, was unsuccessful; he was defeated and slain in the plains of Alcassar, and Muley Mohamet, who was then in his army, was drowned in crossing a river. Muley Abdelmeleck, who had usurped the crown, and was ill before the battle began, expired in his litter, in the very moment of victory; and thus do vast projects vanish in an instant.

Muley Achmet, brother of Abdelmeleck, after having won the battle, was proclaimed king of Fez by the army, and the governors of provinces and cities. His brothers were obliged by him to swear fidelity to his son, Muley Shek, and insure to him the succession. In 1594 this prince

made

made preparations for extending his dominions, when he was informed of the arrival of Muley Nacer, who had long remained in Spain, and who, depending on
promifed aid from Philip II., endeavoured
to incite a revolt in his own favour. Muley Achmet fent one of his fons with a
body of troops againft this ufurper, who,
after having been wounded in the battle,
was obliged to abandon his camp and baggage, and renounce his hopes.

Muley Achmet, beloved and refpected
by his people, was the laft defcendant of
the Sharifs, whofe reign was troubled
by no revolution. He died in 1603, and
left his ftates diftracted by factions, which
greatly increafed the regret felt for his
death.

The hiftory of Spain informs us that
Philip II. maintained a friendly corefpon-
dence with him, and even fent an ambaffador to his court, by whofe intervention
thofe Lords, who had been taken at the
battle of Alcaffar, were recovered from
flavery. Muley Achmet alfo fent the

body

body of the king, Don Sebaſtian, to Philip. From other Spaniſh writers we learn that Philip II. ſent painters to the king of Morocco, who generouſly rewarded them for their works [a]. Hence we may conclude that moſt of the paintings, to be found in the palaces of the Mooriſh kings, are probably the performances of Chriſtians.

After the death of Muley Achmet, Muley Sidan, the youngeſt of his ſons, being preſent with his father, was proclaimed ſucceſſor; but this proclamation did not prevent his three brothers from forming parties to maintain their claims, and, in leſs than two months, all the four were alternately maſters of the empire. In the different actions occaſioned by theſe revolutions, victory always declared for Muley Sidan: this prince having, at length, ſubjected Sallee, which, from its ſituation, gave a balance in favour of its poſſeſſor

---

[a] Viage d'Eſpana, de Don Ant. Pons. Tom. I. Lett. II.

throughout

throughout thefe difputes, remained victorious over his rivals.

His eldeft brother, Muley Shek, had re-
courfe to the king of Spain, Philip III.,
to obtain a fupply of money, and, in November 1610, put into the hands of this
fovereign the city of Laracha, of which he
was poffeffed, as a fecurity, both for his
friendfhip and the fum received. This aid,
however, did not prevent Muley Sidan
from ftill remaining fovereign of the empire.

The repofe of the monarch was difturbed by the Brebes, or inhabitants of the
mountains, near Morocco, who obliged
him to quit his capital, that he might free
himfelf from their inroads. Having found
means to divide thefe tribes, and fubject
them either by his arms or his negotiations, he peacefully paffed the remainder
of his reign, and died at Morocco in 1639,
leaving princes, as his fucceffors, who were
little qualified to govern. It appears that,
in 1622, this fovereign received an ambaffador from Holland, who was accompanied
by

by Golius, the difciple of Erpenius, and profeffor of the Arabic language. Muley Sidan was aftonifhed at the learning of Golius, who wrote Arabic perfectly, but who could not fpeak it with facility *.

· Muley Abdelmeleck, eldeft fon of Muley Sidan, fucceeded his father, and was the firft king of Morocco, who, beholding feveral fmall kingdoms united under his government, affumed the title of Emperor. At the commencement of his reign this prince affected to be religious, but, afterward, yielding to his character, he rendered himfelf fo hateful to the people, by his drunkennefs, cruelty, and a multitude of other vices, that the citizens of Fez called his brother, Muley Achmet, to the throne. The latter, having manifefted fimilar propenfities, was not lefs difagreeable to his fubjects, who perceived they were not bettered by the change.

The public difcontent incited new factions, and Muley El-Valid and Muley

* Bayle Dic. Hift. & Crit. mot Golius.

Semen

Semen both difputed for empire with their brother. But, neither of them infpiring fufficient confidence to raife up a powerful party, they were obliged to defift from their enterprize. After reigning four years, Muley Abdelmeleck, in 1635, was aſſaſſinated in his tent by a diſcontented flave, who, finding him in a ſtate of intoxication, fhot him with a piftol.

Muley Abdelmeleck being dead, Muley El-Valid, his brother, afcended the throne; this came the more unexpectedly becaufe he had been impriſoned by order of his deceafed brother, whofe intention it was to have put out his eyes as a punifhment for the rebellion he had raifed. Such are the fports of fortune. The reign of this prince was diftinguifhed by his mildnefs and affability, which obtained him the efteem and affection of his fubjects, reftlefs as they had been when fuffering under the cruelty of his predeceffors. El-Valid likewife gave proofs of a generous and great mind, by pardoning and releafing ftate prifoners, and by augmenting the pay of his troops.

His

His reign, however, was troubled by an insurrection, which his brother Semen, a restless and ambitious man, had incited, and which was promoted by an Alcaid, whom Muley El-Valid had released from prison. The sedition, however, was soon quelled by the defeat of the troops of Semen, who, together with the Alcaid, was taken; the latter was beheaded in reward for his ingratitude, and Muley Semen strangled; a rigorous judgment for Muley El-Valid, who, in the beginning of his reign, had shewn so much humanity and clemency. This severity, perhaps, contributed to over awe the turbulent, for his reign was no more troubled by rebellion, and he died a natural death, in 1647, after having reigned twelve years. M. Sanson, ambassador from France, who had met so many obstacles under the reign of Muley Abdelmeleck, obtained from Muley El-Valid the ransom of various Frenchmen, who had been held in captivity in the states of Morocco.

Muley Achmet Shek, the last of the sons of Muley Sidan, was elected Emperor,

peror, after the death of his brother, Muley
El-Valid. An enemy to labour, addicted
to pleasures, and ever immured with his
wives, this prince wholly neglected the government of his kingdom, commiting it to
the care of covetous ministers, who abused
their influence and authority.

The indolence and effeminacy in which
this monarch lived, and the oppressions of
the governors of provinces, and cities, excited murmurs among the people, and, at
length, universal discontent. The mountaineers, more restless and more resolute
than his other subjects, consulting their ferocity only, and profiting by the weak state
of the empire, besieged and took Morocco.
After subjecting the inhabitants to all the
calamities of war, they put Muley Achmet
to death, and proclaimed one of their
chiefs, named Crom-El-Hadgy; who had
no right of birth to the crown, and who
reigned some years without the love of
his people.

This prince inhumanly massacred all the
descendants of the Sharifs, who might
                                        any

any way have difturbed his reign, and, by his cruelty, revenged the blood and the rights of the houfe of Merini, whofe monarchs thefe fame Sharifs had deftroyed, after having ftripped them of wealth and fovereignty.

Raifed to the throne by a factious multitude, Crom-El-Hadgy was ever confidered as a ufurper. Having never been proclaimed by the people, his power was limited to the metropolis, and extended not to the remainder of the empire. His furname of Hadgy, which leads us to fuppofe he had been at Mecca, was, perhaps, the only circumftance that produced his election, becaufe of the veneration in which the Moors hold thofe who have performed this pilgrimage. Crowned by the caprice of fortune, this fovereign, having no ideas of government, defpifed the Moors fo much that he confided all his authority to a Jew, as alfo the collecting of his revenues. This Jew, that he might avenge thofe humiliations his nation fo often had fuffered, fometimes abufed his power ; his will was law, and, without his

his confent, nothing could be tranfacted. The conduct of Crom-El-Hadgy, and his misplaced confidence, fo offenfive to the prejudices of the Mahometans, made him the contempt of his fubjects; and, after having reigned about feven years, his end was tragical.

Having fallen in love with the daughter of Muley Labes, whofe brother he had murdered, he determined to make her his wife, notwithftanding the fecret averfion in which fhe held him; and this princefs, like another Judith, facrificed him to the public hatred, and her own refentment. After confenting to efpoufe him, fhe gave him wine to drink on the bridal day, in which was a foporific infufion, took this occafion to poniard him, and avenged, by the murder, the blood of her family, which had ftained the throne of the ufurper.

It appears probable that this princefs had a paffion for Muley Shek, the fon of Crom-El-Hadgy, fince fhe fent him intelligence of his father's death, and afterward

ward married him, which, at leaft, highly
diminifhed a her pretenfions to generofity,
or nobleners of mind. Muley Shék did
not long enjoy royalty, to which he had
not the leaft claim; he was dethréned by
a new revolution, that placed the reigning family on the throne of Morocco, as we
fhall fee in the following book.

BOOK.

BOOK IV.

Sharifs of the reigning family to the acceffion of
Sidy Mahomet — Reign of Muley Sharif, the
founder of this Dynafty — Reign of Muley Mahomet — Reign of Muley Arfhid — Reign of Muley Ifhmael — Reign of Muley Achmet Daiby —
Reign of Muley Abdallah.

CHAP. I.

*Muley Ali brought from Mecca ; held in
veneration, and called, by diftinction, Muley
. Sharif. Reigns peaceably.*

WHEN we attentively confider the
prefent fituation of Africa, and all the
changes that have happened on its northern
boundaries for a fucceffion of ages, we are
led to imagine it was deftined by Providence
ever to remain the theatre of great revolutions ; and thofe which have ravaged the
empire of Morocco, fince the introduction
of Mahometanifm, feem to have been ftill
more fermented by this religion.

After

After the Arabs had subdued the northern coast of Africa, we beheld Edris, the descendant of Mahomet, fly from Medina to its western boundaries, as to the further end of the world, to escape tyranny and persecution. The Moors, who inhabited the mountains where he fixed his abode, edified by his virtues, eagerly embraced his religion; and, respecting his birth, they still further claimed him as their sovereign. By some inexplicable contradiction, Edris, a humane and just prince, the enemy of wars and devastations, became the founder of an empire ever in commotion; and the first acts of a rustic, restless, and ferocious people, were homages paid to virtue.

Mahometanism, which, by the nature of its customs and institutions, must ever be most successful in hot climates, made such a rapid progress, in Africa, that it there invariably stamped the character of despotism, which was the basis on which it first rose, and which, prodigally bestowing on the sovereign unbounded authority, inspires only fear and despondency in the subject.
The

The Moors, more fufceptible of fanaticifm than any other people, becaufe they are more ignorant, and becaufe the heat of the climate more fuddenly inflames their imagination, prefently faw thofe different fects fprout up, that pride and fuperftition have multiplied, and that, fometimes under the veil of exceffive aufterity, at others affuming the mafk of indulgence and reformation, feduce the mind, over which they alternately domineer. Then is religion the cloak of ambitious conquerors, who impofe upon an ever fickle, turbulent, ignorant, and fanatical multitude. Thus has the northern part of Africa, the prey of credulity, oppreffion, and defpotifm, fucceffively groaned under an army of ufurpers, and changed the mafter almoft with the moment.

The Empire of Morocco, which, in the thirteenth century, under Jacob Almonfor, had acquired an extent of power fcarcely credible, loft this power with equal rapidity, becaufe that thofe paffions, which actuate kings, and raife infurrections among the people, neceffarily bring on the fall of empires, that only profper under the protection of certain and fixed laws, and want bafis and fupport where the government is arbitrary.

Having taken a retrofpect of this empire, overturned by a fucceffion of crimes, originating in the ambition of ufurpers and the reftleffnefs of the people, we fhall now fee it, under the reigning houfe, acquire a kind of confiftency by the aid of devaftation and ferocity, which ftill are much more proper to overthrow than to raife up empires; yet have not thefe violent concuffions fhaken the throne of Morocco; nay, its foundation feems to have been further fecured, in proportion as it has been cemented by blood. Equally the inftruments and the victims of tyranny, ever divided by prejudice and hatred, the Moors know not how to make one ftep toward liberty. Confirmed in their belief of irrevocable fate, which impofes upon and over-awes their minds, they only behold, in the will and caprice of a never-fatisfied defpot, the eternal decrees of that Divinity

I   whofe

whofe image and oracle he is fuppofed.
Thus, by prejudice confecrated to flavery,
thefe people never can change their condition, whatever may be the example of
revolution, the progrefs of reafon, or the
power of time. Reafon, indeed, can make
no progrefs in an arbitrary and ever abfolute government, where tyranny and violence prefent inceffant barriers. Their government refembles the brambles of their
deferts, which ftifle, in their firft growth,
thofe genial plants that only flourifh by
care and culture.

After the extinction of the family of the
Sharifs, who had dethroned the houfe of
Merini, and who afterward fell themfelves
the victims of their own ambition and
perfidy, there were feveral years of dearth
at Tafilet, and thefe countries underwent
all the horrors of famine. The Moors of
that province, who then made a pilgrimage
to Mecca, brought back a Sharif, named
Muley Ali, a defcendant of Mahomet,
born at the town of Yambo, near Medina,
whom the people treated with the utmoft

I 2   refpect

refpect. According to Moorifh tradition, the palm trees bore no fruit before the arrival of the Sharif. Seafons having returned to their former courfe, the harvefts became fo abundant that the fimple and fuperftitious people of the country attributed a change fo miraculous to the prefence and religion of the Sharif. All the Moors of the Morocco ftates, difcouraged as they had been by the devaftations which had afflicted the empire, and wondering at fo happy a return of plenty, eafily believed Providence had fent them Muley Ali, to bring their calamities to a period, and this prince, on whom they had beftowed the name of Muley Sharif, as a title of diftinction, was proclaimed king of Tafilet. The remaining provinces of the empire proclaimed him alfo, except Morocco, and its environs, which were then in the power of Crom-El-Hadgy.

The laft of the fons of Muley Sidan having been deftroyed by that ufurper, the princes of the ancient families, who had governed the empire, were all extinct.

1   · Muley

Muley Sharif, therefore, king of Tafilet, was, by the rights of birth, of religion, and the public wifh, the legitimate fovereign.

The Dynafty acquired the furname of Fileli, derived from Tafilet, from this prince, whofe pofterity was fo numerous that he is faid to have had eighty-four fons, and a ftill greater number of daughters; thofe of his male children, who have been moft known to hiftory, are Muley Mohamet, Muley-Quiber, Muley-Haran, Muley-Meheres, Muley-Arfhid, and Muley-Ifhmael-Semein. The firft and the two laft have reigned in fucceffion; the latter, fons of a Negroefs, diftinguifhed their reign by fome warlike actions, but much more by a continuation of tyranny and cruelty that degrade humanity.

The veneration in which the people held Muley Sharif was the moft certain pledge of their fidelity, and he had no need of the aid of armies to make his power refpected; he therefore remained at Ta-

I 3

filet,

filet, without fhewing himfelf throughout his empire; and the provinces, exhaufted by the divifions with which they had been fcourged during the preceding reigns, were governed with equity, by thofe rulers to whom they were affigned by the monarch.

We perceive, notwithftanding, that moft of the Shaiks of the tribes, diftributed among the mountains, filently profited by the troubles which divided the empire, the advantages of fituation, the propenfity of the People, the diftance of the Court, and the indolence of the Emperor, to extend their own authority. This authority would, at length, have become acknowledged, and hereditary in their families, had not the ambition and barbarous policy of Muley Arfhid ftopped its progrefs.

Muley Sharif reigned fome years, undifturbed by the wavering temper of his fubjects, to make whom happy he had dedicated his life. His death was highly regretted,

gretted, and Muley Mohamet, his eldeft fon, who gave hopes of virtues equal to his father's, afcended the throne, and was unanimoufly proclaimed.

I 4   CHAP.

C H A P. II.

Accession of Muley Mohamet. Rebellions and stratagems of Muley Arshid.

MULEY Mohamet peaceably reigned at Tafilet, after his father's example, when a rebellion was raised by his brother Muley Arshid. This prince, intelligent, but ambitious and bloody, knowing the inconstancy of the Moors, projected a division of the empire, and again exposed it to revolutions similar to those by which it had been so long distracted. Retiring toward Dara, he presently found himself at the head of a numerous party; but Muley Mohamet expeditiously followed him with a body of cavalry, seized and threw him into prison, and inflicted exemplary punishment on the rebels.

Muley

Muley Arſhid having eſcaped, and been retaken, he was guarded with greater precaution ; but, by the aid of a negro ſlave, appropriated to ſerve him, and who alone had the liberty of ſeeing him, he effected a breach through the tower, in which he was ſhut up, and, during night, was delivered from his dungeon. The faithful ſlave, after procuring liberty for his maſter, and having prepared horſes for flight, while ſtooping to put on the ſpurs of Muley Arſhid, was cloven down by the inhuman monſter who thought only of his own ſafety.

This black ingratitude, the reward of the labours and fidelity of a ſlave, was alſo the ſignal of new calamities, by which the empire was afflicted. Muley Arſhid haſtily fled to the mountains of Shavoya, eaſt of Temſena, and, without diſcovering himſelf, went and offered his ſervices to Sidi-Mahomet Ben-Buker, who there was abſolute, and held in veneration for his holineſs. Arſhid, diſſembling his birth and projects, ſerved as a common ſoldier,

and

and gained his master's confidence by his
zeal and fidelity.

Some Moors of Tafilet having disco-
vered this prince in the market, the sons
of Ben-Buker took offence, and Muley
Arshid thought proper to fly, went to Quiviana, in the mountains of Rif, and offered his services to Ali-Soliman. This
prince, who reigned as sovereign, remark-
ing his abilities, soon confided to him
the administration of his domains. Arshid
behaved with so much art, and dissimula-
tion, that he obtained the unlimited confidence, both of prince and people. Going
to visit the states dependent on Ali-Soliman, Arshid, under the pretence of restoring order, raised contributions there, took
possession of some castles, cut off the governors, whom he accused of malversation,
and distributed the wealth he had acquired
among his soldiers.

He next proceeded into a district, called
the mountain of the Jew, because a Jew
governed there, and because the Brebes,
whom he had subjected to his laws, respected

fpected him as their fovereign. After
fpreading terror through the country, he
maffacred the Jew as unworthy of com-
manding Mahometans, feized on his wealth,
and rewarded his troops.

Muley Arfhid, having gained the confidence of his foldiers, whofe numbers were
augmented by his courage, generofity, and
ambition, he declared to them whom he
was, no longer concealed the plan he had
formed, but promifed to fubdue the country, and give it a new Lord, if they would
fecond his endeavours, and partake his fortune and fate. The propofition was accepted by all the chiefs of the mountains,
who, induced by his valour and generofity,
fwore fidelity, and acknowledged him their
mafter.

The Shaik, Ali-Soliman, informed of
the perfidious conduct of Arfhid, marched
to give him battle, before his party was
further ftrengthened. The daring Arfhid
waited his approach, and fo artfully fpread
the rumour of his liberality that moft of
the foldiers of the Shaik abandoned him,
and

and deferted to Muley Arſhid. Soliman
was himſelf delivered up to this prince,
who brought him priſoner to Quiviana,
that he might get poſſeſſion of his treaſures, menacing him with death if he did
not diſcover them with the utmoſt exacti-
tude. Abandoned by his troops, and beholding himſelf in the power of a perfidious and furious man, Ali-Soliman did
not heſitate to give up all his concealed
riches; but Muley Arſhid, regardleſs of
his promiſe, put him to death, thus to
confirm his own authority.

The conqueror then called his ſoldiers,
and ſaid to them : "However precious
"theſe metals may be, a prince, who
"buries them in the earth, deſerves not to
"reign. Come, my friends, and divide
"with me what you have merited by
"your activity and affection." The gold
he kept, that it might be of after ſervice ;
but he gave all the ſilver to the officers,
that they might diſtribute it among the
ſoldiers.

The

The fame of Muley Arſhid was extended by this conduct, and was an irreſiſtible recommendation among the Mooriſh tribes. Covetous, poor, and rendered vile by oppreſſion, they forgot the perfidy of a traitor, who had robbed his benefactor of dominion, and afterward of life, remembering thoſe proofs of generoſity by which their avarice was provoked. Muley Mohamet, king of Tafilet, alarmed at this propenſity of the people, in his brother's favour, endeavoured to ſtop his progreſs, and marched with an intent to meet and give him battle. Their armies approached each other among the mountains; and that of Muley Mohamet, twice thrown in diſorder, was at laſt obliged to fly. Muley Arſhid continued the purſuit as far as Tafilet, where Muley Mohamet had ſhut himſelf up, and to which place the former laid ſiege. The king, intimidated by his brother's courage, and ſtill more by his ferocity, fell ill, and died, a few days after, in 1664.

CHAP.

C H A P. III.

Reign of Muley Arſhid ; his politic liberality ; conqueſts ; barbarities and accidental death.

THE city of Tafilet was ſoon taken, after the death of Muley Mohamet ; the face of the whole empire was changed, and Muley Arſhid made the neceſſary diſpoſitions to maintain his ſovereignty. He entered the province of Rif, which he poſſeſſed himſelf of, as likewiſe of the city of Teza, where he paſſed the winter. In the ſpring of 1665 he marched for Fez, which city, having taken by ſurprize, and ſending for the governor, after having obliged him by torments to declare where his wealth was concealed, put him to death. He attempted the ſame practice with the governor of New Fez, who, acquainted with

his

.his perfidy, chose rather to expire in torments than to discover where his treasures were concealed, haughtily telling him, he hoped they would become the instruments of destruction to him, and all his posterity.

All the Shaiks of the neighbouring districts, and the governors of cities, who, during the relaxation of government, had erected themselves into petty sovereigns, terrified by the rapid and bloody progress of Muley Arshid, hastened to render him homage, and offer him presents. The Alcaid Looeti, one of the number, had a beautiful daughter, whom Muley Arshid espoused; and the power she obtained over him gave her father, also, an ascendency over this prince, by which Looeti moderated the severity of his decrees.

Desiring to subdue the province of El-Garb, which extends along the western coast, from the mouth of the Strait to Mamora, the king, before he departed, sent for the richest tradesmen of Fez, and commanded each of them to build a house in

the

the new city, in which to lodge his foldiers ·
at his return.

His army now amounted to forty thoufand men, and he fubdued the people who
inhabited the eaftern part of the province
he had undertaken to conquer. The Alcaid Gailand, a courageous man, who governed in this country, made fruitlefs efforts to oppofe the victor ; abandoned by
his forces, he was conftrained to take refuge in Arzilla, whence he fled by fea to
Algiers, that he might efcape the wild fury
of this prince. The conqueft of El-Garb
induced the inhabitants of Sallee to make
their fubmiffion ; and, from this city, Muley Arfhid fent prefents to thofe Shaiks, of ·
the Shavoya mountains, by whom he was
known, that he might there obtain new
allies, infomuch that, in two campaigns,
Muley Arfhid was mafter of all the north
of the empire. He foon departed for the ·
mountains of Shavoya, fubduing on his
route the Shaiks of different tribes, and
feizing on their riches, which he divided
among his foldiers. He next invaded the
territories of Ben-Buker, under whom he
had

had served as a common soldier, and who waited for him with an army of mountaineers, intending to give him battle; but this Shaik, abandoned by his troops, was delivered up to Muley Arshid, who possessed himself of his treasures, and put him to death.

· After thus having crushed these small rising principalities, Muley Arshid passed the winter among the mountains, where he reinforced his army by a number of volunteers; he then began to march toward Morocco, in 1667, intending to dethrone Crom-El-Hadgy, who, about this time, had been poniarded by his wife, and had left his son, Muley Shaik, the heir of his usurped domains. The latter, intoxicated by his pleasures, troubled himself little concerning Muley Arshid, and did not think of defence till the conqueror was at the gates of his city; he then sallied out with some troops, little inured and ill disposed to war, and that, far from fighting in his defence, were each more eager than the other to desert to Muley Arshid, and acknowledge him their sovereign.

VOL. II.　　　　K　　　　Thus

Thus abandoned by his troops, Muley Shaik endeavoured to fly into the neighbouring mountains, but was taken and brought to Muley Arſhid, who had him dragged into the city on the fortieth day of his reign, tied to the tail of a mule. The city of Morocco was glad to ſubmit itſelf to Muley Arſhid, having for ſome time been under the government of uſurpers, without name, birth, or abilities; they even requeſted the body of Crom-El-Hadgy might be taken from the ſepulchre of their kings, which was granted; and this corpſe, with that of the Jew, who had commanded under him, and all his family, then living, were burnt, to ſtrike terror into the Jewiſh nation, and teach it no more to interfere in the principal adminiſtration of government.

No ſooner was Muley Arſhid maſter of Morocco, than this monarch, whom I ſhall hereafter call Emperor, his predeceſſors having aſſumed that title, received homage in the metropolis from all the neighbouring tribes. He afterward departed for the eaſtern ſide of Mount Atlas, the frontiers

I   of

of Tafilet, to fubjugate the inhabitants of that country. Terrified by the rapid fuccefs of his arms, thefe tribes eagerly haftened to pay him fubmiffion. He next marched toward Tarudant, where the people were equally ready to implore his clemency, and fwear fidelity.

Mafter of all the provinces of the empire, this monarch now returned to Morocco, where he made preparations for two new expeditions. The firft of thefe, intended againft Fez, he was himfelf to command, and the other to be fent againft the Shabanets, or Chabanets, who inhabited various vallies near Mount Atlas, his nephew, Muley Achmet, was to conduct.

It would be difficult at prefent to afcertain the origin of this tribe. From the moft ancient accounts, it appears they were the pofterity of more than forty thoufand flaves, male and female, who, during the reign of Jacob Almonfor, and before his time, had been tranfported from Spain to Africa, who had built the extenfive

K 2 walls

walls of Rabat, and had been employed in various works. To recompence the labour and fidelity of these slaves, Jacob Almonſor determined to grant them their liberty. The principal people of his court remonſtrated concerning the danger there would be in ſetting free ſo great a number of foreigners, who, having made a conqueſt of part of the country, might eaſily return, and vanquiſh the whole.

Jacob Almonſor had pledged his word for their freedom, and was determined to keep it; he therefore offered them the choice of the province they moſt would prefer for their abode; and this choice fell on a diſtrict among the mountains, which the Brebes were obliged to abandon. This emigration took place during the moon called Shaban; and, according to Moorish tradition, the people were for that reaſon called Shabanets.

For ſome generations the deſcendants of theſe ſlaves profeſſed the Chriſtian religion, which they gradually changed for Iſlamiſm, having no place of public worſhip,

ſhip, and becauſe that moſt of the men married Mahometan wives. This caſt long preſerved the reputation of valour, but, confounded with the neighbouring tribes, it has forgotten all remembrance of its origin, which, indeed, would be but a poor recommendation among the Moors, who are much more proud than is imagined of the antiquity and purity of their deſcent.

Muley Arſhid, arriving at Fez in the ſpring with four thouſand horſe, ſummoned, on his arrival, the tradeſmen, whom he had commanded to build houſes, or barracks, for his ſoldiers. This order they had neglecting to execute, truſting to the incertitude of human events, and not ſo ſuddenly expecting the return of their tyrant. He, enraged, commanded them to be tied to orange trees, and began to maſſacre them himſelf with his ſabre, when the Alcaid Looeli, his father-in-law, interceded in their behalf, obtained their pardon, and prevailed on the Emperor to be ſatisfied with a fine of thirty quintals

K 3 of

of filver, or upward of eight thoufand
pounds.

The widows of the tradefmen, who
had been killed, refufing to pay a part of
this contribution, Muley Arfhid obliged
them by torture, himfelf prefiding, a fpectator of their torments * ; he would even
have had them drowned in the river, after
having received their money, had not the
Alcaid Looeti obtained a revocation of this
order. What are kings, if monfters fo
execrable are worthy of the title !

During the time that Muley Arfhid was
thus employed at Fez, Muley Achmet, his
nephew, marched to fubject the Shabanets,
who, at firft, obtained fome trifling victories ; but the prince, having, at length,
been entirely fuccefsful, he compelled
them to render homage to Muley Arfhid.

---

* He had the deteftable barbarity to put the breafts of
thefe women between the lid of a coffer, and to get upon
it himfelf, to oblige them to give up their money.

No sooner did the Emperor hear of the refiftance thefe mountaineers made to his troops, than he departed from Fez to encounter them himfelf; and, although he learnt on his arrival at Morocco that they where fubjugated, he determined to proceed. To prove that he applauded their valour, he offered to entertain and treat thofe among them well who would ferve in his armies. This tribe, abounding with valiant men, beheld, with pleafure, the arrival of Muley Arfhid, whofe warlike deeds they refpected: the chiefs among them again paid homage to him perfonally, and a body of fix thoufand men followed his fortunes.

Inflated with profperity, and projecting the conqueft of Africa, Muley Arfhid entered with his army into the province of Hea; the inhabitants of which, animated by the firft efforts of the Shabanets, had refolved to difpute his paffage. Difcouraged, however, by the defeat and fubmiffion of thefe mountaineers, they went to meet him with rich prefents, and brought

'K 4
him

him their young virgins, as vaffals bring up to their lord their firft fruits.

Muley Arfhid received the deputation favourably, and, without abufing his power, fent the maidens back to their parents with prefents.

He then marched toward the Cape of Aguer, or Santa Cruz, where the inhabitants, difperfed among the mountains, determined to take up arms. The Emperor had then about feventy-five thoufand men under his command, all valiant, armed with fabres, maffy-clubs, and arrows. Irritated by the refiftance he found, he gave no quarter to thefe tribes, but feized on all their riches. His feverity fpread terror fo much, throughout the country, that the town of Santa Cruz made its fubmiffion, previous even to his arrival.

Ambition, and the fuccefs of his arms, determined Muley Arfhid to proceed to Illec, the capital town of the principality of Suz, at that time governed by Sidi Ali, a Maa Marabout, held in great veneration throughout thofe diftricts. The Emperor laid fiege to the town, which was unable to refift for want of provifions. Sidy Ali, preffed by the inhabitants, whofe inconftancy he dreaded, faw the town muft be taken; but, defirous of efcaping the cruelty of the conqueror, he and his whole family fled, by night, through a door in his garden, and efcaped, into the province of Sudan, lying to the north of Senegal, where he claimed an afylum, and the protection of the king.

After the departure of Sidy Ali, Illee having opened its gates to Muley Arfhid, he, covetous of glory, and emulous of furmounting difficulties, refolved to pafs into Sudan, and collected the neceffary provifions for the traverfing of the deferts, which feparated thefe countries.

When he came to the frontiers of the fouth with his cavalry, harraffed by fatigue, he found more than a hundred thoufand negroes in arms to difpute his paffage. Unwilling to rifk the chance of a battle a battle in a country fo barren, and where he had no place of retreat, he fent fome Alcaids to the king, to inform him he was not come to make war, but to requeft he would deliver into his hands the prince of Suz.

The king of Sudan replied, Sidy Ali had fled to him for refuge and protection, confequently he could not deliver him up without violating the laws of hofpitality, a crime impoffible for him to commit; that, having already been deprived of his ftates, it was but juft to preferve his life; and that he further defired, he, Muley Arfhid, would declare, whether he came as as a friend, or an enemy.

Remembering the hazard and peril of his prefent fituation, Muley Arfhid diffembled his anger; and, after having affured the king of Sudan his intentions were friendly, marched back toward his own country. On this occafion he prevailed on many negroes to follow him, to whom, treating them with generofity, he confided the guard of the palace.

Having

Having extended his empire from the Straits of Gibraltar to Cape Non, Muley Arſhid beheld himſelf the moſt puiſſant monarch of Africa; he was equally deſirous of being the moſt wealthy, and beſtowed all his attention on the amaſſing of riches. Detachments were ſent throughout the provinces to levy extraordinary contributions, with orders to pillage on the leaſt refuſal.

A Caſile, compoſed of ſeveral tribes, made ſome reſiſtance, and this emperor ſent a detachment thither, with a command to bring him the heads of the rebels. The news of this expedition having occaſioned the greateſt number to fly among the mountains, the old men, women, and children, only remained, who fell the miſerable victims of this abject, this abhorrent decree. Their heads ſent to Fez, and, expoſed round the walls of the city, ſpread terror throughout the empire.

To maſk his barbarity, under a pretence of paying ſome attention to juſtice, for deſpots, as well in Morocco as elſewhere,

think

think it neceffary thus to colour their capricious cruelties, this Emperor commanded
that thofe who robbed travellers, or granted
any afylum to thieves, fhould be fought
out, and their families exterminated; further ordering, that each province, and each
Douhar, fhould become refponfible for the
crimes committed within their diftrict,
that, by their watchfulnefs, crimes might
be prevented. This ordinance gave the
people impreffions fomewhat more favourable concerning their ferocious tyrant,
and was in itfelf good and ufeful; the
roads became fafe, and the country people
could go and come, without danger, to
their markets, where they might barter
their mutual products.

The law was favourable to the poor,
who were much the moft numerous; but
it alfo ferved to cloak the avidity of the
monarch, who, devoured by the thirft of
accumulating gold and filver, employed
every means his avarice could fuggeft to
ftrip the rich and great of their wealth,
and thus deprive them of the defire, or
the means, of infurrection. This maxim,

fo

fo proper in itfelf to exterminate nations, appears to have become a ftate fyftem in Morocco, and the devaftation of that empire demonftrates what are its wretched confequences.

No longer occupied by projected conquefts, Muley Arfhid commanded various caftles to be built in the provinces of his empire, thereby to give his power ftability, and prevent the effects of inconftancy among the people. The fmall fquare fort, which ftands alone at Rabat, was built for this intent.

The tyrant had now begun to indulge himfelf in eafe, when the fons of his brother Mahomet, king of Tafilet, who had taken refuge among the mountains, entered into a confpiracy there to revenge the death of their father, and to feize on the empire themfelves. They had gained over the governor of Old Fez, who had enjoyed their father's confidence, and him they informed by letter of the place where he was to meet and join their forces. This letter they confided to a renegado, re-

com-

commending him to kill the bearer, that they might be certain of not being difco-vered.

The renegado had fome fufpicions, and, inftead of taking the letter to the governor, went and prefented it to the Emperor, who generoufly rewarded his fidelity. The Emperor immediately went to the place appointed, that he might himfelf furprize his nephews; but, underftanding they were betrayed, they took to flight, and efcaped, though fired after by their purfuers; they, however, were overtaken and brought to their uncle, who fent them prifoners to the caftle of Teza, where he commanded them to be put to death.

Having gone into the province of Rif, in the begining of the year 1672, to amufe himfelf with hunting, Muley Arfhid was there informed, that his nephew, Muley Meheres, whom he had left viceroy at Mo-rocco, profiting by his abfence, had taken up arms. The young prince had confided in the Alcaid Abd-Elhafis Araze, whom the Emperor had appointed to watch over his conduct.

conduct. This governor betrayed him, and, that he might do so the more effectually, promised to second his projects.

. Muley Meheres proposed that he should go and seize on Saffi, whither he might transport his treasure, and take precautions for safety, in case of ill-success. Abd-Elhafis acquiesced in all the wishes of the prince, and departed sooner than was intended, under the pretext of furthering his designs, which, however, he took the best means to circumvent. After having required the Alcaids of Saffi, and the neighbouring towns, to be watchful for their safety, he repaired with all diligence to the Emperor, and informed him of what had passed.

Little suspicious of this, Muley Meheres departed, during night, for Saffi, where he expected he should meet the Alcaid Abd-Elhafis. Finding, on his arrival, that the town persisted in refusing to grant him admittance, the prince, seeing himself betrayed, took the road for Mazagan, to demand refuge from the Portuguese; but, being

being informed that the governor of Azamore was in arms to prevent his paſſage,
he fled toward Sallee that he might eſcape
to Mamora, which was under the dominion
of Spain. As he was croſſing the river
of Sallee he perceived he was known ; he,
therefore, took the road toward Fez, that
he might avoid raiſing any ſuſpicion. He
ſoon, however, ſaw he was followed by the
horſe of the Alcaid of Sallee, who had orders not to loſe ſight of him ; eſcape
was now become impoſſible, for, at three
quarters of a league from the river, and at
the entrance of the foreſt, he encountered
the army of the Emperor, who was returning from Rif, and marching in all haſte to-
word Saffi. Here, therefore, Muley Meheres was arreſted, and gave up his arms.
The Emperor, having his nephew in his
power, immediately marched to Morocco,
that he might prevent any inſurrection in
favour of this adventurous prince, who
was exceedingly beloved there by the people ; but the city having teſtified no inclination to revolt, Muley Arſhid, to recompence the fidelity of the officers, confirmed

firmed them in the places which had been bestowed on them by Muley Meheres.

The Emperor then commanded his nephew to come before him, reproached him for his disloyalty, but, attributing this to his youth and want of proper reflection, ordered him to repair to Tafilet, there to employ himself in the study of the Coran, and in gaining a more perfect knowledge of his duties, as well as in the means of rendering the enterprizes he should in future undertake more succefsful. The feast of sacrifices approached, and, that it might be celebrated with the greater magnificence, Muley Arshid sent for the governors of provinces and cities to be present, according to the custom of that court. On this occasion the Emperor, having drank excessively of wine, in company with some of his confidential friends, a custom to which he was much addicted, took the fancy of mounting his horse, to amuse himself after the manner of the Moors. After prancing about in the allies of his garden, he spurred him forward, as may be well suppofed, with too much ardour, and the horfe ran with him into an alley of orange trees, where he fractured his fkull, and died three days after, on the twenty feventh of March, 1672, in the forty-firft year of his age.

Of all the Emperors who had governed Morocco, Muley Arfhid was the firft who had demonftrated a character natively ferocious; his reign was fhort, but marked by a fucceffion of cruelties, the remembrance of which will not eafily be loft : he had fo far contracted cruelty, by habit, that it was even become one of his amufements.

An Alcaid, returning from a journey, vaunted of the fafety of the high roads throughout the empire, which was fo great that he had feen a fack of walnuts which nobody had taken away. " And " how didft thou know they were wal- " nuts?" faid the Emperor. " I touched " the fack with my foot," replied the Alcaid. " Sever that foot from his body," continued Muley Arfhid, " as a punifh- " ment for his curiofity."

I confine

I confine myfelf to this anecdote, un-willing to afflict the feelings of the humane, by here relating the extravagant and mad actions of a monfter. The relation of fuch events as influence the fate of nations, or the manners of men, are alone abfolutely neceffary to hiftory.

L 2   CHAP.

C H A P. IV.

Muley Ifhmael, equal in policy, and cruelty to, and more avaricious than, his predeceffors : embaffies, rebellions, and fieges, during his reign.

AFTER the death of Muley Arfhid, his brother, Muley Haran, in all diligence, began his journey toward Fez, that he might feize upon the public treafury as a certain means of fecuring empire to himfelf and foldiers for the defence of his power. Muley Ifhmael, however, who was at Teza, and to whom the news was brought by a meffenger on a dromedary *,

was

---

* A dromedary can travel fixty leagues in a day ; his motion is fo rapid that the rider is obliged to be girthed to the faddle, and to have a handkerchief before his mouth to break the current of the wind *.

* Reckoning the league at two miles and a half, and the day at twenty-four hours, this is ftill extraordinary travel

was already at Fez, and even proclaimed
Emperor before the arrival of his brother.
The latter, not daring to enter Fez, went
to Tafilet, there to aid his nephew, Muley
Achmet, with his advice, that he might
make himself master of that part of Morocco where he was beloved. Muley Haran, having formed a party in Tafilet, was
acknowledged king; and this was the first
division of the empire, after it had been
united under Muley Arshid, in consequence
of an unnatural mixture of valour, prudence, and blood-thirsty cruelties.

Muley Ishmael, who possessed the same
qualities, and still greater vices, than his
brother, Muley Arshid, was publicly acknowledged Emperor in the city of Fez.
The Alcaid Carra, governor of the city of

ling; yet M. Saint Olon, ambassador from Louis XIV. to
Muley Ishmael, says, the Moors assured him the Emperor's
uncle had travelled a hundred leagues in one day upon a dro-
dary; which account, however, he held to be exaggerated.
Perhaps it was upon this occasion that the uncle of Muley
Ishmael made such extraordinary haste. T.

St. Olon, Relation de l'Emp. de Mar. p. 24.

Morocco,

Morocco, devoted to Muley Achmet, caufed the gates of the palace, of which he was mafter, to be fhut, and proclaimed Achmet, king of Morocco, at the head of the troops that were under his command. He fent intelligence of his proceedings to the prince, preffing him to come and fecure his election by his prefence.

Muley Achmet immediately departed for Morocco, where he was received moft favourably; he was perfonally beloved, and had alfo married the daughter of Muley Labes, who was born in that city, and who therefore had a claim to the affection of its inhabitants.

Informed of what had happened at Morocco, Muley Ifhmael marched thither with his army in the fpring of 1673, before his nephew had had fufficient time to provide for his fecurity. After paffing the river of the negroes, Muley Ifhmael pitched his camp near the green mountain, to the eaft of the province of Duquella, where he learned that his nephew was encamped within a

league

league of the capital. Receiving advice of this, Muley Ifhmael ftruck his tents, and marched within a fmall diftance of his nephew, pofting himfelf in a vaft plain, where he immediately made preparation for battle.

The two armies did not long remain idle fpectators of each other; fortune, for a time, feemed indecifive; but victory, at length, declared itfelf in favour of Muley Ifhmael, who had the beft troops. Little accuflomed to gunpowder, the inhabitants of Morocco had retired toward their ramparts, there to wait the event of the battle. A profufion of duft, alfo in the plain, had occafioned fo much confufion that numerous foldiers perifhed in the canals, dug in the earth, of which they were not aware.

Muley Achmet difcovered much courage in this action, and was defirous of defying his uncle to fingle combat; but, having been wounded by a ball in the thigh, and in danger of being taken, he retired, for momentary refpite, to the palace of his brother, Muley Talbe; and, after there

L 4

having

having his wound dreſſed, he fled from the city to gain the mountain before the concluſion of the battle.

After Muley Iſhmael had made victory ſure, he entered the caſtle, where he imagined he ſhould have found his nephew : the governor, Carra, informed him, he was fled ; and this Emperor, with one ſtroke of his ſabre, ſevered the head of Carra from his body.

Some horſemen, who had gone in purſuit of Muley Achmet, took him, he being betrayed by the ſon of a Shaik, to whom he had fled for aſylum. Aſhamed of his perfidy, the father purſued the horſemen with a detachment, and once more recovered the young prince, who immediately fled to Tafilet.

We behold with veneration, that, in climates like theſe, deſtined to ſlavery, there are mountains which ſerve as barriers to independency, and people, though ferocious and uncultivated, whoſe fidelity is unſhaken toward the wretched fugitives whom they protect.

Muley

Muley Ifhmael remained fometime at
Morocco to receive homage from the
neighbouring tribes and provinces, and
then made preparations to march into the
north of his empire. Not treating his
foldiers with the fame generofity as Muley
Arfhid had done, they at firft difcovered
marks of difcontent with the monarch's
conduct. The city of Fez, informed of
the fecret difpofition of the foldiers, entered into a confpiracy, the members of
which fent a deputation to Tafilet, to defire Muley Achmet would come and put
himfelf at their head.

The city of Teza fubmitted to this
prince, and the troops, that had partook
the dangers and difficulties of Muley Ifhmael, retired, and deferted from his ftandard in open day. All the provinces were
eager to receive Muley Achmet wherever
he approached. The Alcaid Gayland, who
had fled from Arzilla under Muley Arfhid,
informed of thefe changes and troubles,
folicited and obtained aid from the Algerines to recover his property and his government,

vernment, in which he was prefently re-
inftated at the head of an army.

The old and new cities of Fez, divided
in their inclinations and interefts, daily
combated each other, the old in behalf of
Muley Achmet, the new for Muley Ifhmael ; but, as the latter had the beft general, it had alfo the moft influence among
the neighbouring tribes.

To prevent the mifchiefs that muft refult from the defection of the provinces,
Muley Ifhmael, who had come before
Teza, thought proper to raife the fiege,
and march with twelve thoufand men, the
whole of his remaining forces, to give battle to the Alcaid Gayland, who had encamped near Alcaffar. The Emperor attacked this brave general with fo much intrepidity that he put his forces to flight.
Gayland, notwithftanding the rout of his
army, fought like a man in defpair ; he had
four horfes killed under him, and, having
received a ball in his body, he fell, at
length, the victim of numbers, and his

2   head,

head, carried at the end of a lance, was the most important trophy of victory.

The defeat of this general intimidated the insurgents, who thought proper to submit, beholding fortune declare itself so decidedly for Muley Ishmael. The conqueror pardoned the city of Alcaffar; and, after establishing peace in the province of Garb, he marched toward Old Fez, endeavouring, by promises, threats, and every means which policy could suggest, to gain over the inhabitants. Embarraffed and undecided how to act, the citizens affembled in the mofque, where, following the counfel, and affifted by the good offices of Sidi Abdelcader Feffi, a perfon held in veneration, and whom they fuppofed could penetrate the fecrets of futurity, they refolved to implore the clemency of Muley Ifhmael. Neither, however, confiding in the faith of this Emperor, nor in all the promifes he gave, they demanded that he should folemnly make oath on the body of his brother, which had been tranfported from Morocco to Fez, there to be entombed.

Muley

Muley Ifhmael having concurred with every requifition of the citizens, the deputies repaired to his palace, where, proftrating themfelves to the earth, they fupplicated pardon for the paft. The Emperor raifed, embraced them all, and, after hearing every thing Sidi Abdelcader Fefli had to fay, he took him by the hand, proceeded with him to the fepulchre of his brother, and there folemnly fwore peace, according to the conditions demanded by the deputies : the joyful people again returned to caft themfelves at the feet of the monarch, and thanked him anew ; after which, each man went quietly back to his houfe.

Muley Ifhmael took advantage of this momentary fecurity, cunningly, and without tumult, to fend foldiers into the houfes of the city, and feize on the arms of the inhabitants. This was done with fo much fecrefy, and dexterity, that no individual fufpected what had happened to his nextdoor neighbour. The Emperor remained two months longer at Fez, where he diftributed money among the troops, and thus gained their affection.

In

In the beginning of 1674 Muley Ifhmael went to encounter his nephew, Muley
Achmet, who was encamped at no great
diftance from Fez. Being come in fight
of each other, the armies were obliged to
remain inactive for fome time, becaufe of
the rains that fell; each party likewife
hoped to vanquifh the other by ftratagem.
This fufpence was favourable to Muley
Ifhmael, who beheld a part of his nephew's troops, difcouraged by the ill-
fortune of the latter, defert to his army.
Muley Achmet, at length, retreated, and
took refuge in the province of Dara, there
to wait a more fovourable opportunity of
once more appearing in arms.

Muley Ifhmael, having returned to Fez,
diftributed money among his foldiers, and
marched toward the fouthern provinces,
there to re-eftablifh tranquillity, and relieve the city of Morocco, which was all
but befieged by the mountaineers. The latter, informed of the approach of the Emperor, retired to their mountains, and the
monarch continued his march to Morocco,

rocco, where he was received with demonftrations of joy.

After a temporary repofe, Muley Ifhmael
proceeded to the province of Hea, where
he levied heavy contributions. He next
turned his march toward Mount Atlas,
fubjected the Shabanets, and put numbers
of them to death by torture. He thence
departed into the province 'of Shavoya,
where the people obftinately refufed to pay
tribute. Thefe mountaineers, intrenched
in their vallies, and behind trees that they
had felled, rendered all the efforts of Muley
Ifhmael for a time fruitlefs ; at length, one
of his generals marching round the mountain with four thoufand horfe to put them
between two fires, they, feeing themfelves
thus furrounded, took to flight, and abandoned their wives and children, who were
put to the fword ; the plunder, which was
very confiderable, was diftributed among
the foldiers.

After this expedition, which, in its cir-
cumftances, greatly refembled thofe of
Muley Arfhid, Muley Ifhmael returned to
Fez;

Fez, where he exacted a contribution from the inhabitants of fifty quintals of silver, which he, as a favour, reduced to thirty-three, amounting to two hundred thousand livres (between eight and nine thousand pounds.)

The custom of paying contributions by a determinate weight of silver is very ancient, as we read in Sallust. When Jugurtha, king of Numidia, intreated clemency from Rome, Metellus, who commanded in Africa, first provisionally exacted that he should pay the Romans two hundred thousand pounds weight of silver. The quintal of silver in Morocco, as now understood, is a stated sum of a thousand ducats, amounting to six thousand six hundred livres, although a quintal of coined silver is equal to more than ten thousand livres.

In 1675 an ambassador arrived at the court of Muley Ishmael, from England, who came to demand peace, and who, among his presents, had brought some Moors who had been enslaved. The Emperor,

peror, agreeably to the usual mode and expressions of the court of Morocco, answered, he would act according to his request, and that he should return with satisfaction. At the very moment when the treaty was to be concluded, a Marabout, all in rags, but one of those who are saints by trade, approached the king, and told him, that the Prophet had appeared to him the night before, and had commanded him to inform the Emperor, Mahomet would aid him to vanquish his enemies, if he would not make peace with the English.

The king, pretending to venerate these reveries, kissed the dirty head of the Moor, and informed the ambassador, he was exceedingly sorry he could not make peace with him, for that he durst not incur the wrath of the Prophet. This anecdote perfectly depicts the conduct and instability of the court of Morocco, where the despot never wants a specious pretext to act according to his will, or an excuse for neglecting what he ought to perform, and that which he may have most solemnly promised.

In

In the fame year the feeds of infurrection again began to fprout, in the fouthern
part of the empire. Muley Achmet, for
whom the people ftill had fome predilection, had a momentary hope of afcending
the throne. The Moors of Tarudant, and
fome tribes of mountaineers, fent him their
deputies, fwore obedience, and offered to
combat under him as their leader.

Confiding in this return of profperity,
the prince expedited a courier to the
princefs, his wife, who was at Morocco,
to inform her of what had paffed, and induce her to procure him partifans in the capital. This princefs, by her artful and
kind behaviour to thofe women who vifited her, fo well difpofed the minds of the
citizens, in her hufband's favour, that they
promifed to receive him into the city, and
proclaim him Emperor. Muley Achmet,
pre-informed of thefe events, prefented,
himfelf before Morocco ; the great were all
in his intereft, and the common people, impatient under the oppreffions of their then
governor, were ftill more defirous of this

change. To prevent any tumult which might refult from public proclamation, the night prayer was called on the towers of the mofques, and heaven invoked for the prefervation of Muley Achmet; this occafioned it to be fuppofed that the prince was already in the city, and all infurrection was thereby impeded. Muley Achmet entered in reality, followed by a numerous train; and the Alcaid, who governed in the name of Muley Ifhmael, was obliged to retire.

Muley Ifhmael was at this time proceeding toward Sallee, when he heard of the admiffion of Muley Achmet into Morocco. He fent his general, Meffaoot Gerari, with four thoufand horfe and five hundred foot, whom he had felected at Sallee, to threaten the deftruction of their families if they failed in their duty, and waited himfelf for the remainder of his army from Fez. Meffaoot Gerari paffed the river of the negroes with little refiftance. Muley Achmet, who had only collected a few troops to oppofe him on his paffage, had, with the remainder, lain in ambufcade, and

and fell fo opportunely on the van of the forces of Meſſaoot that he totally defeated the general, and obliged him to repaſs the river in diforder. Muley Achmet gave a favourable reception to the vanquiſhed, and prevailed on many of them to enter into his fervice.

Hearing of the defeat of his general, the Emperor began his march, to come in perfon and attack his nephew. By the treachery of one of his generals, Muley Achmet was perfuaded to return to Morocco, and not march and give battle; it was urged this would but expofe him to the hazard of a defeat, in combating an army which would deftroy itfelf. The army of Muley Iſhmael, in effect, fuffered greatly for want of fubſiſtence, the provinces having been laid defolate; and almoſt rendered defert by the late fucceffion of civil wars. The Emperor approached but flowly toward Morocco, having been informed by the general, who was in his intereft, that his army was inferior to that of his nephew.

Nor

Nor was this incertitude the only difficulty Muley Ifhmael had to encounter during the campaign. The comparifon
which his troops drew, between the character of himfelf and that of his nephew,
was fo highly to the favour of the latter,
that a confpiracy was formed in his camp ;
from the confequences of which the Emperor efcaped almoft by miracle. The
principal Alcaids, fecretly inclined to favour Muley Achmet, entered into a plot to
affaffinate the monarch, who even was
flightly wounded in the arm by the ball of
a mufket, which one of the confpirators
fired. The guilty, however, were feized,
put to death, and their effects confifcated
by the Emperor. A few of them only efcaped, who entered into the fervice of
Muley Achmet.

The treachery of the general of Muley
Achmet having been at this time difcovered, by the intelligence the fugitives
brought, and various intercepted meffages,
he was put to death, and his body, after
being dragged through the city, was denied
the rites of fepulture.,

Muley Ifhmael, unable to meet his nephew with equal forces, determined to
march befide Mount Atlas, and there endeavoured to gain over fome tribes to his
party. He paffed thence toward Santa
Cruz, which place had put itfelf under the
government of Muley Achmet. Not
daring to entangle himfelf among the
mountains, he could only fend letters,
hoping, by gentlenefs and promifes, to
regain the city.

The inhabitants of Santa Cruz, who
were capable of felf-defence, and who ab-
horred Muley Ifhmael for his various cruelties, returned his letters unanfwered, and
even commanded the meffengers to inform
him of the imprecations they uttered on
his head. Obliged to diffemble his refentment, the Emperor retreated, again marching befide the mountains, to wait fome fit
opportunity of furprizing the enemy.

His march was attended with unexpected
fuccefs; his nephew, having fuppofed
him at the diftance of feven days journey
from Morocco, had fent a part of his

M 3 forces,

forces, confifting of hufbandmen, to ga-
ther in the harveft, and remained only with
a few foldiers. Muley Ifhmael, informed
of this, fuddenly advanced, and came and
pitched his camp within a day's march of
Morocco. Muley Achmet haftily affembled the hufbandmen of the environs, and,
finding himfelf at the head of twenty-eight
thoufand men, pitched his camp without
the walls of the city.

Muley Ifhmael approached the camp of
his nephew, where he two days remained,
obferving the enemy's motions, hoping that
the foldiers of Muley Achmet would defert, as the intelligence of fome fugitives
had led him to fuppofe. Defirous of
coming to action, Muley Achmet made a
motion with his army, and Muley Ifhmael
then began the attack. The nephew, who
had made this manœuvre purpofely to
bring on a battle, fought with fo much valour that he routed the forces of Muley
Ifhmael, who loft more than three thoufand
men.

Muley

Muley Achmet, now mafter of the field of battle, had not the prudence to profit by victory; inftead of purfuing the retreating enemy, his army was employed in rejoicings, which gave Muley Ifhmael time to rally his troops, and come to a fecond action, in which victory declared in his favour. The forces of his nephew, who little expected again to be attacked fo fuddenly, were entirely routed, and the prince, obliged to re-enter Morocco, precipitately abandoned a part of his army, which miferably perifhed.

Muley Ifhmael then thought proper to blockade the capital, but the fallies which Muley Achmet occafionally made obliged him not to approach too near; a greater misfortune for him ftill was that, his army not being fufficiently numerous totally to circumvent the city, it received fupplies with facility, while Muley Ifhmael was himfelf in want, becaufe of the deteftation in which he was held by the neighbouring people.

Wearied

Wearied by the length of the fiege, Muley Ifhmael made propofitions of peace to his nephew, offering him the vice royalty of Morocco in perpetuity; but the youthful prince, full of courage, proud of paft fuccefs, and ftill prouder of the fidelity of his foldiers, haughtily anfwered, that he who thrice had been a king never fhould confent to become a fubject, and that it would be his glory to defend fovereignty by feats of arms.

Muley Ifhmael next propofed an interview with him in a neighbouring fanctuary, whither each of them was to repair, accompanied by ten perfons. Muley Achmet confented, and was the firft at the appointed hofpitium. Muley Ifhmael came, but with perfidious intents; he had commanded a detachment of cavalry to come to his aid, and carry off his nephew.

The interview began by mutual compliments. Muley Ifhmael purpofely endeavoured to lengthen the conference, that he might obtain time for the arrival of his
horfe;

horfe ; but one of the attendants of Muley Achmet, who was upon the watch,
perceiving a cloud of duft at a diftance, related his fufpicions to his mafter, and the
young prince accordingly mounted his
horfe, and reproached his uncle with
cowardice and treachery. Lefs irritated
by this juft obloquy than by the failure of the plot he had contrived, Muley
Ifhmael returned to his camp, where he
vented his wrath againft the foldiers ; a
great number of whom forfook him, and
went over to Muley Achmet.

Muley Ifhmael attempted once more to
cut fhort this protracted fiege, by keeping fpies in the city of Morocco, and
making preparations to fcale the city walls
with a fmall detachment, which was to render itfelf mafter of one of the gates.
The project, however, failed ; fome of the
moft determined affailants arrived fafely on
the walls ; but, having been there encountered by the cuftomary patrole, and unable to defcend, becaufe that the fcaling lad-
ders were taken away, they were cut in
pieces.

Muley

Muley Achmet profited by this leſſon, and reſolved to employ none but thoſe ſoldiers of whoſe fidelity he was well aſſured, in guarding the out-works. He alſo forbade the inhabitants to aſſemble, and cut off a number of the Sharifs who were in the city, and who had acted as ſpies for Muley Iſhmael.

·The beſieged continued to make ſome ſallies, which equally enfeebled both parties. Muley Achmet would himſelf have been taken by the generals of his uncle, had they not been moſt fortunately killed by the cannon of the city, at the very moment when it was impoſſible he ſhould have eſcaped. Muley Iſhmael loſt on this occaſion his general, Meſlaoot Gerari, and a confidential Alcaid.

To the length of this ſiege, and the incertitude of ſucceſs, was added a ſtill greater cauſe of vexation; the Emperor had no means of gratifying his troops, that, for ſometime paſt, had received no pay. To extricate himſelf from this difficulty, in 1677, he invited the Shaik Sidi Semagh, Alcaid of the mountains of Tedla, to come

2   and

and pay him a visit; the monarch made
him eat with himself, flattered, caressed
him, gave him hopes of a still better government, and intreated he would lend
him a sum to pay his forces.

Vain of the distinguished manner in
which he was treated, and the benevolent
intentions of the Emperor, the Shaik sent to
his government, and ordered a present of six
hundred negroes, of both sexes, eight hundred horses, a thousand camels, four hundred
mules and twenty-five quintals of silver,
amounting to a hundred and sixty thousand
livres *, (or upward of six thousand six
hundred pounds), which he intreated the
monarch would accept. Muley Ishmael was
astonished at the magnificence of the gift;
it led him to suppose that this Shaik was still
possessed of greater wealth, and, listening

---

* Twenty-five quintals of silver, according to the
former and following estimates of the author, are but a hundred thousand livres; the sum of sixty thousand livres,
therefore, is either appropriated to the remainder of the
present to which it is apparently inadequate, or there is an
error of the press. T.

only

only to his avidity, he arrested him, under the pretence that he intended to revolt, and six months after had him beheaded, having first seized on all his possessions, which, indeed, was the only crime of which he could be accused.

Other Shaiks, coming likewise to visit Muley Ishmael with very considerable presents, met a like favourable reception; but, terrified by the capricious conduct of the Emperor toward the Shaik of Tedla, they knew not how to interpret all the politeness he testified; a thousand times they reiterated their protestations of fidelity, which served but to discover the secret dread by which they were tormented. Artful and treacherous in his nature, Muley Ishmael turned this embarrassment, which the Shaiks, by their conduct, made visible, to his own profit, and exacted from them a hundred and fifty quintals of silver, or a million of livres (upward of forty-one thousand pounds), a number of sheep, oxen, horses, camels, and a thousand negroes, of both sexes. The governors did not fail to raise
this

this contribution, and efteemed themfelves happy in having efcaped fo well.

Similar extortions, and certain homages, which were voluntarily paid, by fome tribes, to the Emperor, enabled him to maintain his army before Morocco, without, however, empowering him to take the city. Muley Achmet, on the contrary, blockaded as he was, found himfelf expofed to the want of fuccour, when a happy incident relieved them both from their perplexity.

Muley Haran, king of Tafilet; the brother of Muley Ifhmael, uncle and father-in-law to Muley Achmet, beheld with regret thefe two princes at war with each other, and determined to repair to Morocco, in the hope of being able once more to eftablifh concord. This Sharif was exceedingly well received by Muley Ifhmael, whom he promifed, a few days after, to enter the city of Morocco, which he accordingly did, and where Muley Achmet received him with all kindnefs.

Muley

Muley Haran took infinite trouble to pacify his brother and nephew, and, by his repeated efforts with them individually, he, at length, accomplished his wished-for purpose; a treaty was concluded, in which it was stipulated that Muley Achmet should preserve the title of king, but retire to Dara, the sovereignty of which he should possess, that the soldiers attached to this prince should be permitted to leave Morocco, and follow him with arms and baggage, and that Muley Ishmael should pardon the city of Morocco, with each and all of its inhabitants, without entering into any enquiries concerning the origin of, or persons concerned in, this war; to which were added, other articles of reciprocal security.

Muley Achmet, not having confulted the citizens of Morocco concerning this treaty, left the place by night, with all his effects and equipage, and accompanied by the most faithful of his troops, under the pretence of going on fome secret expedition.

Informed

Informed on the morrow of the peace
concluded between Muley Ifhmael and his
nephew, the inhabitants of Morocco were
in the utmoft alarm ; the Talbes were de-
puted by the city, followed by all the children, and preceded by white flags, to implore mercy from the Emperor, who apparently granted them pardon.

The Emperor entered the city, in company with his brother Muley Haran ; after
which he vifited the caftle, and there, perceiving that the magazine fcarcely contained provifions fufficient for a week, he
tore his beard up by the roots in his rage,
accufed Muley Haran, his brother, of treachery, caufed him to be feized in his camp,
and fent one of his generals with a large
detachment to deprive him of his kingdom
of Tafilet. He afterward fuffered his troops
to enter the city, permitted them to pillage,
and commit all kinds of licentioufnefs,
and perfonally practifed every violence,
which his own barbarity could infpire,
againft the principal inhabitants, without
refpect to his word, his treaty, or the faith
of

of that capitulation, on which the city had been yielded.

The actions of Muley Ifhmael can only be recollected with horror; his art, his cunning, his falfehood, his contradictions, and all the defpicable means he employed to accomplifh his defires, betokened a mean foul, incapable of elevation, and by nature ignoble.

Scarcely had he reduced Morocco before he received advice of an infurrection, which had fuddenly broken out in the province of Shavoya, and the neighbourhood of Mequinez. The arrival of Mahomet El-Hadgy-Ben-Abdallah, one of the fons of the Alcaid Ben-Buker, who governed this country during the reign of Muley Arfhid, gave occafion to this revolt. The Shaik, after making a long abode at Mecca, had journied to Conftantinople, there to folicit protection from the Grand Signior, who, accordingly, had commanded the divan of Algiers to grant him fuccours.

Mahomet

Mahomet El-Hadgy was received in his domains with tranſports of joy; ſo great was the degree of reſpect that he acquired, among the tribes ſcattered over the mountains, that Muley Iſhmael, conceiving the danger to be conſiderable, ſent various detachments, firſt, and afterward marched himſelf, with the remainder of his army. Mahomet El-Hadgy, having more than ſixty thouſand men under his command, little, it is true, inured to war, made the neceſſary diſpoſitions to encounter Muley Iſhmael, who was marching to give him battle.

Arrived at the foot of the mountain with ſome artillery, the Emperor ſo diſpoſed his cavalry that it might attack the enemy when retreating. His troops received the diſcharge of muſketry, arrows, and ſlings, of this ill-diſciplined army; to which Muley Iſhmael replied by an exploſion from a battery of ten cannon, loaded with balls, which made the inſurgents give ground; the cavalry had time to eſcape, but the infantry, being ſurrounded, was moſt of it put to the

` ſword;

fword ; the Emperor purfued the cavalry
with a detachment for three days, and put all
to death who fell into his power. ·

On his return to the camp, he fell fword
in hand upon the women and children, and
fent ten thoufand heads to Fez and Morocco
to be fixed upon the walls of thofe cities,
thereby to announce his victory, and fpread
terror throughout the whole empire.

Having thus terminated, by events as
fortunate as they were inhuman and deteftable, a war, which had endured three
years, Muley Ifhmael repaired to Mequinez, there to enjoy repofe. During his
abfence, the vaft palace he had begun had
been finifhed, in which he difplayed the utmoft magnificence. On his entrance into
this palace, he received vifits from all the
grandees of his kingdom, who eagerly
came to make him rich prefents.

In full enjoyment, at length, of all the
fweets of eafe, and voluptuoufnefs of vice,
the Emperor indulged himfelf in the native
affections of his temperament, and the im-

I   pulfe

pulfe of his character. That he might add
to the variety of his pleafures, he daily
augmented the number of his concubines;
he kept a nurfery of flaves, ever agitated
by fear, and whom he ill-treated, or cut off,
on the flighteft pretext. The domeftics of
his palace, and thofe Chriftian flaves whom
the fate of arms delivered over to the
power of his Corfairs, underwent a fimilar
treatment.

Wholly regardlefs of the lives of men,
this Emperor made it his paftime to affaffinate them with his own hand. The days
fet apart for prayer were generally dedicated by him to thefe maffacres, and
thus did he eftimate his facrilegious devotion by the number of his murders.

Turn we our eyes from acts fo horrid,
at which nature fhudders; the relation of
them is to be found in fo many books that
it would be fuperfluous, here, to add new
teftimonies of the barbarities of tyranny
and defpotifm.

Afflicted

Afflicted as it had been by a succession of devastations, the empire of Morocco, in 1678, had still new to encounter; the plague, which had been introduced by the communication between Algiers and Tetuan, made dreadful ravages; there are narratives that say this contagion swept away more than four million of people from the empire, which, to me, appears, indeed, very extraordinary. This dreadful scourge of man, the sacrifices which Muley Arshid and Muley Ishmael made to their ambition, their avarice, and wild ferocity, the revolutions which succeeded under Muley Abdallah, and the various other calamities which, beneath a government so arbitrary, continue to destroy the human race, are so many physical and moral causes that account for the present depopulation of the empire.

Notwithstanding the progress of the contagion, which spread still more fatally in the northern parts, the Alcaids of the environs of Tangiers made various attempts on that town, which, at that time, was under the dominion of England. The Alcaid of Alcassar, Amar-Hadoo, in the month of

2   March,

March, made himſelf maſter of two ſmall
advanced forts, in which he ſurprized
twenty ſoldiers, and ſeized a ſingle braſs
cannon, on which was the arms of Portugal.

Conducted to Mequinez with much
pomp, and diſplayed as a trophy, Muley
Iſhmael himſelf left the city, attended by
a numerous train, to go and receive this
cannon. Thrice he proſtrated himſelf to
earth, thanking God for the firſt victory he
had gained over the Chriſtians. The Alcaid, Amar-Hadoo, was made viceroy of
the province of Garb.

This ſame year the Emperor determined
to leave Mequinez ; the plague committed
its ravages in the environs of the city, and
he himſelf was inwardly devoured by that
ſpirit of inquietude which was irreconcil-
able to ſo long a repoſe. He went to paſs
the hot ſeaſon among the mountains, in the
neighbourhood of Atlas, on the banks of
the Mulluvia, whence he ſent to demand
contributions from the neighbouring Brebes.
Theſe mountaineers, favoured as they were

by

by situation, refused to obey the commands of the Emperor; and he, finding himself unable to subject them by force of arms, dissembled his resentment, and thought proper to rest satisfied with such tribute as they should think proper to pay.

About this time there was an insurrection at Tafilet, which was raised by Muley Haran, the brother of the Emperor, whom he had stripped of sovereign power. Muley Ishmael, having repaired thither, routed the insurgents, and restored tranquillity to that part of his empire. Toward the end of the year, leaving Tafilet, he marched beside Mount Atlas to exact contributions from the Brebes, who were dispersed among the mountains. The tribes that were unable to oppose him by force of arms submitted, and paid what he required; but those that, by their situation, were able to resist him, opposed his will with so much resolution that the Emperor was, not only obliged to renounce his enterprize, but, endeavour to make them his friends, promising to leave them in tranquillity.

This

This folemn promife was guaranteed by
the facrifice of a camel, flain at the foot of
the mountain, as a pledge of the faith of
Muley Ifhmael. Thus fecured, the chiefs
left their mountains to falute the Emperor,
and offer him their prefents; and they, alfo,
in turn, received prefents on his part. Thefe
people hold fuch kind of facrifices in fo
much reverence that it is the atteftation
of mutual confidence, which is employed as
a means to calm the anger of the monarch;
or make peace, when any caufe of rancour
exifts among themfelves.

Although it is cuftomary among the
Moors to offer up facrifices to God, in gratitude for favours beftowed, and afterward to
diftribute the animals thus facrificed among
the poor, I do not think fuch oblations
ought to be confounded with the facrifice
performed on this occafion by Muley Ifhmael, and which often are offered up by the
different Moorifh tribes to calm or difpel
their inteftine quarrels. Such facrifices
fhould, I apprehend, be confidered as folemn
vows, which are not to be violated: this is
a cuftom made facred by ages, known in

times more remote than the birth of Mahometanifm, and, perhaps, peculiar to the
nations of Africa. From Livy we learn
that Hannibal, on the eve of giving battle
to Scipio, on the banks of the Po, after
making many promifes to the foldiers of
his army, to encourage them to fight valoroufly, took a lamb, and intreated Jupiter
and the heavenly deities, that, fhould he
break his promife, he might himfelf perifh,
as that lamb was about to perifh. The
foldiers, adds the hiftorian, received the promifed hope, as if it had been fent from the
Gods themfelves *.

The valour with which thefe mountaineers had firft refifted Muley Ifhmael infpired all the people of the neighbourhood
with courage, which, however, could not
make him defift. Impelled by the hope of
booty, he rafhly entered among the mountains, without fufficiently forefeeing all the
dangers of the enterprize. Endeavouring
to terrify thefe Brebes, who lived in brutal

* Liv. lib. XXI.

ignorance,

ignorance, he threatened he would give them to the Chriſtians to eat alive, of whom they had formed fanciful and monſtrous pictures; but this terror had little effect, when they beheld, as they themſelves ſaid, that a Chriſtian had the head, the body, the arms, and the legs, of a man.

The army of the Emperor was detained among the mountains by ſnow, which had cloſed up the roads, and might have expoſed it to periſh with famine. However, he opened himſelf paſſages among theſe precipices, and abandoned his camp to a detachment, which, that it might not miſerably periſh with cold and hunger, afterward abandoned it alſo. In this campaign, Muley Iſhmael loſt about three thouſand tents, the wealth that he had amaſſed, and a part of his army, the rear guard of which was harraſſed by the mountaineers, who took the baggage.

Having gained the plain of Morocco, the Emperor there was joined by the Baſhaw Seroni, who waited for him at the head of the troops of that province. This reinforcement

ment fo far recruited his army that he was enabled to grant repofe to the foldiers, who had efcaped this unfortunate expedition.

Humbled by his imprudence, Muley Ifhmael flowly returned toward Mequinez, and put to death his Vifir, Abdaraman Fileli. Abufing the power committed to him by the monarch, this minifter had indulged himfelf, during the abfence of Ifhmael, in every kind of prevarication, violating the moft facred rights, without refpecting even the wives of the principal Moors, who accufed him publicly in perfon. After breaking the arm of this man with a piftol fhot, Muley Ifhmael commanded him to be dragged through his camp, fewed up in the hide of an ox.

All the perfons in the train of this vifir were put to death, as accomplices of his extortions, and the abufe of his authority, during the abfence of the Emperor. This feverity, which prefents a picture of the violence of arbitrary government, was, perhaps, equally criminal on the part of the

prince

prince with the guilty acts his vifir had committed.

Here it is proper to obferve that the monarchs of Morocco, defirous to imitate the Ottoman court, have fometimes had vifirs; but fuch eminent fituations, in this empire, have neither the fame fplendor nor the fame power as thofe at Conftantinople. Authority cannot be delegated, except when it is founded on rational principles, which it is not in a government truely and abfolutely defpotic, where each act depends on the arbitrary will of one man. A vifir, of Morocco, is called by the fame title occafionally there as in Turkey; but equal puiffance he never can enjoy.

Muley Ifhmael arrived at Mequinez at the feaft of facrifices, whither he had convoked all the grandees, who haftened to bring him prefents; for, at that court, the vifit and the prefent are not only paid together, but, it is, in fome meafure, admiffible to delay the vifit, provided care is taken only to fend the prefent.

The

The ambitious projects of Muley Ifhmael, and the various difficulties he had to encounter in the beginning of his reign, made him fuppofe the neceffity of maintaining a body of confidential troops; he therefore conceived the project of forming a corps of negro foldiers, that fhould immediately be under his command. To accomplifh this the more quickly, exclufive of the negroes that Muley Arfhid already had collected, he purchafed himfelf a great number of blacks, male and female, and accuftomed his grandees to fend them as prefents.

After marrying and fetting apart territories for their habitations, he gave a degree of ftability to this generation of flaves, educated them in the Mahometan religion, accuftomed them to the ufe of arms, and made foldiers of them, who became formidable to the natives. A monarch fo abfolute, and fo capricious, as was Muley Ifhmael, had good reafon to fear the ficklenefs and difcontent of his enflaved fubjects, whom his violent conduct muft continually render liable to revolt, and who could not be kept

peaceable

peaceable but by overawing them with troops, whofe intereft fhould alfo be the intereft of the defpot.

In this precife fituation were the negroes. They were defpifed by the Moors, as well becaufe of the prejudice entertained concerning their colour, which the white men have every where configned to flavery, as becaufe of the idolatrous worfhip they maintained *. They alfo were foreigners. While fighting for the glory of their mafter, they fulfilled their military duty, and at the fame time took vengeance for the hatred in which they were held by the Moors. By this artful policy, and the rivalfhip which Muley Ifhmael knew how to raife between his foldiers and his fubjects, this monarch found the means of holding in fubjection, during a long reign, all the provinces of an empire accuftomed to a change of mafters, and which otherwife

* The negroes adore the Sun, and even mingle this adoration with Mahometanifm ; although this, of all errors, is the moft pardonable, the Moors do not the lefs regard it as idolatrous.

the

the barbarity of the prince muft foon or
late have obliged to rebel.

. After having exercifed his negroes in military dicipline, the Emperor, that he might
add to the ftrength of men the power of
fuperftition, confecrated them, with ceremony, to the profperity of religion. Following the example of the Sultan Amu-
rath, who, when he formed the corps of
Janizaries, fent them to Hadgy Beſtaſch *,
that he might beftow his benediction on
them, Muley Ifhmael appointed his negroes as a patron, and the fignal of rally-
ing, Sidi Boccari, one of the commentators of
the Koran, on which book he made them
take the oath of allegiance. This book,
from that time, was, and is ftill, carried re-
fpectfully in the army. It is depofited in a
diftinguifhed tent, placed in the centre of
the camp, as the image of their worfhip,
and the pledge of their fidelity.

---

* Hadgi Beſtaſch, a Saint, in eſtimation among the
Turks, and the founder of the Dervifes, cut the fleeve
from a felt robe which he wore; that it might ferve as a
model for the bonnet of the Janiffaries.

Herbelot Bib. Orien.

All

All the troops act under the same auspices, but none, except the blacks, the Ludaya, or other tribes, destined personally to guard the Emperor, obtain the surname of El-Boccari, which is thus meant to signify those soldiers who are immediately in the service of the prince; that is to say, who constitute the standing army. This negro corps, from that time, became the individual guard of Muley Ishmael, nor did he ever find guards more faithful. His successors, though they have made some reforms, have nearly followed the same plan.

After the monarch had quieted those troubles, by which his empire had been distracted, he was seized with a passion for building, and the embellishment of his palace became his amusement. Indulging his own instability of temper, and having in the beginning no fixed plan, what he built one day he would pull down the next, giving himself the plans of the works he would have executed. In dedicating himself to this employment, the barbarian found

more

more frequent occasions of indulging his cruelties; these, indeed, he made his sport.

Christian slaves, or other workmen, employed in executing his commands, often fell the victims of his blood-thirsty caprices. If the bricks they made were found too small, they were broken upon the head of the brickmaker. The workmen all were punished, either by pecuniary mulcts, or by chastisements analogous to their profession. Still further to diversify his amusements, and render his idleness more supportable, he sent for various lions, which he ordered to be enclosed in a park; and to these he occasionally delivered the poor wretches he selected, finding an inhuman pleasure in being a spectator of the combat.

In the beginning of April, 1680, Muley Ishmael, ever the enemy of tranquillity, sent forces, under the Alcaid Amar-Hadoo, to lay siege to Tangiers. This general made himself master of a small fort, garrisoned by forty men, who, finding it impossible they should receive succour from

the

the town, rather chofe to capitulate than to expofe themfelves to perifh, by defending their poft.

The governor of fort Charles, alfo, perceiving he could not long defend himfelf for want of provifions, determined to abandon this fort; and, with his troops, to reinforce the garrifon of the caftle. Having concerted his retreat with the commander of the caftle, he cut his way through the intrenchments of the Moors. Of feventy men who had garrifoned fort Charles; and had made this defperate fally, about forty were faved, and attained the caftle ; the reft were either taken, or killed. The commander had undermined fort Charles, and blew it up. The Moors took eighteen cannon, which had been fpiked, and were therefore rendered ufelefs. Muley Ifhmael made great rejoicings for this fuccefs.

In the fame year, the Chevalier de Chateau Renaud, the commander of a French fleet, appeared in the road of Sallee with ten fhips of war. His intent was to

O block

block up this port, and endeavour to make an advantageous peace. The Alcaid Amar-Hadoo, viceroy of Garb, whose duty it was to negotiate with him in the absence of the Emperor, had several conferences with the persons sent by the French commander. These negotiations, however, were all fruitless, and tended to no other purpose than that of multiplying presents, and increasing expences, according to the custom of the court of Morocco, where they will promise any thing, but where no affairs can be brought to a conclusion.

The Emperor, at this time, had marched toward Tremecen, there to chastise the mountaineers who had granted an asylum to his fugitive brothers. He received homage from the tribes inhabiting the lesser Atlas: they made their excuses for having granted the refuge, by which he was offended, and, without difficulty, paid the contributions he thought proper to impose.

As the Moors of Tremecen had often demanded assistance from Muley Ishmael

against

against the Turks of Algiers, who were in possession of that city, he wished himself to examine the condition in which it was; but he found it so well guarded, and in so good a state of defence, that he saw no hope of a successful enterprise. The Divan of Algiers penetrated his intentions, and wrote to him that, if he thought the limits by which they were separated somewhat too confined, he must impose it as a duty on himself, to extend them (i. e. remove himself) far even as from the Ocean to the Desert. Muley Ishmael received this letter, struck his tents, and returned no other answer than that of marching back toward Mequinez.

Having re-entered his capital, the pleasure he took in building again revived, and, under the pretence of enlarging and aggrandizing his palace, he alternately built up and pulled down; partly to indulge the inconstancy of his temper, and partly to occupy those about his person. He remarked, with great acuteness, meaning to picture the restlesness of men, and, perhaps, to justify his own, that, " were a

" number

" number of rats put into a basket, they
" would certainly eat their way out,
" unless the basket were continually
" shaken."

Toward the end of the year 1680, Muley Achmet, the nephew of Muley Ishmael, who had three years before retired from Morocco with the title of King of Dara, having entered into an alliance with a Shaik, of the kingdom of Suz, whose daughter he had married, aided by the advice and troops of his father-in-law, assumed the title of King of Suz. The intention of this prince, whose delight was only in war, was to invade the kingdom of Sudan, he having been promised aid by the Arabs of the desert.

Having assembled his forces, and collected the provisions necessary for crossing the desert, which separates the principality of Suz from the kingdom of Sudan, Muley Achmet began his march, and was joined by the Arabs of the neighbouring provinces. His army suffered much for want of water, and he lost about fifteen hundred

men

men among the moving fands, which he was obliged to crofs, and which, in this defert, vary their form according to the variations of the wind.

Muley Achmet, at length, arrived in Sudan, and layed fiege to Tagaret, the capital of that kingdom. The negroes, who were fhut up in the city, made fome refiftance; but, having only lances and javelins to oppofe to fire arms, their defence was ineffectual, and the place furrendered at difcretion, when it was on the eve of being ftormed. The riches Tagaret contained were fufficient to load fifty camels: a great part of them confifted in gold duft.

Muley Achmet agreed that the fon of the king of Sudan fhould give him ten thoufand negro flaves, for his ranfom, and that they fhould be fent to the frontiers of his ftates; which agreement was accordingly executed. After concluding this treaty, Muley Achmet returned toward Suz, and underwent his former difficulties in traverfing the defert, where many of his

fol-

followers perifhed, and where he loft feveral camels that bore a part of the riches
he had taken. Once more fafely arrived
at Tarudant, he fent meffengers to Muley
Ifhmael, his uncle, announcing the fuccefs
of his expedition, and with them a number of flaves, of both fexes, as a prefent.

Muley Ifhmael, ever forming new projects, and having no other amufement at
Mequinez than what his wives and concubines, his buildings, and the exercife of his
cruelties, could afford, wearied at this uniformity of life, undertook, in 1681, the
conqueft of the caftle of Mamora, which
was in the power of the Spaniards. Informed, by a fugitive, how entirely the place
had been neglected, fince the death of Philip IV., and that the garrifon was daily
weakened, by thofe difeafes which the hu-
midity of the marfhes were the caufes of,
the Emperor fent an order to the Alcaid
Amar-Hadoo to affemble the troops in the
province of Garb, and inveft the caftle.

Arrived before Mamora, that general
foon deftroyed the lines, which were
formed

formed only of ftakes and palifadoes. He likewife took two towers, facing the fea, in which there were only twelve men, who, unequal to ten thoufand, capitulated, on condition their lives fhould be faved. The general did more; he granted them their liberty, fent them into the place, and bade them inform the governor and the garrifon, that, if they did not yield, they would all be put to the fword on the arrival of Muley Ifhmael. The very name of this man fo difcouraged the foldiers that they rather chofe to encounter the lofs of liberty, than to expofe themfelves to his barbarity, by defending a place fo ill provided. In this extremity the governor faw himfelf obliged to furrender, and the garrifon were made prifoners of war.

Muley Ifhmael, who was encamped in the environs of Alcaffar, received advice of the capitulation of Mamora, and marched thither on the morrow. Finding in the place near one hundred pieces of artillery, numerous arms, and much ammunition, he proftrated himfelf to earth, and returned thanks to the Almighty for this

O 4   conqueft.

conqueſt. From this time, ambitious of
ſeizing other places on the coaſt, he ſent
the governor of Mamora to Laracha, there
to inform the commander, and garriſon,
they ſhould be treated with the utmoſt
rigour, if they refuſed to ſurrender.

In the month of June, and the ſame
year, the Chevalier de Chateau Renaud an-
chored once more in the road of Sallee,
with a ſquadron of four ſhips; and, having
deſtroyed ſome Corſairs, Muley Iſhmael
ſent orders to Amar-Hadoo to conclude a
truce. This negotiation, which was one
continued chain of contradictions, not being brought to a concluſion, the Emperor
reſolved to ſend the Hadgi Themin, governor of Tetuan, and Caſſem Menino,
brother to the governor of Sallee, ambaſſadors, into France, on board the royal
ſquadron.

Theſe Ambaſſadors arrived at Paris toward the end of December. It was the
intention of Muley Iſhmael to equivocate;
their miſſion, therefore, went no farther
than to announce the deſire of, without
the

the power to conclude, peace. Every delay, of which this negotiation was susceptible, and every new impediment, being an additional motive for new presents, Muley Ishmael was eager to renew the conferences.

The Emperor, constitutionally ambitious, and admiring the splendour of the reign of Louis XIV., who singly resisted Europe, leagued against him, appeared desirous of concluding a treaty of peace with this monarch. He therefore wrote to Louis XIV., requesting he would commit the negotiation to a confidential person, with whom he might treat, offering likewise to send an ambassador himself, should that be agreeable to the king.

In consequence of this invitation, Monsieur de St. Olon made a voyage to Mequinez, as ambassador of France, which had no other effect than that of demonstrating the instability of the court of Morocco, and the ambiguous character of Muley Ishmael. Eager to seize on the presents sent by the court of France, the Emperor

eluded,

cluded, by various specious pretexts, the motives of an embassy which he disavowed, although it had been made at his own request *.

Much about this time the English parliament, disgusted with the expence of maintaining Tangiers, from which the nation had imagined it should derive great advantages, and which, instead of profitable, was found burdensome, resolved to abandon the place. Consequently, in 1684, the English withdrew their garrison, stores, and artillery, and blew up the mole, and the fortifications which had been constructed by Charles II. This was new cause of triumph to Muley Ishmael, who affected to suppose that England had forsaken Tangiers, and restored it to him, from the dread they entertained of his arms.

Glorying in the conquest of Mamora, and the abandoning of Tangiers, the Emperor made preparations, in 1687, to be-

* Memoires de M. de St. Olon.

siege

siege Laracha. After the necessary stores
were collected, he marched, and laid siege to
the place; in the following year he erected
batteries on the south side, and blockaded
it by land. The town resisted his assaults
during five months, but, at length, capitulated in 1689. It appears that the garrison
remained the prisoners of Muley Ishmael,
and was only allowed to be exchanged, on
condition of restoring ten Moors for one
Christian.

Thus having the towns of Mamora, Laracha, and Tangiers, in his power, the
next attempt of Muley Ishmael was to take
Ceuta. In 1694 he assembled more than
forty thousand men, and layed siege to this
fortress; but, perceiving he should be unable to vanquish it, unless he could render
himself superior by sea, he contented himself with blockading it on the land side, and
securing his camp from surprize.

There were some skirmishes between the
Moors and the Christians, when the Spaniards made occasional sallies, but the loss
on both sides was inconsiderable. The

Moors

Moors being, however, greatly difturbed by the bombs and grenadoes, which were thrown from the town, Muley Ifhmael thought proper to encamp at a greater diftance. He afterward left the command of his army to the viceroy of Garb, who merely lay a fpectator of, without befieging, Ceuta.

The wars which happened in Spain at the beginning of the prefent century, after the death of Charles II., gave Muley Ifhmael the hope of conquering the place with lefs difficulty. He therefore fortified the Moorifh camp, erected houfes for the commanders of his forces, huts for the foldiers, ordered the fiege to be begun anew, and the place never to be forfaken.

The Moors had languidly lain more than twenty years before Ceuta, when Philip V. of Spain determined to drive them to a greater diftance. In 1720 this prince fent an army thither, under the command of the Marquis of Leda, accompanied by a number of gallies and fhips.

The

The Spanish army attacked the centre
of the Moors, while the ships bombarded
the wings, and with so much success that
the Moors were thrown into disorder.
The Marquis pursued his advantage with
so much ardour that, in four hours, he not
only drove them from their intrenchments,
but also from one valley to another, without their daring to make further resistance.
When the Spaniards returned to the
Moorish camp, they found four Mortars,
some pieces of artillery, four pair of co-
lours, and many stores.

I have interrupted the order of the history
of Muley Ishmael that I might present,
under one point of view, all the attempts of
that Emperor against Ceuta. Although the
Moors, after his reign, never made any attack upon this town, their camp of observation has continued to exist, and, in despite of the good understanding which has
lately been reciprocal, between the court of
Spain and that of Morocco, the intercourse,
between the camp of the Moors and the
town of Ceuta, is mutually maintained
with circumspection.

Not

Not by devaſtations, conqueſts, and ambitious projects alone, was the empire of Morocco, under Muley Iſhmael, agitated: as he advanced in years, his ſons whoſe numbers, ambition, and turbulence of character, led to new revolutions, and the commiſſion of new crimes, made him ſenſible, in the beginning of the preſent century, of all thoſe cares and vexations which he well might expect, from that reſtleſſneſs, and ferocity, of which he had given them an example.

Independent of the influence which the young princes began to acquire over provinces, the ſubjects of which, groaning beneath oppreſſion, were ever ready to change their maſter, domeſtic ambition, likewiſe, gave birth to domeſtic troubles. Secret intrigues were carried on by the wives of the Emperor, each of whom endeavoured to favour the intereſt of her own ſon, to the prejudice of the other brothers, and the provinces which theſe princes governed long ſuffered from their factions, and the perſonal animoſities with which ſuch factions were maintained.

Muley

Muley Mahomet, who, of all the fons or
Muley Ifhmael, moft merited to be beloved,
by the qualities he poffeffed, and the hand-
fomenefs of his perfon, was the one who
gave his father the moft chagrin. His
mother was a Georgian, purchafed at Algiers, who, by her accomplifhments and
beauty, had acquired fome empire over
the heart of this barbarous monarch.
The pre-eminence he held in the public
opinion had rendered Muley Mahomet audacious, and, regardlefs of the facred afylum of the palace, confulting only the head-
ftrong and illegitimate paffions of youth,
had entered the feraglio of his father, to
the intrigues and violences of which he
fell a facrifice. A fate that the more certainly attends fuch intruders, becaufe that
thefe intrigues are carried on in filence and
fecrefy.

One of the queens *, of negro origin,
the mother of Muley Zidan, ambitious and

* In Morocco they indifferently give the name of queen,
and that of Lela, or Lady, to the wives of the Emperor;
whom they call Ladies only, and not queens, in the Seraglio of the Grand Signior.

intriguing,

intriguing, and who, by the art with which she could enflame the passions, shared the depraved heart of Muley Ishmael, determined to effect the destruction both of her rival and her rival's son, and, by this means, assertain the affection of the father for Muley Zidan. This queen, by her influence, and the natural ascendancy of her character, had acquired an authority over the other women, who, like herself, were jealous of the Emperor's partiality for the Georgian; she therefore induced them to conspire with her, confirm the suspicions she had raised of infidelity, and they thus obtained from Muley Ishmael, in an atrocious moment of love and rage, permission to have her strangled.

Grown cool, and left to reflection, the Emperor was much affected by her death, and his attachment for Muley Mahomet was increased. In order to remove him from the intrigues of Lela Zidana, whose powers of seduction he himself dreaded, he bestowed on him the government of Tafilet. This prince, who was governor of Fez, and who preferred that city as a place

place of refidence, eluded his departure,
under a pretence of illnefs. His father,
unwilling to control his repugnance, agreed
to fend him into the province of Suz to
Muley Sharif, who had fucceeded Muley
Achmet.

Muley Mahomet had been but a fhort
time in his government before, according
to the Emperor's defire, he appeafed infurrections raifed near Tarudant, and the fuccefs of the prince, on this occafion, became
the caufe of his misfortunes.

Lela Zidana, who, with vexation, beheld that the conduct of Muley Mahomet
gave him a farther claim over the affections of his father, fet every poffible en-
gine in play to accomplifh his deftruction.
She wrote a letter to the prince, to which
fhe affixed the imperial fignet, and therein
commanded him to put a Shaik to death,
who was moft highly in the favour of the
Emperor. The prince executed the order
he received moft reluctantly. Being fummoned to Mequinez, there to juftify him-

felf concerning the death of the Shaik, he prefented his father's letter, to which he had only paid obedience out of refpect to the will of the Emperor.

Beholding his power thus abufed, Muley Ifhmael, at firft, was furious; but Lela Zidana fo fuccefsfully employed her arts that he fent back his fon to Tarudant, and rewarded the children of the Shaik to re-compenfe them for the lofs of their fa-ther.

Muley Mahomet, after having been fummoned to Mequinez, there to anfwer an accufation fo malicious and fo wicked, was inconfolable to behold the facility with which his father gave way to firft impref-fions, and, knowing no means of counter-acting the plots of Lela Zidana, whom he held in abhorrence, he rafhly entertained projects of rebellion. Muley Ifhmael, by let-ters he received, judged what were his fon's intents; but, having undertaken an expedition againft the regency of Algiers, and being on the eve of departure, he would not change his plan.

The

The monarch began his march, toward the commencement of the prefent century, with more than fixty-thoufand men ; the army of the Algerines fcarcely exceeded ten thoufand, but it was compofed of much better troops, and encamped itfelf on the frontiers, there to wait for the army of Muley Ifhmael, which, when it arrived, was harraffed by fatigue, and in want of all neceffaries. The Algerines began the attack with intrepidity, and without lofs of time ; the army of the Emperor was routed, and Muley Ifhmael, who, for more than thirty years, had fought againft the Moors with unfailing fuccefs, was obliged to retire, and re-enter his ftates, after an ignominious battle.

Muley Mahomet took advantage of the impreffion which the defeat of his father had made on the minds of his fubjects, to render himfelf mafter of Morocco. He marched thither with near forty thoufand men, whofe fidelity was fecured by the perfonal qualities, fine figure, and bravery of their leader. The capital at that time was governed by the Alcaid Melek, who

fhut

that the city gates, difpatched meffengers to the king for fuccour, and caufed the treafure of the palace to be fecretly buried.

Muley Mahomet, who had no artillery, found it impoffible to take Morocco, unlefs by furprife ; he therefore divided his army into two corps, the one of which concealed itfelf near the city, while he began his march with the other as if retreating. Deceived by this ftratagem, as the prince had forefeen, the Alcaid Melek made a fally with his forces to attack Muley Mahomet as he retired ; and the other corps, leaving its place of concealment, fell upon the Alcaid in the rear, who was thus furrounded, and his army, in part, flaughtered, while the prince rendered himfelf mafter of the city. Muley Mahomet indulged his troops in pillage, as a reward for their valour, and feized himfelf on the treafures, buried by the Alcaid, which were immediately difcovered to him by a young flave.

Muley

Muley Ifhmael, on receiving the advice fent by the Alcaid of Morocco, ordered an army to march to the fuccour of that city, under the command of Muley Zidan, the fon of that artful queen, who, by her fafcinations, her intrigues, and plots, had occafioned the rebellion of Muley Mahomet. The latter prince, informed of his brother's march, retired to Tarudant, where he provided for his fafety. Among his officers was an Alcaid, the kinfman of Lela Zidana, who informed the court of all tranfactions, and who, having been difcovered, was beheaded.

When Muley Mahomet had affembled fufficient money and troops, he determined to march againft Muley Zidan, who had a fine army. Muley Mahomet gave the command of his van to the Alcaid Melek, the former governor of Morocco, who had entered into his fervice. Melek fuffered himfelf to be furrounded by the troops of Muley Zidan, which occafioned the lofs of the battle.

Seeing

Seeing the van of his army in the power
of the enemy, Muley Mahomet was
obliged to fly. The prifoners were conducted to Morocco, whence the chiefs were
fent to the Emperor, who put them to tor-
menting deaths. The Alcaid Melek himfelf, who had been guilty of treachery
only thereby to obtain pardon, was facrificed to the vengeance of Lela Zidana.
She would not forgive him for having, by
order of the prince, beheaded her relation,
who had acted as a fpy. To render cruelty more infernal, this unhappy man
was fixed to a board, and fawed down the
back.

Muley Zidan, encouraged by victory,
and the flight of Muley Mahomet, determined to march and befiege Tarudant ; but
having been repulfed in various fallies, made
by the befieged, he was obliged to retire.
Every artifice of treachery was then employed by this prince to enfnare his brother, and to corrupt his partifans. Having
placed fome troops in ambufcade to feize
on him, one day, as he rode out, Muley
Mahomet, notwithftanding all his efforts,

was

was taken and brought prisoner to Morocco, whence he was sent by Muley Zidan, under a strong guard, to the Emperor, in the year 1706.

After having afflicted the reader by an uninterrupted succession of crimes and cruelties, I would it were in my power to omit scenes still more tragical, and, under an impenetrable veil, to conceal the atrocious acts of a violent and barbarous father, toward a rash, unfortunate, and guilty son.

Muley Mahomet approached Mequinez on his journey, when the Emperor went to meet him at the river of Beth, there to punish his rebellion, and avoid all intercessions in his behalf. I shall suppress the shocking preparations which Muley Ishmael made for the ferocious exercise of vengeance. They both arrived on the banks of the Beth on the same day. The Emperor passed four-and-twenty hours without admitting him to his presence; when he, at length, sent for him, the prince fell prostrate to the earth, and sup-

plicated

plicated pardon for his errors in the moſt affecting terms. His father preſented him the point of his lance, and the prince, fearing death leſs than thoſe preparations which did but multiply its horrors *, again humbly conjured him to grant him pardon, and ever after to depend on his ſubmiſſion and fidelity.

The inflexible Iſhmael, who had ſo far forgotten all human pity as to be preſent at the puniſhment of his ſon, and the ſon whom he had moſt loved, commanded two men to ſeize him, and a third, a butcher, to cut off his right hand. The latter refuſed, preferring, as he ſaid, death to the ſacrilegious act of bathing his hand in the blood of a Sharif. Enraged at a ſentiment ſo generous, the Emperor ſtruck off the head of the butcher, and called another,

---

* Father Buſnot informs us that the Emperor was preceded by a guard of two thouſand horſe, and one thouſand foot; that fourteen Chriſtian ſlaves carried a cauldron, a hundred weight of tar, or pitch, and as much oil and tallow; and that they were followed by a cart load of wood, and ſix butchers, each with his knife in his hand. T.

who

who executed his will by cutting off the
right hand, and the right foot, of the unfortunate prince.

" Now, doft thou know thy father, wretch !" faid Ifhmael.

He then feized a mufket, and killed the
Moor who had cut off the hand and foot of
his fon. Mahomet, groaning under pain
as he was, could not forbear to remind
him of the guilty inconfiftency of a fovereign, who equally murdered the man,
who refufed to execute his orders, and him
who obeyed. Pitch was then applied to the
leg and arm of the fuffering prince as a
ftyptic, and the Emperor, ftained with the
blood of his fon, commanded his guards
to bring him living, under pain of inftant
execution, to Mequinez.

The recital of this tragical fcene fpread
terror and confternation through the city ;
the palace refounded with lamentaions,
groans, and fhrieks, and Muley Ifhmael,
unable to affuage their grief by the feverity
of his orders, maffacred feveral women
who

who had dared to difobey, till forrow, at length, was obliged to weep in filence.

The children of Muley Mahomet only were allowed to mourn, but were not admitted any more to fee their father. The prince lived thirteen days in torments, and demanded to be buried, not as a prince, but as a flave, for fo he had been treated by his father. Ifhmael, however, built him a maufoleum, and thereby preferved to pofterity a memento of his own barbarity.

After the defeat of his rival, Muley Zidan, with little internal caufe of happinefs, returned to Tarudant once more to befiege that city, in which the remainder of the revolted had fhut themfelves up, which he furrounded fo entirely that famine made dreadful ravages among the citizens, and it was obliged to furrender at difcretion. More ferocious, more avaricious, more inhuman, even than his very father, Muley Zidan, committed every kind of barbarity in Tarudant, and, by his cruelties, juftified the opinion entertained of him in his youth, that in him all the vices of the human heart were united.

The

The horrors, robberies, and maſſacres, commited by Muley Zidan in the city of Tarudant, being publiſhed, ſo terrified the Moors of the neighbouring provinces and towns, that they fled for refuge among the rocks, and no where ſuppoſed themſelves in ſafety. The town of Santa-Cruz was at the ſame time evacuated, that is to ſay, in 1712; and when this prince marched thither, to beſiege it, he found no perſon but an old woman and a blind Jew, who, becauſe of their infirmities, were unable to ſeek a hiding place. The ſoldiers of the prince finding no further reſiſtance, the Moors every where flying, enriched themſelves with pillage, and were indulged in every kind of licentiouſneſs.

The ſucceſs of Muley Zidan, his troops, and his treaſures, began highly to diſturb Muley Iſhmael, who was inceſſantly preyed upon by his paſſions; the Emperor repented ſomewhat too late that he had beſtowed the command of his army on his ſon, and invented various pretexts to recal him to Mequinez; but Muley Zidan, who meditated far other projects, delayed

his

his return from year to year, alledging that his prefence was ftill neceffary, totally to fubdue the infurgents.

The better to deceive his fon, Muley Ifhmael occafioned a report to be fpread that he was ill, and forbore to appear in public, at the fame time that he prevailed on the mother of Muley Zidan artfully to fend for her fon to Mequinez, in order that, in cafe of death, he might the more eafily poffefs himfelf of the government; but the prince, well acquainted with all the fubtleties of his father, fufpected the intelligence, and paid no attention to this advice. His mother wrote a fecond letter, telling him, that his father was at the point of death, and that, if he did not incontinently return, he would be too late to pay the laft duties of a fon. Whether my father live or die, replied the prince, I will not forfake the army, which, in cafe of his deceafe, will but the better afcertain my fucceffion.

The rumours of the illnefs of Muley Ifhmael, and the fear that he was in reality dead,

dead, gave rife to fome commotions in the provinces. The citizens of Mequinez were ripe for revolt, when Lela Zidana, who governed defpotically, under the pretence of the Emperor's illnefs, fallied from the palace with a lance in her hand, attended by a guard of armed foldiers, to re-eftablifh tranquillity, and even arrogantly commanded fome negroes, whom fhe encountered as fhe paffed, to be punifhed.

An event fo fingular, among a people where the women never appear in public, and under a government in which they are fuppofed to have no right to empire, aftonifhed the citizens, who, believing the king dead, imagined that this ambitious princefs, whom they fecretly detefted, intended to feize on the fovereign authority. This fuppofition fpread fo quickly, and excited fo great an alarm, that Lela Zidana was obliged to re-enter the palace.

The Emperor, who had not been feen in public during fifty days, informed of the commotion among the inhabitants of the city, inftantly left his retreat, and overawed

awed the people by his prefence, who tef-
tifyed the fatisfaction they received to behold him alive. The pretended recovery
of Muley Ifhmael was the caufe of public
rejoicings, and he received the vifits of the
Alcaids, the grandees, and deputies of provinces and towns, on the occafion, who
brought with them the cuftomary prefents.

Highly regretting that he had not been
able, by artifice, to inveigle Muley Zidan
to Mequinez, the Emperor, confulting only
the violence and ferocity of his character, now took other means to difencumber
himfelf of this prince. He well knew
how much he was addicted to drunkennefs, and that, in the fury of intoxication,
he fo far abandoned himfelf to his cruelty
that his very wives and concubines were
not in fafety. Thefe he made his inftruments to obtain his purpofe. The wives
of Muley Zidan had little reluctance in
complying with the barbarous defire of
Muley Ifhmael, for they had no other poffible means of freeing themfelves from the
tyranny to which they were hourly fubjected.

jected. Surrounding him in one of his fits of drunkenness, they smothered Muley Zidan between two mattresses, and thus delivered the world of a monster unequalled in depravity.

The body of the prince was taken from Tarudant to Mequinez by the command of his mother, and there interred. The Emperor, that he might conceal the part he had taken in his death, built a mausoleum, and a mosque, to his memory, in which an asylum is given to criminals; and thus, under a supposed idea of sanctity, is the memory of a prince held in veneration, who had abandoned himself to every vice, lived detested by the nation, a rebel to his father and his Emperor, and, contemning the laws of his religion, died in drunkenness.

After being informed of the death of Muley Zidan, Muley Ishmael, governed by that spirit of contradiction which, in him, was a characteristic quality, commanded the seven wives of this prince to be brought from Mequinez, and along with them the

Jew

Jew merchant, who had fupplied them
with the brandy, by drinking which he
had made himfelf drunk. Lela Zidana,
as well worthy to be the wife of Muley
Ifhmael as the mother of Muley Zidan, facrificed thefe eight victims to the barbarity
of her revenge. Her cruelty was detef-
tably atrocious. She ordered the breafts to
be fevered from three of thefe women, and
obliged them to eat them previous to their
being ftrangled.

Nero, Caligula, Heliogabalus, were abhorrent villains; yet Nero, Caligula,
Heliogabalus, themfelves, were unequal
to the fiends of whofe acts I give but a
partial relation.

The death of Muley Zidan happened in
1721, and his brother, Abdelmeleck, fucceeded to the government of the fouth,
where he, at firft, behaved with difcretion;
but the diftance at which he lived from
his father, the ambition of reigning, the
levity of the people, and the internal vices
of the government, which, here combined,
infpire rebellion among fuch princes, foon
rendered

rendered him equally guilty with his brothers. Acting with defpotic authority
over the princes he governed, Abdelmeleck
prefently became fufpected by his father,
and even had the temerity to refufe paying
him tribute.

The Emperor, whofe great age no longer
permitted him to traverfe deferts that he
might punifh infurgents, poffeffing now
no other arms than thofe of artifice, wrote
his fon letters, the moft tender and confidential, that he might perfuade him to return to court, in which he even infinuated
it was his intent to abdicate the empire in
his favour. Well acquainted with his father, Abdelmeleck anfwered with like art,
and in the moft refpectful terms, that he
might remove thofe fufpicions which he
appeared to have entertained. Muley Ifhmael, difembling his vexation, feigned to
be fatisfied with the conduct of his fon, and
made no more intreaties; but, fecretly
nourifhing hatred in his heart againft this
prince, he determined to leave his younger
brother, Muley Achmet Daiby, his fucceffor

in fovereignty. Some have fuppofed it was
the Emperor's intention to make the nation
regret his memory, by leaving a fucceffor
unworthy of the fceptre, and incapable of
government.

After reigning fifty-four years, continually agitated by inquietude, fufpicion, or
revolt, and fullying his fceptre by the moft
tragical fcenes, Muley Ifhmael died on the
22nd of March, 1727, aged eighty one.
Active, enterprizing, and politic, this Emperor has tarnifhed the glory of his reign
by his avarice, his duplicity, his oppreffions, his injuftice, and a continuation of
barbarities, the relation of which would be
dreadful, and the remembrance of which
time only can efface.

Addicted to fenfuality, Muley Ifhmael
had a prodigious number of wives, and, fo
numerous was his pofterity, that, it is
doubted whether he himfelf knew all his
children. If the common opinion may
be credited, he had more than eight hundred fons ; and there ftill remains at Tafilet a confiderable body of the Sharifs,

t   who

who are the defcendants of Muley Ifhmael, of his brothers, or his forefathers.

The Moors relate that the laft child of this fovereign was born eighteen months after the death of his father, and the Talbes decided that child birth, with refpect to him, had departed from the order of nature. The time of geftation, however, is certainly not longer in Morocco than in Europe; but phyficians, in the latter country, are lefs indulgent in their opinions.

Muley Ifhmael, who, among a number of vices, poffeffed fome good qualities, was ardent in the purfuit of his projects, artful in policy, and diftinguifhed his reign by his application to the forming of troops from the negro families, and their defcendants, whom he acquired from the coaft of Guinea. This population of foreign foldiers, whofe intereft was ever oppofite to that of the Moors, but ever connected with that of the monarch, has planted in the heart of the empire a new and diftinct nation. After the death of Muley Ifh-

Q 2

maol,

mael, the number of the negro foldiers capable of bearing arms amounted to about one hundred thoufand. This warlike and infolent foldiery, which was made the inftrument of the avarice of Muley Ifhmael, and by whofe aid he gratified all his paffions, had great influence in the revolutions, which, after the death of this Emperor, have fo much agitated Morocco. The Negroes might have fubjugated the empire in the fame manner as the Tartars have feized on China, had there been found among them ambitious leaders, as capable of forming as they were of executing projects fo great. During fuch tempeftuous intervals the empire became, for feveral years, the prey of this avaricious body, which never gave the fucceffors of Muley Ifhmael time fufficient to fecure their authority. They refembled the Roman legions, during the decline of that empire, they elected Emperors on one day, and dethroned them on the next.

CHAP.

CHAP. V.

Muley Achmet Daiby proclaimed by the Grandees and the Negroes. Duquella fubjetted. Avarice of the Emperor. Revolt of Abdelmeleck. Brutality, drunkennefs, and indolence, of Muley Achmet. Abdelmeleck ftrangled. Death of the Emperor.

MULEY Achmet Daiby, the only fon of Muley Ifhmael who happened to be at Mequinez when his father died, behaved himfelf with fo much prudence, by the council and aid of the governor of that city, that he difconcerted the projects of his brothers, Abdelmeleck and Abdallah, who, being both his feniors, had that claim to empire, and the confidence of the people, which age and experience give. The troops of the latter, while he was waiting

Q 3   fome

some revolution in his favour, voluntarily abandoned his party, which had not afcendancy fufficient to withftand his opponents.

The grandees, and the officers of the Negroes, being affembled, the day after the death of Muley Ifhmael, unanimoufly proclaimed Muley Achmet Daiby, and took the oath of fidelity. The new Emperor gave them two hundred thoufand ducats, about one million three hundred thoufand livres, or fifty-four thoufand pounds fterling, to diftribute among the troops; and they, encouraged by this generofity, marched againft the provinces that gave any tokens of infurrection, and that, after having loft Muley Ifhmael, fuppofed they no longer had a mafter.

The Moors of the province of Duquella, and of its environs, having taken up arms againft Muley Achmet Daiby, were entirely defeated and fubjected. This victory, which added to the afcendancy the Negroes had acquired, re-eftablifhed order and tranquillity in the other provinces.

Muley

Muley Achmet Daiby was only generous
from policy : he was by character as avaricious as his father had been. In the very
beginning of his reign he took all possible
care to know and to increase his treasury. So little respectful was his avidity
that he even stript the wives of his father,
of the gold and silver jewels which they
had received, in the moments of his caprice,
or his liberality. The wealth left by Muley Ishmael was considerable, and Muley
Achmet himself had been an œconomist, so
that the treasury of the Emperor might
amount to one hundred millions of livres,
or near four millions two hundred thousand
pounds. Yet did this mass of money, accumulated by time and oppression, soon
after, disappear in an instant.

Dazzled at beholding such heaps of gold,
Muley Achmet, as avaricious as he was intemperate, neglected the cares of government, and dedicated himself wholly to his
pleasures. He yielded to the debauchery
of drunkenness, without reserve ; and this
passion, which alienated the love of his
people, was the source of his misfortunes.

In

In order to gain the affection of his subjects,
in the beginning of his reign he issued an
edict, by which he reduced all taxation to
that of simply collecting the tenths, as
prescribed by the law of Mahomet. Yet
did not a regulation so wise produce effects
which ought to have been the result, but
rather served to manifest the abuse of authority among the governors, who profited
by the vices of the imperial power to
increase their extortions. The provinces
became so much dissatisfied that the people,
in many parts, took up arms to redress
their grievances, and thus spread confusion
throughout the empire.

The most of these provinces, beholding,
with repugnance, the irregular conduct of
Muley Achmet Daiby, were secretly inclined toward prince Abdelmeleck, who
was a religious observer of the law.
They, however, durst not openly testify
their discontent. Muley Achmet being
informed of the disposition of the people,
and perplexed concerning the manner in
which he ought to act, wished to secure
the fidelity of the Negroes by his gifts, and
almost

almoft wholly confided the imperial adminiftration of government, to the caprice
and fickle avarice of his troops.

Such implicit confidence, prodigally beftowed on foreign foldiers, whom the
Moors detefted, ftill further alienated the
minds of men, and the fermentation became general. Sedition firft manifefted itfelf at Fez, the governor of which, and
near a hundred men of his party, were
maffacred by the people. The city of Tetuan, and its environs, followed the example; the governor was obliged to fly, and
the furious people deftroyed his houfe,
his gardens, and fubjected the city to all
the horrors of a civil war.

Muley Achmet, funken in brutal intoxication, was incapable of yielding any re-
medy to fuch diforders, of which the people
round him even kept him in igorance. So
cruel was this emperor, when he was
fober, that his attendants and wives had
no other means of fafety than that of
making him drunk. The governor of Mequinez, on whom he principally depended

for

for the administration of affairs, only rendered his master the more odious by his own negligence. Indolence and neglect pervaded the court. The debauched life of the king, the contempt in which his inactive government was held, and the murmurs of the people, rendered discontent so universal that it ended in revolt.

The provinces of the south were the first that reared the standard of rebellion. Muley Abdelmeleck, who had gained the hearts of the people, finding himself at the head of a powerful army between Suz and Morocco, was, of all those who aspired to empire, he who seemed to have the best founded claims; but he was guilty of an error, which became an obstacle to his good fortune and future elevation.. In order to flatter his own army, composed of the inhabitants of the mountains and volunteers, who held the Negroes in abhorrence, this prince declared, that, should he ever arrive at empire, he would maintain no negro troops.

A decla-

, A declaration like this, which was exceedingly impolitic at such a moment,
when the Negroes, accustomed to war, were
in possession of all power, was for a time
exceedingly favourable to the party of Muley Achmet, whose authority these same
Negroes, proscribed by Abdelmeleck, saw
themselves necessitated to maintain. The
latter was not long before he felt the effects of his indiscretion, and the resentment of these troops. . Morocco was already in his power; after having gained a
battle, the provinces of the south were in
his interest, as were the cities of Fez and
Tetuan in the north, insomuch that he
was almost master of the empire; but,
having been defeated by the Negroes,
whom he had provoked, he was obliged to
abandon Morocco, and retreat, after having
received three wounds, which occasioned
the report of his death to be spread.

Having sustained some attacks from the
forces of Muley Achmet Daiby, the city
of Fez made peace with this prince, and
acknowledged him Emperor. Muley Abdelmeleck made a proposition to lay down
his

his arms, if his brother would cede him
the half of the empire ; and Muley Achmet was himfelf inclined to acquiefce,
that he might have nothing farther to do,
but drink and fleep. His minifters, however, his courtiers, and particularly his
troops, who had great influence in thefe
deliberations, firmly oppofed any fuch di-
vifion.

The diflike of the people to Muley
Achmet continued the fame, after he was
thus recalled to empire, for his manner of
life underwent no alteration. Totally
neglectful of government, he knew not of
thofe troubles which were incited in his
provinces. His days were wholly fpent in
drinking, and his debauches were carried
to fuch excefs, that, to conceal them, from
the public, was no longer poffible. Going
one Friday to the mofque to prayer, he was
fo drunk, that, when he proftrated himfelf,
according to the cuftom of the Mahometans, he vomited up his wine ; an inde-
cency which was every where rumoured,
and every where gave offence.

When

When he was brought back to his palace he treated his wives with exceſſive cruelty, becauſe they made him ſóme remonſtrances, till, impatient at ſuffering his violence, they left the place, and uttered their clamors aloud, in the ſtreets, againſt the indolence and diſſimulation of his miniſters, and the commanders of his forces, who had no reſpect whatever for religion. So general was the diſcontent, that the ſoldiers themſelves, prejudiced as they were againſt Abdelmeleck, joined the natives, and Abdelmeleck was once more proclaimed.

This proclamation made, which happened in the month of March, 1728, the principal Alcaides, aſſembled at Mequinez, ſent deputies to Abdelmeleck, preſſing him to haſten his arrival. His ſon, who was at that time in Mequinez, was appointed regent, in expectation of the coming of his father; and the young prince, by ſome well-timed gifts, very prudently ſmothered thoſe diſcontents which the party of Muley Achmet at firſt teſtified, in conſequence of this election.

Muley

Muley Abdelmeleck arrived at Mequinez, and made his public entry on the
10th of April. In the barbarity of his
religious zeal, it was his intention to have
put out the eyes of his brother, but he fatisfied himself with banifhing him to Tafilet, remonftrances having been made to
him that, Muley Achmet having been
found unworthy of the throne only in
confequence of his debauchery and indolent conduct, he did not merit any other
chaftifement than that of being depofed.

After this firft act, Abdelmeleck,
auftere, arrogant, and choleric, began to
treat his minifters, and the Moors in general, with fo much feverity, haughtinefs,
and contempt, that he univerfally alienated
the minds of his fubjects. Scarcely had
he reigned three months before the Negroes, recollecting the declaration which
Abdelmeleck had publicly made concerning them, formed a party, and fent a detachment to Tafilet to folicit pardon of
Muley Achmet Daiby, and to invite him
once more to put himfelf at their head, and
affume the reins of government.

Attended

Attended by some troops in addition to the Negroes, the Emperor began his march, and presently found himself at the head of eighty thousand men. Abdelmeleck, who, by the excess of his pride, had deprived himself of partisans, was obliged to shut himself up in Mequinez, where he was besieged, and the city, taken by assault, was exposed to pillage, and every horror which vengeance and barbarity could inspire.

During the confusion, Muley Abdelmeleck escaped to the city of Fez, where he was again besieged. Unable to take this city by storm, Muley Achmet resolved on a blockade, and, as there were not sufficient provisions in Fez to sustain a siege, the inhabitants, at the end of three months, determined to capitulate. The sole condition which the Emperor exacted from them was, to yield up his brother. Abdelmeleck was accordingly delivered over to the conqueror, who, for a moment, dissembling the ferocity of his character, thought proper to send him, under a strong guard, to Mequinez, where he some-fometime after commanded him to be ftrangled.

Muley Abdelmeleck had been executed but a few days before Muley Achmet Daiby himfelf died, in March, 1729, of an incurable dropfy. Such was the end of a prince, become brutal by indolence and intemperance, and who, defpifed by his fubjects, never was capable of making his power refpected.

CHAP.

C H A P. VI.

*Accession of Muley Abdallah, his cruelties;
power of the Negroes, their insatiable avidity, and consequent revolutions. Muley
Abdallah a sixth time proclaimed Emperor; the negro troops enfeebled, and the
power of the Emperor rendered more
stable. Character of Muley Abdallah,
his depravity, vices, and intolerable barbarities.*

AFTER the death of Muley Achmet
Daiby, the sceptre, which the army difpofed of at will, was frequently removed
from prince to prince; and the empire of
Morocco, which, in its birth, had fo often
been the prey of fanaticifm, was now at
the mercy of the negro foldiers. Muley
Booffer, the fon of Muley Achmet, who

was the immediate heir to the throne, first presented himself as his father's successor; but his party was not sufficiently powerful. Lena Coneta, the mother of Muley Abdallah, an artful and intelligent princess, knew so well how to gain the minds of the people, and treated the Negroes with so much generosity, that her son was by her means proclaimed.

Muley Abdallah, though, perhaps, as capricious as, and not less cruel than, his father, Muley Ishmael, was generous even to excess. Six times deposed, and six times remounting the throne, in the commencement of his reign he was the sport of fortune, the victim of his people's fickleness, and the avarice of his soldiers. Muley Booffer, his nephew, contested with him for empire; but Booffer's sole resources were in a Marabout, held in veneration by some followers, whom the spirit of fanaticism had assembled; his faction therefore was soon defeated and dispersed by the Negroes, and he was himself taken, as was the Marabout, who had become his counsellor, protector, and guide.

Muley

Muley Abdallah pardoned his nephew, and granted him his liberty; but, regardless of the prejudices of the Moors, he commanded the Marabout to be beheaded, and treated him as an impostor; for, said he, had this Marabout been really a Saint, the sabre that struck at him would have been edgeless.

Muley Abdallah afterward marched against Fez, which had declared in favour of Muley Booffer, and laid siege to the city. It sustained a blockade of six months before it surrendered; and, irritated at the obstinacy of the inhabitants, the Emperor intended to have destroyed and wholly erased its foundations. Remonstrances, however, were made to him, that it had been built by a descendant of Mahomet, and a founder of the empire, and that he would expose himself, by such profanation, to the wrath of Heaven, and the hatred of the people.

The little religion Muley Abdallah demonstrated, in thus manifesting his intention to destroy a city consecrated by the

Moors

Moors to devotion, and the violent and fanguinary character his actions already had
announced, fo alienated the minds of
men that there were indications of fedition in various provinces of the empire ; the Brebes of the mountains of
Tedla were the firſt who took up arms.
Prompt and vindicative, Muley Abdallah
haſtily aſſembled ſome native Moors to
march and reduce thefe mountaineers,
without reflecting that he endangered his
own glory, and difguſted his other troops
by fo ill-judged a felection.

Having attacked the mountaineers at the
head of twenty-five thouſand men, the
Emperor loſt the half of his army in the
battle, and returned to Mequinez to wreak
his vengeance, and add to the ſhame of his
defeat, by odious exhibitions of barbarity.
A multitude of the inhabitants were put to
death on the flighteſt pretext, himſelf aiding
the murderers. Defirous of ſhewing him the
deteſtable abſurdity and inhumanity of ſuch
actions, his mother remonſtrated, and he replied — " My ſubjects have no other right to
" their lives than that which I think pro-

I   " per

" per to leave them, nor have I any other
" pleafure fo great as that of killing them
" myfelf." More abominable in cruelty
than even his predeceffors were, this Emperor feemed anxious to add to the infamy
of his hereditary ferocity.

The tragical barbarities of Muley Abdallah occafioned the tribes of the mountains of Tedla to revolt; and, proud of the
advantage they had already gained againft
the monarch, they drew over the neighbouring provinces to their party. Grown
prudent by experience, and liftening to the
advice of his mother, the Emperor engaged
the Negroes to take part in his meditated
vengeance, and, by fome acts of liberality,
induced them to forget the neglect with
which they had been treated. He now
marched at the head of thirty thoufand
new-raifed troops, who were followed by
as many Negoes. In July, 1730, he arrived among the mountains of Tedla, and
proceeded through a country full of brambles and underwood. Unfortunately thefe
took fire near his camp, and he loft many
men, horfes, and camels, with all his pro-

vifions,

vifions, and was himfelf in danger. The
fuperftitious foldiers confidered this accident as an evil prognoftic, and the Negroes,
who had teftified fome indications of inconftancy, were difgufted. Muley Abdallah, however, prevented them from abandoning him, by promifing them three hundred thoufand ducats (or upward of eighty
thoufand pounds fterling) at the end of
the campaign.

The army having received a new fupply
of provifions, it once more began its march,
in two columns, each at fome diftance from
the other, thereby to furround the infurgents. The Emperor who commanded the
van attacked them with the greateft valour; and the Negroes, who followed, feconded this attack fo effectually that the
rebels were cut off, and their country totally ravaged. The troops of Muley Abdallah took a vaft number of horfes, camels, herds, and flocks, contenting themfelves with killing the fheep, that they
might carry off the wool. The very women and children were ftripped of their
clothing, and turned naked into the country;

try; but the Emperor gave them wherewith to cover their nakednefs; and this
was the firft act of humanity he had ever
been known to perform.

Muley Abdallah paffed the remainder of
the campaign in the province of Hea,
where his troops were indulged in repofe,
and whence he fent a detachment into that
of Dara. His arms here were unfuccefsful;
the commander, who had been fent on this
expedition, brought back to Mcquinez, to
which place the king had returned, not
more than the tenth part of the forces,
with which he had been entrufted; he
had fought with equal prudence and valour, and was vanquifhed, becaufe over-
powered by numbers.

Muley Abdallah bafely put this general
to death, together with the foldiers who
had returned with him, and not only prefided himfelf a witnefs of, but was the chief
executioner at, this fcene of blood. Perceiving that thofe who put thefe wretches
to death performed their tafk ill, he took
the fabre himfelf, to fhew them the manner

R 4　　　　　　　　in

in which it ought to be ufed. Thus perifhed, by the hand of a vile executioner,
called an Emperor, men who, in any other
country, would have met the rewards due
to their fervices.

To keep his fubjefts bufy, and not give
them time to réflect on his barbarities,
Muley Abdallah built new fortifications
and new walls at Mcquinez, to fecure it
from the incurfions of the Brebes. The
inhabitants, be their rank or condition
what it would, were all obliged to affift at
raifing thefe walls. At the conclufion of
the year 1732, he left this work to march
againft the mountaineers of the environs
of Tetuan, who gave tokens of infurrection, and who, intrenched among their
mountains and precipices, firmly waited
his approach, without even defending the
paffes. Having imprudently entangled
himfelf in a defile with thirty thoufand
men, the Brebes fuddenly appeared on the
heights, and attacked the army of the Emperor with fo much fuccefs that it was put
to the rout, and Muley Abdallah could with
difficulty fecure himfelf and a few foldiers,

leaving

leaving his baggage the prey of the victors.

The spirit of insurrection having spread itself almost throughout the whole empire, Muley Abdallah passed the following year in the province of Tafilet, there to quell a revolt. The success of this campaign was by no means prosperous; the Emperor wanted not intrepidity, but was unskilful and imprudent; and, having rashly attacked the rebels before he had been joined by his whole army, he was vanquished, and obliged to retreat. As the remainder of his forces advanced to join his army, he caused their officers to be seized, and commanded them to be dragged by mules along the road, that he might revenge upon them the disgrace of his own imprudence and defeat.

The mother of Muley Abdallah, perceiving she had lost all influence over the mind of her son, and seeing herself exposed to his contempt, unwilling longer to be a witness of his blood-thirsty acts, asked permission to quit the court, and go on pilgrimage

grimage to Mecca. The Emperor, on her
return, teftified little affection for this
princefs, nor did he fulfil thofe duties prefcribed by propriety and cuftom, after a
journey confecrated to religion. His mother, however, fhewed much tendernefs
for him, and prefented him with four
beautiful flaves whom fhe had bought,
hoping, by their means, to infpire him
with the love of women, and extirpate an
unnatural paffion, to which this depraved
wretch had addicted himfelf. This worthy mother continued to give her fon advice, concerning his government; but,
deaf to her counfels, and liftening only
to his own impetuofity and caprice, he
wholly loft the affection of his fubjects.

That he might the more eafily fubjugate
the Negroes, who, in confequence of his
diffipation, had become intractable, and
whofe avarice and ficklenefs he dreaded,
Muley Abdallah formed the project of cutting off their general, and thofe among
their officers who moft influenced the refo-
lutions of this foldiery. The fecret, however, having been difcovered by the inter-
ception

ception of letters, the negro corps, ever in
arms, and conscious of its own power,
rendered the project of Muley Abdallah
abortive, by publicly deposing him, on the
29th of September, 1734; and Muley
Ali, one of his brothers, was elected in his
stead.

Being informed of what were the intentions of these troops, Muley Abdallah sent
them three hundred thousand ducats, hoping
thereby to appease them; but the Negroes
received the money in part of payment of
what had been promised, and no way
changed their determination. The Emperor then, as a last expedient, shut himself
up in Mequinez, there to defend himself;
but, after having made his preparations, he
fled among the mountains, accompanied by
six hundred horsemen, and left his mother,
his wives, and children, to the mercy of his
enemies.

From Mequinez to Tarudant, Muley
Abdallah visited all the mountains, among
the inhabitants of which the Negroes were
held in aversion, and by this means raised
himself

himfelf a party. Had he been fufceptible of reflection and prudence, he might have re-eftablifhed his power ; but, equally impetuous in profperity and adverfity, he continually acted with violence : the very tribes that had teftified their attachment to him foon felt the caprices of his character, and cruelty ; he, with his own hands, illtreating and killing thofe among them who came to make him remonftrances : fo that, at length, he was detefted and execrated by all the provinces, which no longer would intereft themfelves in his behalf.

Muley Ali, who was at Tafilet when he was called to empire, arrived at Mequinez, in October 1735. The firft of his cares, after his entrance, was to inform himfelf concerning the ftate of the treafury, which he knew had been left rich by his brother, Muley Achmet Daiby. Seeing it reduced to a very trifle, he, avaricious and barbarous like his predeceffors, indulged his ferocity ; and the mother of Muley Abdallah, beholding one of her own female attendants affaffinated in her arms, and fearing herfelf to fall the victim of his fury, gave him fome infor-

information concerning a part that had been concealed, but which, however, was of small value.

Anxious to preserve a crown, for which he was indebted to the preponderating power of the Negroes, this prince distributed among them all the money that remained in the treasury; and, without foreseeing the consequences, further promised them, as soon as he should be able to pay it, the sum of two hundred thousand ducats, or between fifty and sixty thousand pounds sterling. Hitherto the cities of Fez and Mequinez, and their dependencies only, were under the obedience of Muley Ali; the remainder of the empire was to be acquired by the valour of the Negroes.

Their general, the same whom Abdallah intended to have cut off, went, at the head of thirty thousand men, to besiege Morocco, took it by assault, put the garrison to the sword, and gave up the city to be pillaged by his soldiers. Actuated by resentment, this general proposed to march

and

and give battle to Muley Abdallah himfelf; but, perceiving indications of irrefolution among his troops, that had fo often
experienced the capricious generofity of
this Emperor, he was determined to march
with his army into the province of Beni-
Haffen, whence it carried off the flocks
and herds, and ravaged the environs of Sallee; which place refufed to open its gates.

However high the refentment of the
Negroes might be againft Muley Abdallah,
ftill their defire of money foon made them
forget his cruelties, recollecting only the
profufion of his gifts. Muley Ali was
poor, and this to them was a feeble recommendation; their general, who was in the
interefts of the latter, infenfibly loft the
confidence of his foldiers. Influenced by
their own avidity, and the intrigues of the
mother of Muley Abdallah, who promifed
each man thirty ducats if they would proclaim the Emperor once more, they, in
May, 1736, depofed Muley Ali, who had
for fome time paft ftupified himfelf by the
immoderate ufe of the Achicha, which had
benum-

benumbed his powers of body and mind*.

Informed of the reftoration of Muley Abdallah, Muley Ali retreated in his turn among the neighbouring mountains of Tremecen, accompanied by his family, and only fome forty men, who refolved to follow his fortunes.

A fecond time called to the throne, Muley Abdallah received at Teza, where he then was, a deputation of the officers of the Negroes, at the head of two thoufand men, to announce the revolution, and efcort him to Mequinez. Although the Emperor treated this deputation with demonftrations of gratitude, he ftill refufed to return to Mequinez, unlefs the Negroes would deliver up their general, Selim Doo-

* This plant greatly refembles hemp, and, mixed with other drugs, produces the fame kind of intoxication as opium. Some of the Moors take it continually ; it infpires them with agreeable reveries, and, though exceffively heating, it benumbs the fenfes. In fome conftitutions, it renders thofe who take it furious.

quelli; and he then promifed to recompenfe them by a gift of four hundred thoufand ducats, (or upward of a hundred thoufand pound fterling) which he had concealed.

Covetous as they were of money, yet the delivering up of their general was repugnant to the Negroes; befide, they perceived that the plan of Muley Abdallah was to weaken their power, and no longer to remain dependent on the influence they had acquired in the election of Emperor. Selim Dooquelli, an artful man, and beloved by the foldiers, was fo powerful in perfuading them that they did not hefitate once more to renounce their election of Muley Abdallah, and to proclaim Muley Mahomet, Ool Del Ariba *. The general expedited a courier to the latter at Tafilet, and fent him a detachment to efcort him to Mequinez. Thus was Muley Abdallah, by his imprudence, depofed

* That is to fay, the fon of the Ariba, which was the family name of the queen, his mother.

either

either the fame, or nearly the fame day,
on which he was once more elected.

This precipitate proceeding, notwithftanding, gave birth to quarrels among the
foldiers, who were not all of the fame
opinion. They took to their arms, the
party of Muley Abdallah became victorious,
and he was a third time proclaimed before the arrival of Muley Mahomet. The
latter, being then on the road, found himfelf obliged to ftop at Old Fez, where he
was received and treated as Emperor.
Sovereignty, in times fo perilous, was a
very precarious and temporary poffeffion,
which depended entirely on the moment
and its accidents, on the character of the
commanders and the caprices of the foldiery.

The officers of the Negroes, having re-
inftated Muley Abdallah on the throne,
interefted themfelves in behalf of their
general, and obtained a promife of pardon
by the mediation of the Emperor's mother. Selim Dooquelli, who had taken

refuge in an afylum, left this hofpitium on the word of the Emperor; but he informed his foldiers of the fear he had, that he fhould become " the victim of the de-
" ceit of this fubtle and fanguinary fox,
" who, faid he to them, only wifhes to de-
" prive you of your chief, that he may
" deftroy you with the greater facility."

His fears and forbodings were juftified by the event. Having been conducted to Teza, covered by the cloth of the fanctuary, to which he had fled, he proftrated himfelf before Muley Abdallah ; the Emperor kiffed the holy cloth, that far paying refpect to cuftom, and ordered it to be taken from the general, but, regardlefs of the afylum of religion, or his pledged faith, buried his lance in his body, and called for a cup that he might drink his blood. He afterward cut off the perfons attached to this general, and even his children, whom he caufed to be ftrangled in his prefence.

This thirft of blood, this difrefpect of his word, and of the prejudices of the nation, incited general indignation againft

I   Muley

Muley Abdallah. Not only is the fanctu-
aries of their Saints confidered, among the
Moors, as a certain afylum, which guards
the culprit againft the firft efforts of authority, and yields him the means of jufti-
fying himfelf, but a like refpect is alfo
paid to the very habit of the faint, to whom
any fuch hofpitium is confecrated. To
act contrary to this cuftom, to treat the
public opinion with contempt, and thus to
violate the facred rights of the holy place
of refuge, was to deprive the nation of all
protection from the power of defpotifm;
yet Muley Abdallah, acknowledging no
other rule than his arbitrary will, took a
pleafure in contemning thefe hofpitiums
and their Marabouts, for which and whom
the Moors have fo much veneration. Defirous of preventing the refentment which
his ill faith muft infpire among the Negroes, the Emperor departed from Teza
for Mequinez, under the pretext of paying them the four hundred thoufand ducats which they had been promifed. In
order to gain time, and the better to deceive the foldiers, he commanded the earth
to be dug up, in certain places which he

defcribed

defcribed, and affected the utmoft aftonifhment when no money was found.
Having, neverthelefs, promifed to pay the
Negroes before he made his entrance into
Mequinez, and being arrived there without the power of fulfilling his promife,
Muley Abdallah knew not how to act.
The fum of four hundred thoufand ducats, and the gratification which had
been before ftipulated with his mother,
amounted to near two millions of ducats ;
all the money he had poflefled had before
been difperfed, and he was obliged to fell
his arms, his horfes, and jewels; but,
though this facrifice proved his defire to
pay, it did not produce the quarter of the
fum he had promifed.

Never had Muley Abdallah more need
of circumfpection, and refource in his
own underftanding, than at this inftant.
Secretly detefted by his foldiers, who were
enamoured only of his prodigality, he had
the more to dread from their inconftancy
becaufe that he was at no great diftance
from Muley Mahomet, and to whom only
he had been preferred in fhe hope of reward.

ward. The Emperor once more entered
into treaty with the Negroes, and promised
to pay them in the space of two months,
while these soldiers, on their part, determined to remain neuter during that in-
terval, and neither interest themselves in
his behalf nor in behalf of Muley Mahomet, who was shut up in Fez.

Thus we behold a despotic sovereign
capitulating with his soldiers; yet, being
themselves the instruments of despotism, it
is no wise astonishing to see them sometimes thus acting as arbitrators.

This resolution of the Negroes determined Muley Abdallah to lay siege to Fez,
accompanied by the Brebes of his party.
The city made a most vigorous resistance,
and the sallies of Muley Mahomet were
so successful that the Brebes, wearied and
and disheartened, determined to raise the
siege.

The two months, which the Negroes
had granted to Muley Abdallah, being expired, they sent to demand their money,

as

as a creditor sends to demand a debt.
The Emperor made excuses, pleaded present circumstances, and once more paid
them with promises. The Negroes, whom
money alone might render tractable, now
recollected all the vices of Muley Abdallah, his cruelties, his ill faith, and hatred
to them; nor could they find any being
so odious as this Emperor, when he no
longer had any thing to give.

The murmurs of this turbulent body,
whose resentment and ferocity were
dreaded by Muley Abdallah, determined
him to escape with what he could collect
most precious, and retire among the mountains, accompanied by his mother, his
son, and a few soldiers. Astonished at the
flight of the Emperor, and irresolute themselves concerning the manner in which
they ought to act, the Negroes, in October
1736, once more named Muley Mahomet
Ool Del Ariba, at the solicitations of the
deputies of Fez, who engaged to pay, in
behalf of this prince, the four hundred
thousand ducats, which had been promised
them by Muley Abdallah.

Muley

Muley Mahomet, dreading his brother as a rival, and the ficklenefs of the foldiery, fent an army, againft Muley Abdallah, among the mountains in which he had taken refuge; but this army dared not to attack the Brebes in their faftnefies, and was impelled to retreat. After raifing a more numerous army, Muley Mahomet marched thither in perfon, but with no better fuccefs; his cavalry being incapable of acting, among mountains and precipices, he was obliged to renounce his enterprize, and to content himfelf with ravaging the country, and deftroying fome caftles in the environs. His army, having afterward been attacked by the Brebes in a defile, was beaten, and thrown into diforder. Muley Mahomet was himfelf wounded in the arm, and in danger of being taken, having fought perfonally, and with great valour.

After thefe acts of hoftility, the Negroes, much more occupied concerning their own interefts than the maintenance of the fove-reign power, began to make remonftrances concerning the four hundred thoufand ducats, which the deputies of Fez had

under-

undertaken to pay ; the latter having eluded
the payment of this fum, the foldiers no
longer could diffemble their refentment.
Thefe reftlefs and avaricious troops indi-
cated fo much indifference concerning
Muley Mahomet, that this prince, who was
mild, juft, and the enemy of tyranny, was
on the eve of laying down his authority
voluntarily, that he might no longer fubject himfelf to the phantafies of thefe
forces*. The Negroes, perceiving the fovereign they had chofen poffeffed not that
fpirit of vexation which alone might gratify their rapacity, fuddenly ftripped him
of the authority they had beftowed, and,
in 1738, named his brother, Muley Zin
Lahabdin, as his fucceffor.

The reign of Muley Zin was but momentary. Muley Abdallah, who had gone

* This prince has been dead about ten years ; he lived
like a private man near Mequinez, where I had the honour of being acquainted with him and his fons. Like
the princes of the Arabs, they fupported themfelves on the
revenues of their lands, flocks, and herds. They were very
polite, and exceedingly affable in fociety.

toward Morocco, where he had made himself a powerful party, was a fourth time proclaimed Emperor by the provinces of the South, that had taken arms to counteract the power of the Negroes. Made wife by the viciffitudes of fortune, to which he had been expofed by his own vices and diffipations, and by the avidity and inconftancy of his troops, the Emperor felt the neceffity of weakening thefe infolent Negroes, who difpofed of empire at their pleafure.

He long remained encamped under Mount Atlas with an army of Brebes, fuppofing that the Negroes would march to attack him, and intending there to give them battle: but, finding this project did not fucceed, he began his march for Mequinez, where, on his arrival, his election was confirmed. The Negroes had confented to this, becaufe they perceived no better means of acting; they, neverthelefs, did not behold with pleafure a monarch on the throne, who, prodigal as he had been in his gifts, had yet fo often deceived them, and who, contrary to the faith of promifes pledged,

pledged, had facrificed their general and principal chiefs to his policy and his vengeance; but they were obliged to diffemble their difcontent.

As the avarice of thefe troops favoured the intrigues of all thofe who afpired to fovereign power, the fecret diffatisfaction of the Negroes foon found an opportunity of making itfelf manifeft. The mother of Muley Muftadi, who clandeftinely negotiated with their general, fo well fucceeded that fhe difpofed them to favour her fon, who, in 1740, was proclaimed Emperor, and Muley Abdallah was once more obliged to retire among the mountains. Such and fo inceffant were thefe revolutions; for, as they depended on the cupidity and inconftancy of an armed mob, the e raifed up Emperors and pulled them down, almoft in the fame moment.

Muley Muftadi, unwilling to depend on the caprice of his foldiers, thought he acted wifely in uniting himfelf with the province of Beni-Haffen, and with the Bafhaw of Tangiers, who governed that

of

of Garb. This alliance, by which a union was again effected between all the north of the empire, infpired the troops with jealoufy; and, that they might not give Muley Muftadi time fufficient to ftrengthen his party, they once more recalled Muley Abdallah.

Muley Muftadi, however, was not depofed with the fame eafe as his predeceffors had been. Each party maintained and defended his election by the force of arms. Various actions happened between the two armies, and many fell on both fides. At length, Muley Abdallah, fupported by the Negroes, the Ludaya, and the moft warlike tribes, was victorious over the factions of the two provinces, which, powerful as they were, could not withftand an army compofed of foldiers inured to war. Muley Muftadi, on his part, without wholly renouncing empire, thought proper to retire to Arzilla, where he carried on a confiderable commerce in grain with the Spaniards.

The

The empire at this time was, for a
fhort fpace, divided between Muley Muftadi and Muley Abdallah ; the latter, defirous of obliging his brother wholly to
abdicate the throne, marched with an
army to poffefs himfelf of Tangiers, and
to cut off the Bafhaw, Achmet Ben Ali,
who was governer of the city, and who
fuftained Muley Muftadi, by his credit, his
money, and his troops. The Bafhaw having been killed in battle, the city was
taken, and his palace was pillaged ; but
his fon, Mahomet Ben Achmet, had time
to efcape to Gibralter, whither he carried
all his wealth.

Muley Muftadi profited by this momentary diverfion to go and ravage the environs of Fez. On his return from this
expedition, he was attacked near Alcaffar by
Muley Abdallah, and, having been deferted
in the battle by a part of his forces, he
found himfelf obliged to retreat to Sallee,
where, notwithftanding his defeat, he was
received and acknowledged Emperor.

The

The town of Rabat, which is only feparated from Sallee by a river, having refufed to own his authority, a civil war arofe
between the two places, which long continued, and which was equally ruinous to
both by the facility they mutually had to
injure each other. Sallee and Rabat, having become feudatory towns of the empire,
under Muley Ifhmael, formed at that time
a kind of republic, under a municipal government: reftored to the monarchy, they
might, by their wealth, and the character
of their inhabitants, favour the factions
that diftracted the empire.

Muley Muftadi, for fourteen months,
befieged Rabat; but, finding himfelf unable to take the place, he retired to Tedla,
where he was arrefted and put in chains
by the Brebes, of the party of Muley Abdallah. The Brebes of the cafile of Oor-
dega carried him off in the night, and
tranfported him into the hofpitium of
Sidi El Mati, a facred afylum, the faints
of which family had inherited the venera-
ration of the people. Sidi El Mati efcorted
Muley Muftadi to Sallee, where the Ba-

2   fhaw,

shaw, Fenis, received him with so much
the more eagerness inasmuch as that town,
devoted to this prince, was totally averse to
Muley Abdallah.

Muley Mustadi, however, finding that
he was incapable of resisting the faction
of the Negroes, or of restoring tranquillity
to an empire ever in revolt, renounced the
throne, and once more went to Arzilla,
where he lived like a private person, and
continued to trade with Europe.

Muley Abdallah thus, at length, was for
the sixth time, master of the empire, and
the Negroes, enfeebled by so many divisions, became less insolent in proportion as
there were fewer candidates for sovereign
power; beside, it was no longer possible to
set up the crown to the best bidder, or to
gratify the avarice of the soldiers, because
of the exhausted state of the treasury, and
of the difficulty with which contributions
might any longer be raised in the provinces, which had been entirely laid deso-
late by such a succession of revolutions.

Become

Become more prudent and circumspect by experience, and full of resentment against the Negroes, the inconstancy of whom he had so often experienced, Muley Abdallah determined to suppress this audacious soldiery, from whose aid he had nothing more to hope, and from whose insolence he had every thing to fear. He artfully took every occasion to involve the Negroes in quarrels with the mountaineers, and, by his secret intrigues, endeavoured to render them odious to all the provinces. Under the pretence of forced contributions, the amount of which he was to receive, he often set the Negroes at variance with the Brebes, by whom they were held in abhorrence; keeping up a correspondence with these mountaineers, the Emperor himself would send faithful troops, that the Negroes might be put between two fires, and thus sacrificed to the public hatred, his private vengeance, and his future repose. By such acts of barbarous policy, which had, in some sort, become necessary, in consequence of the avarice, fickleness, and preponderance of the Negroes, these turbulent forces, that had so
often

often put up the empire at auction, loft
that afcendancy they had acquired.

The Negroes being thus reduced, the
Emperor recovered his power, and the empire a part of its tranquillity. Muley Abdallah was firmly eftablifhed on the throne,
and remained thus in peaceable poffeffion
till his death. Yet did not all the varieties
of fortune he had felt make any change
in the manners of this Moor; he ftill preferved the fanguinary and cruel character
he from the firft had teftified, and ftill infpired nb other fentiments than thofe of
fear and terror. Ingenious in refining on
barbarity, not a week paffed, perhaps not a
day, that did not behold fome one immo-
lated to his choler, or his caprice.

It muft, notwithftanding, be acknowledged that, cruel and frantic as were the
acts which difgraced his reign, he ftill gave
tokens of fome principles of equity and
difintereftednefs, which, though they cannot excufe, feem, in fome degree, to foften
his ferocity. When any Moor whatever had
committed a crime, Muley Abdallah caufed
him

him to be punished with the utmost severity, without seizing on his wealth. An Alcaid, after having been imprisoned and condemded to death, offered to give him his riches, which were very considerable, would he only grant him his life. "Thy riches," answered the Emperor, " belong to thy " children, who are not guilty; but, as " thou art, it is but just that thou shouldest " perish."

Muley Abdallah having, at length, suppressed those revolutions, by which his reign had so often been disturbed, he alternately made Mequinez and Morocco his places of residence, that he might occasionally be present at each boundary of his empire, and overawe, with the greater ease, the provinces, whose inconstancy he feared. He afterward commanded the palace, called Arbiba, to be built near New Fez, in which he passed the latter years of his life.

Heir to all the caprices and barbarities of Muley Ithmael, he neither possessed his

Vol. II.   T   prudence

prudence nor his policy. More generous than his father, and less a slave to the prejudices of his religion, he did not resemble him in his dislike of Europeans: he soon concluded treaties of peace with the English and the Dutch, who, in the beginning of the present century, enjoyed almost the exclusive commerce of Europe; the confidence of foreign powers, under his reign, was so far established that several commercial houses were settled at Tetuan, Sallee, Saffi, and Santa Cruz; and the merchants, as well as the ships of nations that were not at peace with the empire of Morocco, there enjoyed all the rights and good faith of asylum.

After the example of his father, Muley Abdallah employed the slaves, whom the fate of battles gave into the power of his corsairs, on the public works; and, though he treated them with barbarous rigour, chastising and putting them to death on the slightest pretence, he still held it contrary to the principles of humanity to refuse their being redeemed; many of them were released under his reign, and thus, amidst

amidst the most excessive cruelties, did
he seem to be impressed with some sentiments of humanity and justice.

The plague, which had laid waste the
states of Morocco, under the reign of Muley Ishmael, again committed new ravages
under that of Muley Abdallah, and made
its appearance in 1752, being communicated to the Moors from Algiers and Tunis,
whither it had been brought from Turkey *.

It was at the commencement of the
reign of Muley Abdallah, in 1732, that

---

* The plague was almost general in Turkey in the year
1751, and Constantinople lost a third of its inhabitants.
The ravages of this scourge of man were, in some degree,
foretold by the old people, who, seeing the quantity of
snow that fell in the winter of 1750 and 1751, foreboded,
from experience, that the plague would become very fatal.
Their prophecy was justified by the event, though it had by
many been regarded as vague and idle. It might happen
that the nitrous particles, with which the air was impreg-
nated, increased the fermentation of the blood, and rendered the contagion more quick and poisonous. I have
allowed myself to write this note, which, perhaps, may
deserve indulgence from the accurate observers of nature.

the

the Duke de Riperda, renowned for his high rank and adventures, paſſed over to the court of Morocco. Born in the province of Groningen, and become miniſter of Spain, under Philip V., this Duke, after his difgrace, was expoſed for a time to numerous viciſſitudes of fortune. After eſcaping from Segovia, where he was impriſoned, he went to England and Holland; his reſtleſs and turbulent temper made him liſten to the inſtigations of the Alcaid, Perez, who, at that time, reſided as ambaſſador at the Hague, and turn his thoughts toward Morocco.

Full of animoſity againſt the court of Madrid, the Duke formed the project of beſieging Ceuta, thinking he ſhould thereby involve the court of Morocco in his reſentment. He met a very kind reception from Muley Abdallah; but the ſtates of the Emperor being conſtantly a prey to revolutions, and he himſelf inconſiſtent, the Duke went to Tetuan, and made that the place of his reſidence.

Here

Here he formed various projects to diffi-
pate his wearinefs, and animate the Moors
againft Spain; but his motives of refentment, and plans of revenge, were wholly
ineffectual at a court which never acted
from any fixed fyftem, and which was itfelf too much divided to concern itfelf
with foreign interefts. By nature turbulent, the Duke afterward entered into the
projects of Baron Neuhof, who, under the
name of Theodore, was for a moment king
of Corfica.

Defirous of prevailing on the court of
Morocco to unite itfelf with the people of
Tunis, who were difpofed to give aid to
this rifing kingdom, he made many jour-
nies to the court at Mequinez, where his
plan appeared to be approved; but he was
amufed only with hopes, in order to obtain
prefents, and his political views were very
little regarded. It is not, however, true
that the Duke de Riperda became a profe-
lyte to Mahometanifm; nor did he ever
command the armies of Morocco, as fome
writers have affirmed. Some Moors of
the country, who were particularly ac-

T 3   quainted

quainted with him, have affured me that he ended his life and romantic adventures at Tetuan, toward the end of the year 1737, without either changing his drefs or his religion.

Muley Abdallah having paffed the greater part of his life in one continued agitation, never, during the firft years of his reign, tafting repofe, it may be that this erratic and troublefome life might contribute to the brutal ferocity of his character, and to that depravation of manners which made him contemned by his fubjects. His whole pofterity confifted but of two male children; the eldeft having died in the caftle of Rabat, while heading his father's party againft Muley Muftadi, there only remained Sidi Mahomet, the prefent reigning Emperor.

This circumftance prevented the divifions, which always arife on the death of an Emperor, to obtain the fucceffion; for, as the rights of feniority and birth are not fufficiently eftablifhed to give unequivocal claim, all the fons of the late fovereign, anxious to
                                        poffefs

poſſeſs a crown, form parties ; and the empire becomes the inheritance of him who
is the ſtrongeſt and moſt wealthy.

Sidi Mahomet, deſirous of fixing the
public opinion concerning himſelf and ac-
cuſtoming the people to obedience, obtained from his father the government of
Saffi, where he paſſed a part of his youth.
Several European merchants had ſettled in
this city, which, at that time, was the
moſt commercial on the whole coaſt ; and
this prince, who was exceedingly eaſy of
acceſs, and whoſe views were equally to
employ his time agreeably and to gain va-
luable information, frequently converſed
with theſe merchants concerning the cuftoms of Europe, the commerce of its nations, their taxes, and their mode of adminiſtration. At this time it was that Sidi
Mahomet acquired thoſe general, vague,
and imperfect ideas, which ſince have un-
folded themſelves during the courſe of his
reign, and which have given Europeans an
advantageous opinion of his abilities. Theſe
are, perhaps, held in higher conſideration
among foreign nations than in his own

empire,

empire, where, however, the beſt judgement may be formed of his principles, by an actual view of their conſequences.

Deſirous of ſhewing himſelf in the provinces of the empire, Sidi Mahomet, while prince, pretended it was neceſſary he ſhould journey through them, in order to make the ſovereign authority reſpectable, which authority he inſenſibly appropriated to himſelf: he traverſed thoſe of Duquella, Tedla, and Temſena, where he levied many contributions, to his own profit, with a high hand. At his return, his father, who had retired to Fez, entruſted him with the government of Morocco, and there he reſided with one of his couſins, Muley Dris, an enlightened prince, who, in the firſt advances of Sidi Mahomet toward empire, aided him by his advice and abilities.

Of all the princes who had diſputed ſovereign power with Muley Abdallah, Muley Muſtadi was the only one who, whenever his brother ſhould die, might raiſe an inſurrection in the provinces of the North.

Sidi

Sidi Mahomet, in order to prevent any such attempts, sent him notice to quit Arzilla, and to go and reside at Fez, where he, a short time after, died.

The better to establish his authority in the north of the empire, Sidi Mahomet left Morocco, in 1755, accompanied by an army, and presented himself, during the month of August, before Rabat and Sallee, which places, since the reign of Muley Ishmael, had been governed by a special administration of their own, and formed a kind of republic. This regency, though feudatory to the empire, appeared to prescribe limits to the sovereign authority. The inhabitants of these combined towns, known by the name of Saletines, or Sallee rovers, fitted out corsairs at their own expence, and were in possession of the gains of piracy, and the advantages of commerce, which, by the situation of those towns on the sea shore, and the industry of the people, had become confiderable.

The wealth and independence of these two cities afforded motives sufficiently powerful to enflame the ambition of the prince, covetous as he was of riches, and defirous of empire. Sidi Mahomet had further caufe of enmity againft thefe places, arifing from the wavering ftate in which they remained during the revolutions that had difturbed the reign of his father. This was remembered with rancour by the prince, and thus had the recollection of the wealth they contained, their independence, and the part they had taken in behalf of Muley Muftadi, long excited his avidity and his refentment.

Rabat and Sallee, though united by a confederation, which fituation, mutual convenience, and contiguity, rendered neceffary, were, neverthelefs, difturbed by that fpirit of reftleffnefs fo natural to the Moors, and by a diverfity of interefts, which were continual and unceafing caufes of quarrels and diffenfions. On the approach of Sidi Mahomet, however, they united their forces, and refolved to refufe entrance to the prince.

Rabat,

Rabat, faithful to its engagements, obstinately defended its walls; but the Bashaw, Fenis, who commanded at Sallee, desirous of obtaining the favours of the prince, and by his submission of conferring an obligation on Sidi Mahomet, as he had before done on Muley Muftadi, repaired, in company with the principal men of the city, to the camp of the prince, on the 26th of August, there to supplicate for clemency and reward. Sidi Mahomet pardoned the Bashaw, Fenis, and sent him back exceedingly well satisfied, but, some time after, took an opportunity to effect his destruction, and had him stoned to death in his presence.

After the reduction of the city of Sallee, that of Rabat, which found a difficulty of preventing communication by the river, was also obliged to submit. Sidi Mahomet imprisoned the principal persons in the government, behaved to them like a haughty victor, and obliged them to pay heavy contributions. One of the inhabitants, whose name was Mifteri, exceedingly wealthy, and at the head of the confederants, engaged

gaged to fupply the place with food himfelf during a year; but the brother of this republican betrayed him to the prince, whom he informed of the ftate of the place. Mifteri was ftripped of his property, as a punifhment for his firm refiftance; and his brother was made governor of Rabat, as a reward for his treachery,

All the inhabitants of the city were made to feel the refentment of the prince. Three merchant's houfes, two French, one Englifh, and a Spanifh convent, were not excepted. The monks, who had no property, were made flaves, and where afterward ranfomed. The merchants themfelves were not releafed till each of them had firft paid ten thoufand piaftres, and thefe were paid in effects, which were eftimated at fo low a price that their ranfom amounted to double the fum. The Englifh merchant, for having fold gunpowder to Muley Muftadi, was treated with ftill greater rigour; and, after having been expofed to various humiliations and violences, hung himfelf in defpair. The taking of Rabat and Sallee expofed exposed the inhabitants of these two places to very confiderable impofitions, but coft none of them their lives, the Bafhaw, Fenis, alone excepted, who was put to death fome time afterward, and who was the fole victim the prince appears to have facrificed to his refentment. Perhaps this is the only act of cruelty with which he can be reproached; and, for the commiffion of which, he has himfelf teftified his repentance.

By that contradiction which is either natural to man, to the character of this prince, or, perhaps, to arbitrary power, Sidi Mahomet chaftifed Sallee for having received, and Rabat for not having received, Muley Muftadi. He, with greater reafon, reproached the inhabitants of the latter place for their conduct toward his brother, whom they had befieged and almoft ftarved to death, in the caftle where he had fhut himfelf up, when defending the rights and interefts of his father, Muley Abdallah.

After

After having subjected the cities of Rabat and Sallee, Sidi Mahomet marched into the North of the empire, where he obliged the Alcaid, Lucas, Governor of Tetuan, to render up an account of his administration. This Alcaid, who had taken advantage of the distance of the court, and the feebleness of the government, in the latter part of the reign of Muley Abdallah, to extend his own authority, was stripped of his property and power.

Sidi Mahomet reformed various abuses during the life of his father, with whom he almost divided the empire, till, at last, Muley Abdallah, worn out by age, and still more by the troubles he had met with during his reign, died on the 12th of November, 1757, in his palace at Fez, where he had only preserved the shadow of authority.

Exposed as he was himself, in the first years of his reign, to all the caprices of fortune, and as his subjects were to all those of his own temper, this Emperor still had some good qualities, which were clouded by
a much

a much greater number of vices. He possessed courage, judgment, and generosity; but was violent, sanguinary, and addicted to drunkenness, and to a depraved and infamous vice, which he made fashionable at his court. The ferocity of his character seemed to be the consequence of an atrabilarious constitution, and which displayed itself periodically, occasioned, perhaps, by the greater or less agitation of the blood.

He one day made a present of two thousand ducats to a confidential domestic, and advised him to go and live far from his presence, that he might not be exposed to the effects of his fury. The attachment to his master was so great that the servant refused, and, in one of his barbarous fits, Muley Abdallah shot this faithful servant, reproaching him with his folly for not having left him as he had been advised.

As he was passing the river of Beth on horseback, at the place where it falls into the Seboo, the Emperor was in danger of being drowned, when one of his Negroes

ran

ran to his fuccour and preferved his life.
The flave congratulated himfelf for having faved his mafter, when the Emperor,
drawing his fabre clave him down, and ex-
claimed, " Here is an infidel! To fuppofe
" that he had faved me! As if God flood
" in need of his intervention to fave a
" fharif."

Without publicly neglecting the rites
of the law, Muley Abdallah paid little refpect to popular prejudices, and put to
death feveral Moors, whofe fanctity had
been held in veneration. He one day
killed two Marabouts, who came from the
neighbourhood of Tunis, and who informed him they were faints. " You
" faints!" faid the Emperor. " You are
" no faints. You are impoftors, who,
" abufing the credulity of the people,
" come here as fpies." After which he
fired a mufket at each, and laid them dead
at his feet.

A faint, revered throughout the country,
having come to the court of this prince to
remonftrate to him concerning his mode of
life,

life, so contrary to the laws of Mahomet,
said to the Emperor : " The prophet him-
" self has ordained me to come, on his part,
" and speak to thee thus ——And did the
" prophet tell thee in what manner I
" should receive thee ?— Yes, he told me
" that you would be affected by the words
" which he commanded me to speak, and
" that you would employ them to your
" advantage—Then he has deceived thee,"
said the Emperor, discharging at the same
moment his piece, which laid the saint
lifeless; and, farther to punish his temerity, he would not permit his body to be
buried.

An Alcaid, who had been guilty of difobedience, having come to the court of
Muley Abdallah to implore pardon, the
Emperor commanded him to be beheaded.
He then ordered dinner to be served to the
officers who had accompanied this Alcaid,
and to place in the dish of Coofcoofoo, out
of which they were to eat, this bloody
head, that they might not soon forget the
punishment disobedience merited.

　　　　Thus

Thus did this prince make his crimes and executions his amusement. Enough has been said of him; it were but to insult humanity to dd more traits of the cruelty of his character.

BOOK

B O O K   V.

The reign of Sidi Mahomet—Commercial regulations—Adminiftration, public and domeftic—Infurrections—Wars, Locufts, Famine—Character
of the Emperor—Commerce of the Empire—
Duties, Coins, Weights, and Meafures.

*

—————————————

I N T R O D U C T I O N.

After the death of Muley Abdallah, his
only fon, Sidi Mahomet, who, during
the life of his father, had already accuftomed the people to refpect his authority, fucceeded to the empire without
oppofition.

The

The reign of this Emperor has not been varied by revolutions, or victories; neither is it sullied by those acts of violence, and barbarity, which so dreadfully stained the sceptre of his predecessors. I have imagined, the best mode of giving a clear idea of his reign would be briefly to examine the several regulations attending it, and the principal events. These combined will present a faithful picture of the character, the genius, and the views of Sidi Mahomet, and of the present state of the empire of Morocco. I shall therefore speak separately of the dispositions and plans of this Emperor, relative to commerce and taxation, to the general administration of the government, the domestic and œconomical affairs of the palace, the few insurrections that have happened during his reign, and the events by which it has been distinguished.

CHAP.

CHAP. I.

The dispositions and views of Sidi Mahomet relative to commerce and taxation.

THE empire having been so long disturbed by revolutions, under the reign of Muley Abdallah, the distant provinces lived in a kind of independence. The governors had usurped more authority, and the treasury had been exhausted by the avidity of the soldiers, and the capricious manner in which money was squandered by that Emperor. Sidi Mahomet, ripened by age and experience when he ascended the throne, applied himself to find means of quickly re-establishing the finances, and supplying the state treasury, and with the care of making arbitrary power respected throughout the provinces, which power had

U 3

been

been somewhat enfeebled by the concuffions of the late troublefome reign.

The information he had acquired, concerning commerce and taxation, occafioned
the Emperor to perceive that, of all political advantages, that which tended to re-
vive commerce in a nation could alone augment its revenues, and repair its loffes.
The profits arifing from piracy, an occupa-
tion which was expofed to real loffes and
uncertain gains, might, on the one part,
provoke the refentment of nations, the
maritime forces of which were daily augmenting, while, on the other, the barter
of the productions of the empire would
afcertain to him thofe more abundant refources of wealth which accrue from agriculture.

Reflexions like thefe determined Sidi
Mahomet to make peace with the powers
of Europe. After confirming that already
made between Morocco, England, and
Holland, he, in the beginning of his reign,
concluded treaties with Denmark and
Sweden fucceffively ; and, in the following
years,

years, with the republic of Venice, France, Spain, and Portugal. In 1782, the Emperor and the Grand Duke of Tuscany made peace, and the other powers of Italy enjoy a kind of truce with the empire of Morocco.

Before the reign of Sidi Mahomet the nations of Europe had formed commercial connections on the coast of Morocco, and those who were not at peace with the empire still enjoyed the safety of asylum. True it is that the instability of the government somewhat diminished the confidence of nations; and the little security the roads of Morocco afforded, in winter, was an obstacle to the increase of navigation. At that time there were only a few safe ports on the coast of the empire. They were dangerous from the impediments of bars, and the ignorance, avarice, or evil intentions, of the pilots.

In order to aid commerce, and encrease the glory of his reign, Sidi Mahomet caused the town of Mogodor to be built in the south part of his empire, where nature had formed

U 4   a port

a port acceffible in all feafons. The Emperor encouraged foreign merchants to erect houfes in this new city, by giving them to fuppofe the duties of the cuftoms fhould be leffened. The Moors and the Jews alfo built houfes there to pleafe their Mafter; and Mogodor, as I have already obferved, is built with more regularity than any other city of the empire.

After having thus founded Mogodor, the principal expence of which was fupported by foreign commerce, the Emperor, who began to take delight in building, ordered the fortreffes of Laracha and Rabat to be repaired, embellifhed each of thefe cities with fome edifices and public markets, and, at the fame time, made additions to his palace at Morocco, for which he has a degree of predilection. After he had extended the circumference of this palace, he caufed new pavillions to be added, built with tafle by European mafons.

In 1773, Sidi Mahomet commanded the foundation of the town of Fedale to be laid, which was then begun, but which has never

never been finished. These undertakings have been neglected, pursued, or again abandoned, according to the temporary change of circumstances, or, perhaps, because the revenues of the Emperor are insufficient to support such expences. Neither do cities seem so necessary, in these temperate climates, where the people are habituated to a solitary country life, as they are in latitudes less mild.

The confidence which the regulations, political views, and personal character, of Sidi Mahomet inspired, among foreign nations, at first multiplied mercantile establishments on the coast of Morocco. Merchants settled at Santa Cruz, Mogodor, Saffi, Rabat, Laracha, and Tetuan. There were even too many, and their purposes were subverted by their own eagerness. The Emperor successively increased the duties, hoping thereby to augment his revenues; but this oppression, however, produced an effect the very reverse. Shackled thus by taxation, commerce grew languid.

The

The Emperor, pretending to give it new animation, became a merchant himfelf; and this did but increafe the evil, for it did but increafe reftraint. Obliged to fell their wares and to purchafe the country products at fuch prices as the defpot pleafed to fix, merchants became merely his factors, and were conftrained to remove from port to port in his empire, wherever he chofe to indicate, as beft fuited his convenience, or to thofe to which he gave the preference.

By this means the channel of trade was interrupted. The farmer and the foreign trader, reaping no fruit from the labours of their induftry, and unable to refift the current of authority, are wholly difcouraged; the fields lie wafte, the markets are deferted, and, of all the mercantile houfes difperfed over the coaft of Morocco, there fcarcely remain fix. United at Mogodor, and accuftomed to the variations of the government, they have to ftruggle againft the extortions excited by the fpirit of intereft, and which, at one moment increafed,

creafed, at the next relaxed, are never certain.

More enlightened than his predeceffors,
Sidi Mahomet, in 1766, made a regulation
which betokened extenfive views; but, not
being directed by invariable principles, its
effect was merely momentary. At that time
there was a confiderable quantity of corn
amaffed, in the maritime provinces, which
long had been inclofed in Matamores *,
and there expofed to perifh, exportation
being prohibited by the law. The Emperor, whofe fyftem was more humane and
more œconomical, wifhing to conciliate
the wants of the nation with its prejudices, and give his plan a legal fanction, affembled the learned in the law, and propofed to them his difficulties concerning
the exportation of corn.

* Corn can only be preferved in fuch kind of pits in
hot countries; and it appears probable that the reafon
is becaufe the corn, there, is firm and hard. The wheat
reaped in the northern countries of Europe, which is called
foft corn, could not be fo preferved. Yet this difference in
the grain is accidental, and relative to the nature of the foil
and the climate, and not to its own inherent qualities.

" I have

" I have need," faid the Emperor, " of
" arms and ammunition, for the defence of
" our religion ; but, by purchafing them,
" I muft exhauft the treafures of the ftate.
" Would it be contrary to our law to pro-
" cure thefe things, by giving in exchange
" corn which we cannot eat ourfelves, and
" which, in time, muft perifh ?"

The propofition was fo clear, and the
neceffity alfo of approving the will of the
defpot fo great, that the affembly concluded
fuch barter would be entirely legal, and the
exportation of corn was permitted in exchange for mortars, cannon, and gunpowder. The Emperor, at length, received
money for it, becaufe that, with money,
arms and ammunition may be bought.
In a fhort time he had collected not
only artillery, bombs, and mortars, but
fome millions of livres, while the provinces that had fold their corn had this additional refource to pay their enforced contributions, which, in the Empire of Morocco, is the ufual confequence of wealth,
a tax on their ficklenefs, and the pledge of
their

their fidelity. Thus did this excellent regulation benefit the Emperor alone.

The exportation of corn from the coast
of Morocco would become an inexhauftible
fource of barter and wealth, to the fubject
and to the ftate, were only a moderate taxation impofed, which might encourage
agriculture. But, in free ftates only, and
governments that ferioufly are active to
procure happinefs to man, are fuch advantages well underftood; therefore do we
only behold the lands rich and fruitful
in thofe happy countries where agriculture is encouraged; while the provinces of
Morocco, naturally fertile, yet overrun
with brambles, are little better than deferts,
and where the generations of men lan-
guifh and infenfibly diminifh.

CHAP.

CHAP. II.

Of the public Administration under Sidi Mahomet.

IT has before been shewn that the government of Morocco is wholly subordinate to the will of the despot, and that he confides the regulation of the provinces and cities of his empire to his Aicaids and Bashaws. It has likewise been observed that the Emperor himself, three times a week, gives public audiences to enforce justice, and at which all his subjects, without exception, are heard. This system, which cannot be too much admired, prevents malverfation, and the abuse of authority among the chiefs. It gives the sovereign an opportunity of knowing the truth, which it is the interest of his courtiers to conceal, of becoming acquainted with

whatever

whatever paffes in his ftates, even to their utmoft boundaries, and enables him to fuperintend the adminiftration of juftice.

After the acceffion of Sidi Mahomet, this judicious Emperor, defirous of effacing all recollection of the caprices of his father, wholly employed himfelf in the reftoration of order, of re-eftablifhing rules for government, and uniformity in the decifions of juftice. Well knowing the talents and penetration of Mulcy Dris, his relation, with whom he had paffed a part of his youth, he made him his friend, repofed entire confidence in him, and almoft raifed him to the rank of his affociate in the empire.

Mulcy Dris was a penetrating and enlightened prince. Though covetous of riches, he ftill was generous to his Mafter. Subtle, fagacious, and fertile in expedients, he foon brought all affairs to pafs through his hands, and almoft governed the empire under the fhadow of the monarch. That he might conform to the tafte of the Emperor, he appeared in public with the utmoft

moſt ſimplicity. But, for this abſtinence, he amply recompenſed himſelf in his palace and in his gardens, where he lived voluptuouſly.

Muley Dris almoſt excluſively appropriated to himſelf the adminiſtration of European affairs. This was to him a ſecret ſource of wealth, which, by his management and addreſs, became inexhauſtible. Not one perſon at the court of Morocco could treat ſuch ſubjects with greater dexterity, or could ſo artfully varniſh, or give effect to, his good or his ill offices. Full of diſſimulation with foreigners, who came to viſit him, he oſtentatiouſly diſplayed his cabinets, richly ornamented with ſilver plate, china, and jewels, which he had received as preſents from various courts. Like a cunning courtezan, who knows artfully to ſtimulate the generoſity of her lover, he, with ſubtlety, inſinuated to one nation how much he had received from another, to excite emulation, and the deſire of pleaſing him, by the largeneſs of their gifts. Thus acquainted with the human heart, he ſported with the vanity of individuals,

individuals, and raifed a rivalſhip between nations.

The wealth which Muley Dris had thus accumulated has had a ſimilar fate to that of all other individuals, in Morocco, who have preceded him, or ſurvived. Acquired as it was by the influence of the ſovereign, it has become a part of the treaſures of the ſtate, which muſt, at length, inſenſibly engulph the whole riches of the empire. This prince was, various times before his death, ſtripped of a part of his property, and the Emperor took care to ſecure what remained after his deceaſe, fearing leſt his children, who were young, might make an ill uſe of their money.

Muley Dris, after having indulged in pleaſure to exceſs, died in March, 1772, of a dropſy, which appeared to be the conſe-quence of his irregularities. He made an immoderate uſe of the Achlcha, which is of a nature ſo heating, and which rendered him ſo choleric and ferocious, that there was no barbarity he was not capable to

VOL. II. X commit

commit during his intoxication. He had inherited the vices of his anceftors, was intemperate, covetous, and cruel; and, had fortune raifed him to power, he would have walked in the paths of Muley Arfhid, Muley Ifhmael, and Muley Abdallah.

After the death of this prince, Sidi Mahomet having no confidential perfon whom he entrufted, indulged his own character more freely. Some of his felfifh agents, whom he appoints or depofes at pleafure, are charged with the execution of his orders. They are become the inftruments by whom all bufinefs muft be tranfacted, and negociations are now more tedious and more uncertain. Each new refolution is expofed to thofe variations which muft be the refult, under a government the fyftem of which is to confult the intereft of the moment.

CHAP.

C H A P. III.

Of the domeſtic affairs and interior œconomy of the palace.

SIDI Mahomet does not awe the ſpectator by any oſtentation of magnificence. The friend of ſimplicity, and without the leaſt inclination for luxury, this Emperor is only diſtinguiſhed from the grandees of his court by being on horſeback, and protected from the ſunbeams by an umbrella, which, in Morocco, is the diſtinctive mark of ſovereignty. The numerous retinue of officers, ſoldiers, pages, and ſecretaries, who appertain to the court, beſpeak the preſence of the monarch, who never appears in public but on horſeback, or in his caleſh. He is never ſeen on foot, except in his palace, at his devotions, or, on ſome few occaſions, in his gardens. He

never

never travels in a carriage, becaufe of the bad ftate of the roads.

The Emperor of Morocco, only on days of ceremony, or when he holds his Me-fhooar, that is, his. council, or audience, appears with all his pomp, which then rather confifts in the number than in the fplendour of his train. When he leaves his palace, for his amufement or to vifit the public works, he difplays no pomp; and he has been fometimes feen in a fhallop, on the Sallee river, with not more than two attendants.

The cuftoms of the court of Morocco, and thofe of the Ottoman court, bear no refemblance. The latter is remarkable for its magnificence, the former for its ruftic fimplicity. At the court of the Grand Seignior, the adminiftration of the govern-ment, and that of the palace, are entrufted to a number of minifters, who themfelves live in great ftate, and poffefs great power. At Morocco, the Defpot grants his fubjcéts only fleeting and momentary confi-dence. They attend on him but to execute

cute his commands, without poffeffing any ftable or permanent authority.

Female negro flaves have the care of the palace, and of the kitchen. The Emperor has occafionally fent for European cooks and bakers; but, wanting the conveniences to which they had been accuftomed, unacquainted with the manners of the Moors, ignorant of the language, and not eafily habituating themfelves to a kind of wandering life, thefe Europeans never fettled at the court of Morocco. The monarch being, alfo, naturally temperate, troubles himfelf little concerning fuch things. He has not fo much as any fixed hour of dinner.

The table of the palace is ferved with great uniformity. The Moors eat only to live, and are unacquainted with that multitude of difhes, and that variety of fauces, which, in Europe, are objects of fo much induftry and expence. Sidi Mahomet generally eats alone, and thofe officers who perfonally attend on him are afterward ferved from his table. Each of the Emperor's

X 3

wives

wives has a separate table, which is sufficiently supplied to suffice for all her
attendants. Coofcoofoo, which has been
described in its proper place, is the chief
dish of the Moors, as well in the palace of
the Emperor as in the hovel of the subject; and this is dressed in such quantities
that the vessel that contains it is sometimes
carried on a kind of chairman's horse.

The palace of the Emperor contains numerous servants of both sexes, who are
new cloathed once a year. On this occasion all the taylors in the city are summoned, who usually are Jews, and they are
obliged to labour gratis. This is a species of
corvée, or tax, for which they indemnify
themselves, when they can, by filching.
Most trades are obliged to work gratis for
the Emperor. The proprietor of a lime kiln
must set apart a tenth for the service of the
monarch; each article of merchandize, or
industry, which is subjected to a like taxation, becomes more dear in proportion, and
what the prince does not pay the purchaser
must. The Emperor is served by slaves,
who receive no other wages than what arise
from

from the profits or perquifites of the bufinefs they tranfact. He is at no expence,
except that of feeding and cloathing his family, and which yet is defrayed out of the
product of the tenths, and the cuftom-houfe
duties, fo that he feldom has any occafion
to difburfe money.

In the palace of the Emperor is a guard
of women, with their female commanders,
who are called Harriffa, and who form a
kind of court, the province of which is
the chaftifement of women. Thefe Harriffa are fent over the country to put the
wives of the grandees to the torture, when
the latter are imprifoned, and to make them
confefs all they know concerning the wealth
of their hufbands.

The luxury of the ladies of the palace is
not very great. They depend on the generofity of the fovereign, which, in Sidi
Mahomet, is wholly actuated by the greater
or lefs degree of love they infpire. Such
women as have not greatly pleafed the monarch are often neglected, forgotten, and
left in one imperial city, when the Em-

peror

peror removes to another. This practice
gives credibility to the opinion that accefs
to the palace of the Emperor, in Morocco,
is not fo difficult as at Conftantinople,
where the women are fhut up, and guarded
with greater aufterity. The women at
the court of the Grand Seignior are kept in
much greater fplendor, and are held in
much higher efteem than in thefe fouthern
climates, where the Seraglio is renewed fo
often that they can only infpire a fleeting
paffion. The prefent Emperor has been
known to fend back to a Bafhaw one of his
daughters, to whom he had been only married fix months.

The wives of the Emperor of Morocco,
who are legally efpoufed, are not flaves, but
are generally either princeffes, the daughters of Sharifs, the daughters of the governors of provinces, or of private individuals. The Great Queen, for fuch is the
title they give to the firft wife, was the
daughter of Muley Soliman, and grand
daughter of Muley Arfhid. This princefs,
who, by right of priority, had precedence
over all the other women of the palace,
enjoyed,

enjoyed, during her life, by the rights of birth and perfonal merit, a very high afcendancy over the mind of the Emperor. The very fame reafon, alfo, enfured to her the attachment and veneration of the people, fhe having ever, with the utmoft prudence, attended to the government of Morocco, when the monarch was abfent. The regret of the empire, at her death, was equal to her merit and her virtues.

Sidi Mahomet has a great number of children. His daughters, married to fharifs, have diftricts affigned them, and, during the life of the Emperor, refide in the palace, where they are miftreffes of their own actions. In order to provide for his fons, as foon as they are married the Emperor beftows upon them the governments of provinces and cities, where thefe young princes, indulging all the intemperance and follies of youth, and yielding to the advice and rapacity of their fervants, inflict every kind of vexation, while the fubjects have neither the fortitude nor the liberty to complain. Thus, in the adminiftration of their offices do they imbibe the art of oppreffing the

people,

people ; and, when their extortions raife univerfal difcontent, which can no longer be concealed, they are punifhed by confifcation for the benefit of the public treafury. After this difplay of juftice, oppreffion once more recommences ; the treafury fwells, and the miferable people are the eternal victims.

CHAP.

C H A P. IV.

Revolutions that have happened during the reign of Sidi Mahomet.

NOTWITHSTANDING the reftlefs fpirit of the provinces, under the ever-agitated reign of Muley Abdallah, the tranquillity became great, when Sidi Mahomet afcended the throne. That difcontent, which ever muft arife from public wretchednefs, may often have brooded in fecret, but has fince feldom burft forth. This Emperor has maintained a calm throughout his ftates, by occafionally going in perfon to their utmoft boundaries. Wherever he appeared, fome pretext for levying contributions generally has attended him; either originating in complaints againft the governors, or in the prejudices and divifions which are unceafing, among thofe tribes which

which inhabit the provinces. The paffions by which the Moors are tormented are never ending motives for inflicting pecuniary punifhment. All their quarrels, their reconciliations, all acts of authority, of mercy, or of juftice, are inceffantly concluded by the payment of fome quintals of filver. Such trifling difputes give the monarch no inquietude; they do but draw his attention for a moment. It is even a part of his policy to maintain and provoke thefe mifunderftandings; they are the fafeguard of the defpot, and feldom fail to turn to the advantage of his treafury.

Sidi Mahomet had reigned fifteen years, when, in 1772, fome feeds of thofe revolutions, which had fo often overthrown this empire in its birth, began to appear. A Marabout, whofe enthufiaftic imagination was enflamed by pride and fanaticifm, departed from the fouth, which had been the cradle of all the ancient dynafties, accompanied by a number of his difciples, united by the fpirit of bigottry.

Thefe

These visionaries, amounting to about three thousand, went to Morocco, and informed the Emperor that the end of his reign approached, and that their chief was to become the sovereign. The only arms of the companions of this Marabout were fanatic predictions, and clubs, which they, in the extravagance of their phrenzy, prophesied should be transformed into guns, while the arms of their adversaries should, on the contrary, be metamorphosed into clubs.

It so happened, however, that their prophecies were not fulfilled. The enthusiasts were hewn down, and put to flight, like cowards, by a few soldiers; and their chief, who had encouraged them in their reveries, having been seized in a mosque, was led before the Emperor at his public audience. The Marabout answered all interrogatories with the fortitude and impudence of an inspired person, and the Emperor commanded him to be put to death, at the Meshooar, as a disturber of the public peace.

From

From that time, till the year 1778, the provinces gave no figns of fedition fufficient to infpire fear. Thofe of the north, according to the cuftom of this people, began to be a little troublefome when the Emperor was in the fouth, and thofe of the fouth did juft the fame when he was in the north ; but the prefence, of the monarch, and pecuniary fines, brought them back to obedience ; and thus did the Emperor at once increafe his wealth and confirm his authority.

The treafury was exhaufted, in 1774, by the fiege of Melilla, and a fucceffion of calamities having prevented the Emperor proportioning his expences to his revenues, and again filling his coffers, he found himfelf obliged to increafe the old taxes, and even to add new. The Negroes, the arrears of whofe pay progreffively increafed, murmured againft thefe new taxes, and, at length, in October 1778, drove the tax gatherers from Mequinez, and feized on the city.

After

After an act of such open rebellion, the Negroes sent a deputation to Muley Ali, at Fez, the eldest son of Sidi Mahomet, to offer him the empire. This wise prince, incapable of failing in the respect he owed to his father, rejected the proposal, endeavoured ineffectually to calm the minds of the people, and thought proper to retire to Rabat, that he might not provoke the insolence of the Negroes by a more obstinate refusal.

Muley Ali having thus declined, the Negroes determined to apply to Muley Yezid, who did not betoken the like repugnance to the throne, and this prince, beloved by the soldiers, was publicly proclaimed at the hour of prayer. This revolution caused an insurrection at Mequinez. The governor of that city found a difficulty in escaping, amid the firing of muskets, and his house was pillaged and pulled down.

Muley Yezid, notwithstanding, thought proper to inform his father of what had happened, and make excuses concerning the facility with which he had yielded to
the

the defire of the foldiers, hoping by that means once more to reduce them to obedience. This conduct of Muley Yezid, and fome mifintelligence among the Negroes, relaxed the progrefs of the revolution, which would have been effected, had the prince, who was neither poffeffed of money nor credit, marched at the head of his troops to Rabat. Reinforced as he would have been by eight thoufand Negroes, who were there affembled, he might eafily have made himfelf mafter of the treafury, which had, very injudicioufly, for fome years, been diftributed in the cities of Rabat, Laracha, and Tangiers. The poffeffion of thefe places, which might have been taken in a week, would have rendered Muley Yezid mafter of the empire. The firft effervefcence of tumult over, as is the cafe in all popular commotions, fedition weakened in confequence of reflection, of the inexperience of the prince, and the irrefolution of the foldiers, who, themfelves, had only a confufed idea of the infurrections their predeceffors had fo often raifed, in the beginning of this century. A calm fucceeded this flight tempeft, and the revolt

volt at Mequinez ceafed of itfelf without farther progrefs.

Informed of this rebellion, the Emperor departed from Morocco with his troops, and, on his march, fecured the fidelity of thofe who were at Rabat. He then continued his way to Mequinez, where he was received as a fovereign. Each party, equally agitated by fear, gave contradictory relations of what had paffed.

From Mequinez the Emperor went to Fez. This city, which, from its extent and antiquity, has fome preponderance in the affairs of the empire, had adopted fimilar ideas to thofe of the foldiers, had ftrengthened their diffatisfaction, and given it importance. The principal citizens, and men of the law, being reproached by the Emperor for their difobedience to his orders, replied, with like firmnefs and refpect, " That the city of Fez meaned not to dif- " obey him, nor ever fo could mean, but " that the taxes laid on provifions, the in- " creafe of duties on merchants, and the

VOL. II.   Y   " new

" new imposts which had been laid, and
" which Muffelmen regarded as contrary
" to their cuftoms, and inimical to reli-
" gion, were confiderations that, to a
" prince fo juft and fo religious, might ex-
" cufe the general murmur and difcontent
" of the people."

Sidi Mahomet, yielding to circumftances,
prudently diffembled all refentment; but,
being convinced by intercepted letters that
his fon, Muley Yezid, maintained a correfpondence with the Brebes, which was
fufceptible of dangerous interpretation, he
caufed him to be confined, and afterward
fent him on pilgrimage to Mecca, by that
means to calm his unbridled paffions, and
render him more circumfpect. Grown
wifer by age and experience, the prince
reaped thofe fruits from this voyage which
are the ufual confequences of the ftudy of
men, and the knowledge gained by vifiting
foreign nations.

However inclined to clemency, Sidi Mahomet could not forget the audacious conduct of his negro foldiers at Mequinez,

and accordingly took measures to rid himself of these turbulent troops, the impatience of which daily became more burdensome, and whose ficklenefs and avarice had so frequently been experienced by his father.

The exhaufted treafury could with difficulty fupply the pay of the troops. The country, ravaged as it had been by locufts, in 1779, and by three fucceffive years of dearth for want of rain, which increafed its wretchednefs, no longer permitted the people to pay thofe impofts which time and circumftances had multiplied. There were not above ten millions of livres, or somewhat more than four hundred thoufand pounds, in the treafury, and four of thefe millions were neceffary for the fupport, in thefe calamitous times, of thirty, or thirtyfive thoufand negro cavalry.

In this embarraffing fituation the Emperor determined, in 1780, to reduce a part of thefe forces, from whofe unquiet fpirit he had every thing to dread. That he might difguife his intention, and prevent thofe inconveniences which might other-

wife

wife have been the refult, he fent thefe
Negroes away by detachments, pretending
they muft go and be quartered in the provinces; and, by an after order, fent ftill
ftronger detachments to difarm the firft,
and appoint them lands, in different countries, fufficiently diftant from each other
for him not to live in fear of their communication. A part of them, the fidelity of
whofe chiefs he was affured of, were ftill
maintained; thus, in the courfe of fixty
years, the hundred thoufand armed Negroes, whom Muley Ifhmael had left, and
their pofterity, are reduced to about fifteen
thoufand foldiers. All the remainder have
difappeared.

C H A P.

C H A P. V.

Of the Wars, Locusts, Famine, and other events, under the reign of Sidi Mahomet.

THE Emperor having employed the beginning of his reign to re-establish commerce throughout his states, he afterward made various incursions into the provinces bordering on the mountains, there to confirm and render his power respectable. These expeditions, undertaken from motives of interest, conciliation, and peace, never were of that impetuous and cruel kind with those by which the people had so often been afflicted, under the barbarous government of his predecessors.

Scarcely had this Emperor collected, in 1767 and 1768, a quantity of artillery, than,

Y 3

in

in the beginning of 1769, he made preparations for the siege of Mazagan, which
the Portuguese had resolved to evacuate,
and which surrendered in the month of
march, in the same year.

Flattered by this conquest, Sidi Mahomet, who thus inspired Europe with a
greater idea of his puissance, and his people
with higher awe, meditated projects still
more ambitious. Having permitted farther
exportations of corn, from the year 1771 to
the close of 1773, he still farther increased
his train of artillery ; and, in order to conceal his intentions, he went into the north
of his empire, and took up his residence
for some time at Rabat and Sallee. The
dislike which the Emperor had entertained
to these two cities, which, in times of former revolutions, had thrown off their allegiance to his father, served as a pretence to
make researches concerning the effects and
houses that had appertained to the royal
domain, and he recovered that vast inclosure which, since the reign of Jacob Almonsor, after having so often had new
masters,

masters, had been embellished by gardens and a fine vineyard,

When this vineyard flourished, six pounds of exceeding good grapes might have been bought for a blanquil, worth about seven farthings. In 1775 a single pound of grapes cost six blanquils, or ten pence, so that the price was increased in the proportion of thirty six to one,

Beside this estimable inclosure, the inhabitants of Rabat farther lost several houses, and were even exposed to the licentiousness of the soldiery, which, during this time of prejudice, stole, with impunity, their flocks, their fruits, and corn. Sidi Mahomet caused the ground plot of a new town to be marked out, in a place called Guadel, which, in the idiom of the country, signifies reserve, and to which town he gave this same name, and caused it to be inhabited by five thousand of his Negro troops.

Guadel, which this monarch caused to be embellished with various mosques and

Y 4

public

public edifices, is at prefent deferted, and the houfes have all gone to ruin fince the time when, from political motives, the Negroes were reduced and difperfed. Scarcely buil: i: 1776, this town was no more, in 1781, than a frightful heap of ruins, which feemed to have efcap-d the fury of men and of the elements. The monarch afterward, more juft, fuffered each individual to reclaim his property. But the remembrance of oppreffion fo recent has difgufted the inhabitants of Rabat, who are little anxious to recover poffeffions the limits of which they do not know, and the titles to which are no longer in their own power.

The project which the Emperor fecretly meditated was not difcovered till the year 1774. He then affembled, in the heart of his empire, troops, artillery, and ammunition, and, after having mafked his views, under pretext of hoftilities, at one time againft the city of Fez, at another againft the mountaineers, he began his march to lay fiege to Melilla. The Emperor pretended, for fuch were his expreffions, that

I   he

he was only at peace by fea with his friend Don Carlos, which he was very defirous to maintain, but that they were not at peace by land.

This diftinction, characteriftic of the Moors, and which originated in the hope of fuccefs, gave great offence to the court of Spain, which fent fpeedy fuccour for the defence of Melilla, and broke off all correfpondence with the court of Morocco. Sidi Mahomet might eafily have taken the place, had he at firft attacked it vigoroufly, becaufe that, depending on the faith of treaties, it was then but feebly garrifoned. But General Sherlof, having entered Melilla with between feven and eight hundred men, made fo courageous a defence that the Emperor had caufe to repent of an enterprife, the fuccefs of which failed, which had coft him vaft fums, and which the Moors feemed fecretly to have difapproved.

Sidi Mahomet was obliged to remove his camp farther from the walls, the cannon of
which

which thundered upon his army. It was also annoyed by some frigates, which, notwithstanding the narrow space they had to act in, manœuvred very ably. The Moors were so discouraged that, could the Spaniards have attacked them with any considerable force, they must have put them to flight, and taken the baggage and artillery.

The siege of Melilla had occasioned expences, and met with impediments that had not been foreseen. The cannon and ammunition were to be transported across the lesser Atlas, a mixture of vallies and mountains, among which there scarcely was a path. These stoney and ill-cultivated countries were also unable to supply provender, and this was obliged to be brought at such an excessive expence that the keep of a horse amounted to half a crown per day. The soldiery must likewise be encouraged by gratifications, so that the whole of these expences sunk more than thirty millions of livres, or one million two hundred and fifty thousand pounds sterling, which was an immense sum for a
state

state so poor and exhausted. The Emperor saw himself obliged to abandon his under-taking; and, that he might prevent those impressions which his retreat might make on the Moors, he caused it to be rumoured, through the provinces, that the King of Spain would yield him up Melilla, as soon as he could quell the discontents of the Monks, who highly disliked the cession of that place. Rejoicings were made on the receiving of this news, and Sidi Maho-met returned to Mequinez, in the be-ginning of 1775, exceedingly chagrined with his own proceedings, and highly dreading the resentment of the court of Spain, and the formidable armament that was then preparing, not knowing that it was intended against Algiers. The Emperor was, in effect, in the utmost perplexity, and with reason, at beholding the gathering storm; nor was he more tranquil till he knew the true destination of that fleet, and heard of its failure.

After having thus provoked the resent-ment of the court of Madrid, the mo-narch employed all possible means to ef-

fect

fect a reconciliation ; but the Spaniards, for
some time, preferved that rancour which a
conduct fo perfidious had infpired. A
change in the affairs of Europe having occafioned explanations between the courts,
peace was re-eftablifhed in 1780, and; during its negociation, Sidi Mahomet did
every thing which he fuppofed might be
moft agreeable to the king of Spain, and
might induce him to forget the paft.

When Sidi Mahomet prepared for the
fiege of Melilla, he declared war againft
Holland, finding the prefent fent by the
republic, on fome extraordinary occafion,
not equal to his expectations. Hence it
may be judged how little confidence ought
to be placed in the friendfhip of a monarch
who fets his friendfhip up to fale, as actuated by whim, or intereft. Holland
fitted out fhips for the protection of her
commerce, and, after a defenfive war,
when fhe might have done much better,
renewed the peace in 1778, and increafed
her largefs.

During

During the reign of Sidi Mahomet, the locusts, which so often afflict the southern climates, have various times ravaged the empire of Morocco; but never so generally or so fatally as after the year 1778. In the summer of that same year, such clouds of locusts came from the south that they darkened the air, and devoured a part of the harvest. Their offspring, which they left on the ground, committed still much greater mischief. Locusts appeared and bred anew in the following year, so that in the spring the country was wholly covered, and they crawled one over the other in search of their subsistence.

It has before been remarked, in speaking of the climate of Morocco, that the young locusts are those which are the most mischievous; and that it seems almost impossible to rid the land of these insects, and their ravages, when the country once becomes thus afflicted. In order to preserve the houses and gardens in the neighbourhood of cities, they dig a ditch two feet in depth, and as much in width. This they pallisade with reeds close to each other,

and

and inclined inward toward the ditch; fo
that the infects, unable to climb up the
flippery reed, fall back into the ditch;
where they devour one another.

This was the means by which the gardens and vineyards of Rabat, and the city
itfelf, were delivered from this fcourge, in
1779. , The intrenchment, which was, at
leaft, a league in extent, formed à femicircle
from the fea to the river, which feparates
Rabat from Sallee. The quantity of
young locufts here affembled was fo prodigious that, on the third day, the ditch
could not be approached becaufe of the
ftench. The whole country was eaten up,
the very bark of the fig, pomegranate, and
orange tree, bitter, hard, and corrofive as
it was, could not efcape the voracity of
thefe infects.

The lands, ravaged throughout all the
weftern provinces, produced no harveft, and
the Moors, being obliged to live on their
ftores, which the exportation of corn (permitted till 1774) had drained, began to feel
a dearth. Their cattle, for which they
make

make no provision, and which, in thefe climates, have no other fubfiftance than that of daily grazing, died with hunger; nor could any be preferved but thofe which were in the neighbourhood of mountains, or in marfhy grounds, where the re-growth of pafturage is more rapid.

In 1780, the diftrefs was ftill farther increafed. The dry winter had checked the products of the earth, and given birth to a new generation of locufts, that devoured whatever had efcaped from the inclemency of the feafon. The hufbandman did not reap even what he had fowed, and found himfelf deftitute of food, cattle, or feed corn. In this time of extreme wretchednefs, the poor felt all the horrors of famine. They were feen wandering over the country to devour roots, and, perhaps, abridged their days by digging into the entrails of the earth in fearch of the crude means by which they might be preferved.

Vaft numbers perifhed of indigeftible food and want. I have beheld country people in the roads, and in the ftreets, who had

had died of hunger, and who were thrown acrofs affes to be taken and buried. Fathers fold their children. The hufband, with the confent of his wife, would take her into another province, there to beftow her in marriage as if fhe were his fifter, and afterward come and reclaim her, when his wants were no longer fo great. I have feen women and children run after camels, and rake in their dung to feek for fome indigefted grain of barley, which, if they found, they devoured with avidity.

Let us not dwell too long on woes which thus afflict humanity, and of which fo many thoufands, whofe hearts are rendered infenfible of pity by plenty, have no conception. The mifery would have been much greater, had not Spain and Portugal, where the harvefts had been tolerably abundant, permitted the exportation of oil, butter, dried fruits, and other provifions, and particularly the corn of the north, which happily, at that time, was plentiful at Cadiz and at Lifbon. This corn, which had paffed through fo many hands, was fold in the markets of Sallee at one hundred
dred

dred and twenty livres, or five pounds, the
meafure, which meafure correfponds with
the Setier of Paris *. Bad oil and rancid
butter were worth one hundred and eighty
livres, or feven pounds ten fhillings, the
quintal. Peas, beans, and lentils, which
abound in thefe countries, were become
objeĉts of fo much luxury that they were
counted out by grains, and twelve or
fifteen were fold for a denier. During
three or four years of dearth, the people
ate bread which, by the mixture of the fpe-
cies of grain, and its bad quality, was exceedingly heavy, and difficult of digeftion.
Good bread was worth from fix-pence to
feven-pence halfpenny the pound, and
other articles of fubfiftence in proportion.

Afflicting and extreme as the calamities
of the empire at this time were, the awful
refignation of thefe unhappy people, to the

---

* According to the author's eftimate (See page 328 of
Vol. I.) that the Setier of Paris weighs two hundred and a
half, this meafure will contain fomewhat under four
bufhels. T.

decrees of Providence, could not be beheld
but with aftonifhment ; they fupported
their afflictions without complaint, becaufe
that, according to their faith, all things are
decreed by the Moft High, and nothing
happens but as pre-ordained by his will.
Europeans, lefs refigned, more reftlefs, or,
perhaps, more accuftomed to confide in the
cares of an adminiftration the province of
which is to provide for all their wants, are
impatient and clamorous during times of
fcarcity ; and, fufpecting abufes, which
fufpicions may be fometimes well founded,
they charge their governors with carelefs-
nefs or guilt. Plenty, or fcarcity, neverthelefs, depend moft evidently on the fertility or intemperance of feafons ; when not
occafioned by monopolies, or the excefs of
exportation and importation.

The miferies the empire of Morocco
underwent, in confequence of the fore-
going evils, made it impoffible for the
Moors to pay their taxes ; the efforts of
commerce flackened, and the revenues of
the ftates diminifhed in proportion.

The

The roads foon became unfafe, travellers were obliged to be provided with efcorts, the provinces were in a ftate of warfare, reciprocally to rob each other of what had efcaped from the ravages of locufts, and the unfavourablenefs of the feafons. From the diftricts of Rabat and Sallee to the Morbeya, the whole of the provinces of Temfena and Tedla were, for the fpace of two or three years, expofed to depredations, which the public calamity might excufe, fince they were not excited by the fpirit of fedition. Such troubles, which refemble paffing ftorms, are foon appeafed, without the interference of government, when plenty reftores tranquillity, and once more cools and bridles the reftlefsnefs and rapacity of the people.

In the year 1783, the Emperor made an excurfion to Tafilet, with a detachment of troops ; that city, and its environs, inhabited by numerous Sharifs defirous of power, had for fome time been expofed to civil commotions, which were entirely appeafed by the prefence of the fovereign. Sidi Mahomet levied, in the province and

on

on the eastern borders of the greater Atlas, heavy contributions, to punish the turbulence of the people.

While the Emperor was at Tafilet, the whole empire suffered a great loss by the death of Muley Ali, the eldest of his sons, who died at Fez, at the age of forty four, in consequence of a relapse of a neglected or ill-cured fever. This prince possessed all the qualities necessary to render his people happy; he had not inherited from his ancestors that impetuous and cruel character which, without constituting the happiness of kings, never fails to render nations miserable. Appointed by his father to the government of Fez, which is one of the most considerable in the empire, Muley had behaved with so much prudence, and disinterestedness, that, the Emperor having commanded him to render up an account of all he possessed, the city of Fez consented to pay the sum the sovereign exacted, that the prince might be maintained in his government, and continue in the good graces of his father.

The

The difinterestedness of Muley Ali,
which was a very high recommendation
to him among the people, had, perhaps,
weakened the affection of his father, who
had not the same manner of thinking. Sidi
Mahomet having laid a tax on his son,
which was to be paid for the benefit of his
brothers, commanded him to raife the fum
required on the community of the Jews,
who, not being, he faid, in the road to fal-
vation, merited no pity.—" Sire," replied
Muley Ali, " the Jews are fo poor that they
" are incapable of fupporting their prefent
" taxes, and it is impoffible I fhould exact
" from them new ones. Should you fo
" pleafe, you may difpofe of the revenues
" of my government for the benefit of
" my brothers; but I earneftly fuppli-
" cate you will not require me to op-
" prefs thefe people, and thus oblige
" me to increafe wretchednefs already
" too great."

Such anecdotes prove with how much
reafon the people regretted the lofs of this
prince. I was well acquainted with his

worth;

worth ; the confidence with which he ho-
noured me often made me a witnefs of his
benevolence, and a judge of his heart.

C H A P.

CHAP. VI.

Character of the reigning Emperor.

SIDI Mahomet, endowed with penetration and judgement, would have been susceptible of all the high qualities necessary to govern men, had education brought to perfection those gifts which nature had bestowed. His age is somewhere about seventy six *, his heighth five feet eight inches

---

* It is not customary among the Moors to register the birth of children, not even that of princes; their age is remembered by certain accidents, or events, which the parents commit to memory. A Moor very naturally says, he was born in the dry summer, the wet winter, or mentions any other similar accident.

The reigning Emperor was at Mecca, in 1737, when Muley Ishmael died; he was not then married, and, as he has always perfectly remembered this journey, it may well be supposed he was at that time about sixteen or eighteen,

and

inches, his fymmetry tolerable ; he fquints
a little, which gives his afpect fome feverity ; his conftitution being naturally
ftrong, and his mode of life fober and
frugal, his body is become very capable of
fupporting the fatigue of a life fo laborious
as the government of this empire requires.
He is tolerably eafy of accefs ; foreigners
he receives with politenefs, and converfes
with them willingly ; but the cool, or
warm, reception he gives, alike, are directed
by fome motive of perfonal intereft. His
favour is not conftant, but varies according
as fuch like interefted fenfations vary.

However marked the attachment of Sidi
Mahomet to riches may have been, he has
feldom employed thofe means, for the accu-
mulation of them, which violence or cruelty might have fuggefted. This Emperor
will not leave fo rich a treafury at his deceafe as his love for œconomy might fore-

and that he muft have been born in or near the year 1710.
This is the mode I have taken to calculate his age, in which
I am confirmed by the oldeft people in the country.

bode.

bode, and that becaufe his reign has been expofed to heavy expences; his empire, gradually exhaufted, has no longer in itfelf the fame refources. Independent of the heavy fums expended on the fiege of Mazagan, that of Melilla, and the maintenance of his forces, Sidi Mahomet has alfo built towns and fortreffes, mofques and public markets, exclufive of his palaces, which he has embellifhed. He likewife purchafed, in Malta and the Italian ftates, numerous Mahometan flaves, in 1782, the greateft part of whom were not his fubjects; and he has further fent to Conftantinople, in 1784, more than four million of livres, (or a hundred and fixty-fix thoufand pounds) which it is fuppofed he, out of refpect to his religion, either appropriated to the temple of Mecca or the defence of the Ottoman empire, for which, knowing the ambition of its neighbours, he feems to have fome fears.

Covetous as he appears to have been of wealth, Sidi Mahomet will leave little to pofterity, except thefe monuments of his devotion, his charity, and his precaution.

More

More humane, more acceffible, and lefs
exigent than his anceftors, Sidi Mahomet
has ever treated the Chriftians, whom the
fate of war has put into his power, with
compaffion, and on fome among them he
has beftowed marks of his confidence.
After the taking of Mazagan, he fent
thirty-eight flaves to the Grand Mafter of
the knights of Malta, who were fubjects
of the Grand Duke of Tufcany, and the
Grand Mafter, returned a like number of
Moors.

Quick and penetrating, this Emperor
has often made very juft obfervations on
the characters of nations, judging by the
flaves whom he had in his poffeffion, and
who happened to be about his perfon. Perceiving how active the French were in
their labours, he chofe them in preference
for the execution of any fudden project;
obferving, at the fame time, that they were
reftlefs and turbulent, he held it neceffary
they fhould be employed, that they might
neither quarrel among themfelves nor with
the other flaves. It cannot be faid that,
under his government, flaves have been
worked

worked to excefs; it will likewife be perceived that monarchs, who number the ranfom of flaves as one part of their revenues, have an intereft in their prefervation.

During thirty years that Sidi Mahomet has fat on the throne, his reign has been happy. It would be rafh to prophefy what fhall happen after his death: although it be true that fimilar caufes will produce fimilar effects, we muft not always judge of the future by the paft; the fmalleft difference of circumftances, either in the times, or the characters of thofe men who head infurrections, will change the ftate of things, and decide on the deftiny of nations. Neverthelefs, when we behold in Morocco a multitude of princes, each defirous of governing, each having nearly an equal claim to govern, it fhould feem that like diffentions may well again be feared, and like revolutious to thofe which, under preceding reigns, fo often have rent this empire.

The

The fucceffion is not fixed in Morocco, either by law or cuftom, but depends entirely on concurring accidents. It is well underftood, among the Moors, that the eldeft fon ought to inherit the crown, becaufe that his experience renders him the moft proper to govern; but, as there is no determinate law on this head, and as there is neither divan nor council in the empire to deliberate on affairs of ftate, the election of the Emperor depends entirely on chance, on the character of the candidates, the opinion of the people, the influence of the foldiery, the fupport of the provinces, and moft particularly on the poffeffion of the treafury. He who has money may have foldiers, and he who has foldiers can make himfelf feared.

We have feen that, under Muley Abdallah, one province and one faction would elect this fovereign, another that; and like anarchy may well be expected, whenever there are a great number of candidates for the throne; at leaft, unlefs the governors of provinces fhould all unite to protect one alone. This is a thing moft difficult to be

accom-

accomplished, among the Moors, where men do nothing, and where Providence regulates all.

Of ten or twelve male children, to whom the Emperor is father, there are several who are capable of government; nor can I doubt but that, informed as they must be of former revolutions, they all aspire with equal confidence to that crown to which birth, the voice of the people, or a concatenation of incidents, may give each an equal right.

CHAP.

C H A P. VII.

Of the commercial intercourse between the Empire of Morocco and the nations of Europe.

WHEN the spirit of industry began to effect a change in Europe, in the power of kingdoms, and the manners of their inhabitants, monarchs felt the necessity of naval armaments, and, by their maritime forces, to secure to their subjects the progress of their commerce, and the freedom of the seas.

Before the discovery of the rout to the East Indies, round the Cape of Good Hope, and even for some time after, Europe had no communication with Asia, except by the Mediterranean, and over this sea a considerable trade was carried on through Spain, France,

France, Italy, the Levant, and the northern shores of Africa, which latter, even
at that time, were invaded by bands of
freebooters. Tripoli, Tunis, Algiers,
Morocco, usurped by multitudes of soldiers, whom religion had armed, enemies
as they were of the Christian religion,
from bigotry, became still more so from interest; their inhabitants were poor, little
addicted to labour, without commerce, pirates from inclination and necessity, and
had no means of becoming of some importance, except by the licentiousness of
freebooting.

Europe, which had formerly been armed
against these common enemies by the zeal
of religion, presently found itself divided
in its own political interests. Nations, ambitious of power and of wealth, individually employed by the efforts of industry,
and the barter of their products, consulted
only their individual conveniency, and, in
the hope of acquiring a greater ascendancy
in commercial and maritime affairs, determined to make treaties with these usurpers
of the shores of Africa; which treaties
have

have been more or lefs obferved, according to the opinion entertained of their refpective force, and the reciprocity of their interefts.

Such were the motives, fuch the princi-ples, of friendfhip, between the powers of Europe and the regencies of Barbary. The rivality, or the feeblenefs, of fuch com-mercial nations, occafioned thefe regencies afterward to acquire thofe means of power, the difadvantage and incumbrance of which have fince been fo often felt; the condi-tions by which their friendfhip muft be purchafed have imperceptibly become more humiliating, more intolerable, and lefs ftable.

It was not fo much for the promotion of trade, on the northern fhores of Africa, as to favour the growth of maritime power, and commerce in a different channel, that the nations of Europe have entered into thefe friendly treaties with the Barbary re-gencies, and the empire of Morocco. This empire itfelf, though rich in its native products, is not capable of any extenfive trade; the inftability of its laws is an ob-

ftacle

ftacle to the induftry of its inhabitants,
and to the confidence of foreigners. Neither are the wants of the Moors multiplied by their mode of education, or by the
temperature of a climate where nature requires but little; and imaginary wants
have been further fuppreffed by government, which, by depriving the people of
the means of luxury, muft neceffarily enfeeble the activity of commerce, of which
luxury is the Primum Mobile.

Thus, fome trifling barter excepted, the
fafety of the fea has been the caufe why
the nations of Europe have made treaties
with the empire of Morocco. I fhall fpeak
more particularly of thefe their treaties, and
their interefts, according to the priority of
their dates, and fhall beftow a feparate
chapter on thofe that relate to France.

England is the firft power which concluded treaties of friendfhip and commerce
with the Emperors of Morocco. Being in
poffeffion of Tangiers, which had been
ceded to her by Portugal in 1662, fhe oc-

cafionally felt thofe inconveniences that refult from the turbulency of the Moors, which fhe overlooked, and even gave up certain points, that fhe might, with the greater eafe, maintain the garrifon of that town, which, becaufe of its diftance, at length became a burthen to the nation.

England having, even at that time, acquired an extenfive foreign commerce, fhe made propofitions of peace to Muley Ifhmael in 1675, which the caprices and contradictions of that Emperor rendered ineffectual. A truce, however, was concluded for four years in 1681, but was broken before the term expired; the Moors pretended that the peace had only related to the garrifon of Tangiers, and did not extend to the protection of the Britifh flag.

A diftinction like this, worthy an Empire where treachery is native, gave birth to explanations. Muley Ifhmael fent ambaffadors to London at the commencement of the prefent century. This was a new pretext for new prefents, and the treaty of peace was, at length, renewed under George

George I. After the death of Muley Iſhmael this treaty was confirmed, and renewed, in 1728, by Muley Achmet Daiby,
and a little time after by Muley Abdallah.

The immenſe navigation and trade of the
Engliſh gave them ſufficient motives to
make peace with the Emperor of Morocco; and they had further a political reaſon, which was, to re-victual, with freſh
proviſions, their garriſon of Gibraltar with
facility, which place has been under their
government from the beginning of the preſent century. Sidi Mahomet, more intelligent than his predeceſſors, has derived all
poſſible profit from this circumſtance; and
the Engliſh nation, haughty, jealous, and
ever ready to take offence, has continued, and
ſtill continues, to overlook all that inequality
of conduct to which the ſpirit of avarice
gives birth, on the part of the court of Morocco. The Engliſh have long maintained
a trade on the coaſt of that empire, where
they ſell coarſe cloths, ſerges, linens, pew-
ter, lead, mercer's commodities, and the
iron which their ſhips bring from Biſcay.

A a 2   They

They receive in return fometimes oils, gums, wax, elephants-teeth, and have often fent, in French bottoms, to Marfeilles, oils, raw hides, and wool, the confumption of which is greater in our fouthern provinces than among the more northern nations.

They have alfo exported a number of Mules to North America; but the difmemberment of that part of their dominions has greatly decreafed their trade with Morocco, which before was not very confiderable. England can only have a confined trade with Morocco, not having a fufficient market for the commodities fhe returns. The commercial relations which exift between kingdoms always depend on their mutual wants, and the facility with which barter can be made to mutual advantage.

In 1732 an ambaffador was fent by Muley Abdallah into Holland, and the republic then made its peace with that Emperor: but the revolutions by which his reign was difturbed gave but little ftability to the treaty. Holland was the firft power which

renewed

renewed treaties of peace with Sidi Mahomet, who then was only prince and governor of Saffi, but who, being the sole heir of the empire, had arrogated to himself the chief part of the authority. Independent of the safety of navigation, Holland had further a political motive, which was early to make peace with the Emperor, that she might the better profit by her neutrality during the war of 1755.

Having been informed that this republic treated the regency of Algiers with greater generosity than himself, Sidi Mahomet complained of the States General; and, notwithstanding the compliance that was shewn, the Emperor declared war against the Dutch toward the end of 1774, pretending that an extraordinary present, which they had sent him, and which he kept, was not sufficiently magnificent.

The republic sent numerous vessels into the Straits for the protection of trade and navigation; few of them appeared upon the coast, and that so seldom that the corsairs of Morocco took three Dutch ships,

two

two of them as they left the port of San Lucar, within fight of Cadiz. These advantages were counterbalanced by the losses of the Emperor of Morocco. A Dutch frigate, which did but begin to chace two Corsairs of Sallee, caused them to be shipwrecked, even without following them, the one at the entrance of the river of Laracha, and the other at the mouth of that of Mamora. Holland renewed the peace in 1778, was more generous in her gifts, and, if so she shall please, may continue it by the like means.

Holland carries on a certain trade with the coast of Morocco, and custom has almost rendered her importations necessary. She there vends quantities of Silesian linens, called platillas, many of the coarse linens of the Baltic, and others, some few spices, drugs, tea, timber, iron of Biscay, and quantities of the cutlery and mercery wares of Germany.

Holland receives from the coast of Morocco, in return, sometimes oils, wax, gums, and elephants-teeth; but, as those returns,

returns, which fuit the Dutch merchants, are infufficient to balance the quantity of merchandize they fend thither, they have almoft continually profited by the facility with which they can run for the French ports, to fend oils to Marfeilles, wools, and raw hides, which there find a readier fale than in the north. Had not Holland this liberty, fhe would imperceptibly have been obliged to renounce a trade, which muft have become difadvantageous, when fhe could no longer freight her fhips by barter, or be paid in money,

The court of Denmark began to nego-tiate with Sidi Mahomet in 1755. That kingdom is fo diftant from Morocco that the Danifh miniftry had not any juft ideas concerning the government of this empire, Deceived by a Jew, who was the inftru-ment and interpreter of the negotiations of Denmark, fhe fuppofed fhe might, without impediment, build a fortrefs at Santa Cruz, that fhe might there protect a mercantile fettlement, which fhe intend-ed to eftablifh. The Jew agent difguifed the intentions of the court of Denmark;

nor

nor was there any knowledge in Morocco of the intended fort, till the materials for building it were landed. The Emperor, offended at feeing himself treated like the princes of Senegal, imprifoned the ambaffador of Denmark, and his retinue, pretending he would treat them as flaves. Some time was neceffary to rectify this miftake. Denmark again undertook to negotiate in 1757, a ranfom was agreed upon, new prefents were made, and a new peace concluded.

The late king of Denmark, occupied by commercial projects, gave his confent at that time for the forming of a royal African company, which, on paying an annual tribute of fifty thoufand piaftres, obtained from the Emperor of Morocco the excluive commerce of his coaft, for the term of ten years, in the ports of Sallee and of Saffi, where two mercantile fettlements were made. The oppreffions and embarraffments which this monopoly incited, the expences occafioned by the forming of thefe eftablifhments, and the want of œconomy in fome foreign directors, to whom the administration

miniftration of the company's affairs were
confided, rendered this attempt unfuccefsful. The monopoly extended only to the
ports of Saffi and Sallee, the trade of
which declined in confequence of other
eftablifhments, at the ports of Mogodor
and Laracha, whither, by leffening the
duties of the cuftoms, the Emperor had
drawn the chief products of his domains,
which freighted the returning European
fhips,

This company, befide, were merely concerned in a carrying trade, as uncertain in
its fuccefs as ill judged in its principles.
Denmark itfelf contains no product neceffary for the coaft of Morocco, nor can the
products of that empire find any market in
Denmark ; fo that this company was but a
clog upon the induftry of the intermediate
nations, and could derive no other advantage than that of affording employment to
fome Danifh fhips, which often arrived on
the coaft of Morocco loaded, and returned
empty back. The Danifh African company foon faw its capital funk by ill-timed
fpeculations, and by the gifts which the
compli-

compliance of its directors, and the neceſ-
ſity of ſatisfying the Emperor, did but
multiply.

This company continued buſied in the
liquidation of its debts, after the acceſſion
of Chriſtian VII. to the throne of Denmark; it was ſuppreſſed in 1767, at which
time the court of Denmark freed itſelf
from the annual burthen of fifty thouſand
piaſtres, a price paid for a monoply, which
the royal African company ought to have
enjoyed, but did not. The Danes only,
however, could obtain the continuation of
peace by annually paying the ſum of
twenty-five thouſand piaſtres. Denmark
has not itſelf any direct trade with that coaſt.

The Swedes concluded peace with the
Emperor of Morocco in 1763. The preſent Sweden ſent conſiſted of cannon, maſts,
and timber; ſhe likewiſe agreed to make
an annual preſent of twenty-thouſand piaſtres, which ſhe meant to pay in her own
native products, but which the Emperor
inſiſted on receiving in ready money. In the
year 1771, Guſtavus III., who then
afcended

afcended the throne of Sweden, refufed all kind of tribute, referving to himfelf the liberty of making voluntary prefents, without any determinate time or value. It was, at length, agreed, as a means of continuing the former good underftanding between the courts, that the king of Sweden fhould fend an ambaffador and a prefent once in two years, to the Emperor of Morocco. The Swedes have no commercial intercourfe with this empire.

The republic of Venice made peace with the Emperor of Morocco in 1765. She fent a very handfome prefent in money, and agreed to pay an annual tribute of about a hundred thoufand livres, (or upward of four thoufand pounds.) This republic having treated the regency of Algiers ftill more liberally, the Emperor was offended at the diftinction, and fent a Genoefe, who was in his fervice, to Venice to complain. His envoy having been received with great coolnefs by the Senate, and having returned with an anfwer that did not fatisfy Sidi Mahomet, he gave further tokens of his difcontent to the republic in 1780,

1780, and, inventing certain imputations, obliged the Venetian conful to depart from his ftates ; but the republic having acquiefced in the wifhes of the Emperor, in 1781, the conful returned, and was very favourably received at the court of Morocco. The republic of Venice has no commercial intercourfe with this empire, and therefore, like the courts of Denmark and Sweden, pays this tribute folely for the fafety of navigation.

The court of Spain, as well as that of France, made peace with the Emperor of of Morocco in 1767. Sidi Mahomet was the firft to fend an ambaffador to Spain, and affected to give this kingdom fo much the preference that the confidence placed in his profeffions were too great. After having received very high proofs of the generofity of the court of Spain, and having, in fome meafure, difpofed of his arfenals for the repair of her fhips, this monarch took occafion to deftroy the good harmony which then exifted between the two powers, without breaking the peace, which, according to him, was merely confined

fined to the liberty of navigation. He marched with an army, about the end of 1774, to lay siege to Melilla, which place, instead of defending, he supposed Spain would abandon.

This proceeding, contrary to the faith of treaties, was the occasion of a rupture, between the court of Spain and that of Morocco. The Moor, having failed in his enterprize, took every possible means to re-establish peace; but the court of Madrid, deeply resenting his conduct, deferred concluding any treaty, and was satisfied with remaining in a kind of truce.

The quarrel between France and England having changed the political situation of Europe, the court of Spain thought that a favourable moment to treat with the Emperor of Morocco; and Sidi Mahomet renewed peace, in 1780, by the mediation of his ambassador, Ben-Otman, eagerly acquiescing in whatever the Spanish court demanded. The Emperor not only consented to refuse revictualing the garrison of Gibraltar, the siege of which was medi-

tated

tated by Spain, but the Spaniards were, in a manner, masters of Tangiers, where they victualed their army, and which place served as an asylum to such of their ships as were stationed near the Straits. Their posts of observation beyond the castle, and as far as Cape Spartel, were so well regulated, that their signals from place to place communicated along the whole coast of Andalusia.

Their can be no continued trade between the coast of Spain and that of Morocco, for the corn trade, which varies according to circumstances and seasons, must only be considered as casual. The products of Morocco, their provisions excepted, are wholly useless in Spain; nor does Spain itself afford many articles of consumption for Morocco, cochineal excepted, which is used to dye Morocco leather, and the exclusive trade in which the Emperor has reserved to himself. The iron of Biscay, and the Barcelona handkerchiefs, which are in general use, might, indeed, be imported, but foreign nations buy up the first in exchange for their several products,

and

and the trade in the second is not of sufficient extent to maintain a continual intercourfe.

For fome years after the peace, conluded
in 1767, the harvefts having failed in
Spain, the Spaniards bought up confiderable quantities of wheat and barley on the
coaft of Morocco. This, however, was a
forced trade, and not reciprocal ; they took
their money thither to buy provifions,
poultry, and fruits, wherewith to fupply
Andalufia, where, becaufe of the heat of
the climate, men are little inclined to labour, and where the inequality of the feafons renders their harvefts very uncertain.

Politically confidered, this trade was
only advantageous to the Emperor of Morocco, fince Spain was not only dependent on
him for fupplies, but that, likewife, the facility with which thefe fupplies were obtained
did but further increafe the indolence of
the farmers of Andalufia. Hence refulted
a great circulation of piaftres in the empire
of Morocco, and, perhaps, two million of

livres

livres (or upward of eighty thousand pounds sterling) of increase to the revenue. Between the years 1770 and 1774, Spain transported from Morocco, quantities of wheat and barley; but she again rendered the very same aid to Morocco, from 1779 to 1781, when a part of that empire was afflicted by famine.

In February, 1769, the court of Portugal lost the town of Mazagan, on the western side of Morocco, which it had preserved, and where the arms and the commerce of Portugal were so eminently successful at the beginning of the fixteenth century. This town, situated in the centre of a fertile province, clandestinely supplied Portugal with some provisions and cattle. After the loss of Mazagan, the court of Lisbon, desirous of possessing its former resources, and wishing to acquire greater safety for its flag and guard its ships from the corsairs of Morocco, to which the peace between Spain and Morocco gave more frequent opportunities of approach to the coast of Portugal, thought proper, in 1773, to conclude a treaty with the Emperor.

peror. There is no continued trade between Portugal and Morocco, and the intercourse of the two courts is fimply confined to teftimonies of friendfhip. The Emperor of Morocco fends a few horfes, and many compliments, to the court of Lifbon, which returns demonftrations of good will fomewhat more fubftantial.

Toward the end of the year 1782, Sidi Mahomet fent an ambaffador into Tufcany, who, in 1783, departed thence for Vienna to conclude a peace with both thefe courts; but the trade between Morocco and thefe nations is only accidental, and the treaty has no other utility than that of the fafety of navigation for Tufcan and Imperial fhips, and of thus giving a greater degree of ftability to commerce, which thefe powers wifh to encourage throughout their ftates.

The republic of Genoa enjoys only a kind of truce with the empire of Morocco, which is wholly unfupported by any treaty. A Jew fubject of Morocco, whofe name was Ben-Amor, made a voyage to Genoa by order of his master, and treated with a noble Genoese concerning commercial connections with the Emperor, who on this occasion, voluntarily made very great advances. The senator formed a commercial company, and sent his agents, in 1769, with splendid presents, and a numerous train. This company enjoyed a momentary fame, and afterward as suddenly declined. It did but resemble a flash of lightning in a clouded and gloomy night.

The Emperor of Morocco, thus at peace with the principal commercial nations, and desirous of being so with all the Christian powers, hoping thereby to extend the commerce of his empire, and to profit by the rival spirit of nations, publicly manifested, by letters, in 1777, " That he granted " entire liberty to all ships to trade with, " and enter, his ports, being desirous of " peace with the whole world." This general notice produced no effect, either because those nations which it most interested had not sufficient confidence in his promises, or because they wanted such products and resources as were necessary to
maintain

maintain a trade with the coaſt of Morocco.

Notwithſtanding that the Emperor had
declared he held himſelf to be at peace with
all Europe, he neverthelefs pronounced a
ſhip from Raguſa, taken by one of his corſairs, in 1779, a legal capture. The cargo,
worth more than a hundred thouſand livres,
(or upward of four thouſand pounds) was
the property of the Malteſe, and was con-
fiſcated; and yet, from ſome inexplicable
caprice, the Malteſe ſailors were reſtored to
their freedom, while thoſe of Raguſa were
made ſlaves.

The diſpute this occaſioned, and which
was rendered ſtill more intricate by a diverſity of intereſts, was very tedious, and
liable to numerous incongruities. The
Ottoman Porte claimed the ſailors of Raguſa as its vaſſals, and by the ſame title
protected the freedom of the Raguſan flag.
The diſpatches of the Porte, written in
the Turkiſh language, although the Moors
could not read them, were not received
with the lefs deference; the Raguſan ſai-

lors,

lors, detained in flavery, were reflored to the Envoy of the republic, and the Emperor dictated fuch terms of peace as Ragufa could neither accept nor durft refufe. The fufpence and inconveniences that arofe gave occafion to new explanations, which did not filence the fears of the Senate of Ragufa; a ftate fo feeble, and in fo precarious a fituation, can enjoy but little certainty.

The United States of North America, after fecuring their independence by wife laws, and concluding various commercial treaties with the powers of Europe, were further defirous of adding new means of advantage, and increafe, to their induftry and navigation. In confequence of this, they, during the year 1786, profiting by the pacific difpofition which the Emperor of Morocco announced to all commercial nations, concluded a treaty of peace with this monarch.

C H A P.

C H A P. VIII.

Of the commercial intercourse between the kingdom of France, and the empire of Morocco.

IN the beginning of the prefent century, France was poffeffed of colonies, manufactures, mercantile eftablifhments, in foreign nations, and a maritime commerce, which, in its birth, betokened the extent of which it was fufceptible, from national induftry, and the vigilance of the miniftry ; her navigation began to appear refpeɗable, in confequence of her naval forces, under the reign of Louis XIV. ; but the wars fhe was obliged to maintain, toward the conclufion of this reign, greatly retarded the progrefs of her foreign trade.

So

So rapid was the growth of this trade, under the following reign, that her rivals, jealous of the empire of the fea, took umbrage at her maritime profperity. The late fuccefs of her arms has effaced the remembrance of thofe humiliations to which fhe was fubjected, in confequence of the war of 1756; and the influence which this fuccefs ought naturally to acquire fhould, each returning day, give new ftrength to her commerce.

The firft efforts of France to extend her navigation incited the cupidity of the regencies of Barbary, that were in the neighbourhood of her fouthern ports. After having feveral times chaftifed their temerity, France, at length, made peace with Algiers, Tunis, and Tripoli. She alfo held momentary negotiations with Muley Ifhmael, but found no poffible means of fixing the wavering temper of that Emperor, and of obviating thofe difficulties which might well be feared from his want of good faith. This monarch being dead, the empire of Morocco, become the prey of rebellions, was continually changing
its

its mafters. Its ports, alfo, were under the
government of particular and local laws,
and the difficulties of treaties of peace
were increafed, becaufe that, during a ftate
of fuch anarchy, it was impoffible to affign
any duration to fuch treaties.

These obftacles were removed when
Sidi Mahomet afcended the throne, and
France profited by the difpofitions of this
Emperor to enter on new negotiations ; but
they were fubject to fo much inceritude,
and fo many variations, that, in order ulti-
mately to bring the Moor to a firm determination, fhe thought proper, in 1765, to
fend a fquadron, of one fhip of the line,
eight frigates, three zebecks, one bark,
and two bombketches, to the weftern coaft
of Morocco. This fquadron, of greater
force than was neceffary, was impeded by
a concatenation of circumftances, which
were not fufficiently forefeen, becaufe a
fufficient knowledge of the coaft had not
been obtained. The bomb ketches played
upon Rabat and Sallee with little fuccefs.
The fquadron next proceeded to Laracha ;
the frigates occafioned a corfair to be

ftranded

ſtranded upon the coaſt, and the ſmaller veſſels of the ſquadron, after being detained two or three nights by a diverſity of opinions among the captains, and the difficulties of the paſſage, at length entered the river of Laracha, and there burned a ſhip.

This advantage was balanced by the loſs of many brave men. Obliged, in the river, to give battle to a multitude of Mooriſh ſoldiers, who had had time to aſſemble, becauſe of the delays to which this expedition had been ſubjected, the French loſt near two hundred men on that occaſion, forty-five of whom were made ſlaves, without enumerating the wounded. But this loſs was no ſufficient counterpoiſe to that of the Emperor of Morocco, many of whoſe ſoldiers alſo fell. This monarch was enabled to judge, by the valorous defence of the French, that, on ſome future opportunity, this valour might be more ſucceſsful, and he propoſed a ſuſpenſion of arms. A truce was, at length, agreed on, and this truce was prolonged that reciprocal explanation might be more preciſe. The preliminaries of peace were definitively

tively concluded toward the end of the year 1766, by the intervention of the Sieur Jean Jacques Salva, a French merchant, settled at Saffi.

In the spring of 1767, the Comte de Breugnon, a captain in the navy, was appointed ambassador to conclude the peace, and sailed to Saffi with a squadron under his command. The Comte took with him a present, worthy of the magnificence of his monarch, for the Emperor of Morocco. The French flag was saluted at Saffi by the whole artillery of the castle; and the ambassador met, on shore, and during the rest of his voyage, the most distinguished reception, according to the custom of those people.

France, however, had proof that, though the character of a nation may vary according to circumstances, in reality it is ever the same. At the very moment when the Moors made those warm professions, which an interested court will ever testify for its new friends, a corsair of the Emperor took three French merchant ships in

the

the Straits, which, though there was no difficulty in proving the injury, were sometime before they were reftored. The Emperor difclaimed this act of hoftility, and the corfair was condemned never to fail more. The figning of the peace was itfelf delayed, becaufe that explanations were neceffary, and the preliminaries, which had been agreed on between the two courts, and fent to Verfailles, written in Arabic, to be figned, were laid afide: proceedings were all again to be begun, and the treaty, concerning which the two powers had been mutually agreed, was once more to be difcuffed, and almoft wholly altered.

Previous to the peace between France and Morocco, the French had two mercantile eftablifhments fettled there on the faith of afylum. After the peace their mercantile houfes became numerous. This was the error of the French; there were too many of them for the trade, and their numbers were not only injurious to their own interefts but, probably, excited the avarice of the Emperor, who, eftimating the

the advantages of their trade by their eagerness, was defirous it might become
more profitable to himfelf, and therefore
impofed heavier duties. The trade then
began to decline ; merchants were difcouraged by thefe new fhackles, by rules which
defpotifm prefcribed, by the neceffity of
conforming to thefe rules, by the removal
of their trade from one port to another,
and by all the various means which the
abufe of power, the fpirit of avarice,
and the convenience of the moment, could
fuggeft.

France, perhaps, is the only nation which
is capable to maintain an uninterrupted
trade with the empire of Morocco, mutually beneficial. She is enabled herfelf to
fupply all the wants of that empire, and
the products of Morocco find at Marfeilles
a more certain fale than at any other port.
According to the beft and moft exact information, it is demonftrated that her
trade, on the coaft of Morocco, might not
only become capable of increafe, but that
the reciprocal conveniences, which muft
refult to the two powers by the barter of
their

their respective products, ought to be considered as a political motive for the mutual maintenance of peace.

If France, by living in good harmony with Morocco, should unite to the benefits of commerce that of the safety of her flag, Morocco would, on her part, acquire a very effential advantage from this connection, by the great facility with which she could vend her native products, which constitute the sole wealth of nations, and the ultimate refources of a flate. It must be acknowledged that, at first, it would not be possible to give any degree of stability to this trade, because of the difficulty there must be of fixing the ideas of a despot, whose motives all originate in momentary conveniences, on any determinate point. This, however, may be remedied in time; wants and circumstances every where prescribe laws, and every where, soon or late, teach men the necessity of conforming to thefe laws.

France would insensibly and exclusively engrofs the trade of Morocco, if, profiting by by her advantages, she should subject that trade to the same laws which have so successfully procured her the exclusive trade of the Levant, and the republics of Barbary. Endeavours at improvement, and, perhaps, the spirit of innovation, have caused the voice of freedom to raise itself against prohibitory laws. Such laws may be wrong, in particular cases; but the application of this rule should not be universal; they may, in general, be beneficial to a nation, which, possessed of native products and colonies, having a maritime force to preserve, manufacturers to encourage, and multitudes of workmen to employ, is interested to procure to itself, exclusively, such branches of commerce as may best obtain these ends. She would act contrary to her interests, were she to suffer her rivals to become the carriers of her products, while they refuse her a similar and reciprocal freedom.

The French vend, on the coast of Morocco, much of the linnen of Brittany, and of other places, some raw silk for the manufactures of Fez, unspun cotton, Biscay iron, common papers, mercery goods, some

few

filks, cloths, fugars, and coffee, and as
much fulphur as the Emperor requires,
the trade in which he has referved to himfelf.

They receive in exchange, wool, oil,
raw hides, wax, gums, and elephants' teeth.
The balance, being againft France, is paid
in Spanifh piaftres, or in merchandize
brought from fome foreign nations; yet
we ought not to fuppofe the trade of Morocco difadvantageous to France, fince fhe
does not fend her fhips thither for objects
of luxury, but fupplies neceffary to her
manufactures, and fuch as may animate
national induftry, by renewing the materials cf exportation, and procuring the
commodities of trade and commerce.

After having explained the commercial
intercourfe of the European nations with the
empire of Morocco, enumerated what fhackles are impofed by government, and what
refult from local circumftances, I think it
proper to fpeak a word concerning the cuftom which the Emperors of Morocco have in
fuffering the fhips of nations, with whom
they

are at war, to trade to their coast. This political toleration appears to do honour to these monarchs; but the absurdity of the Europeans, in making use of this permission, is not the less evident, since Morocco enjoys the double advantage of trade and of piracy.

Neither can it be said Europe, in this respect, has a like advantage, for there is the following difference. The empire of Morocco cannot supply its own wants, yet has the balance in its favour, by its commerce with Europe; therefore it grants the freedom of its ports only from necessity, and that it may disencumber itself of products, for which it has no consumption, and receive others, of which it is in absolute need. Hence, it would be much wiser, were the European nations, especially those that find the quickest market for the products of Morocco, to renounce this freedom, and to avail themselves of the necessity of that empire to barter its commodities, and thereby oblige it to remain quiet. For one nation to supply another, with which it is at war, and to carry on a trade beneficial

to

to that other, is, by fair deduction, to
pay tribute, without enjoying the advantages of peace.

CHAP.

CHAP. IX.

*Cuſtom-houſe duties, coins, weights, and
meaſures.*

THE duties, coins, weights, and meaſures, in Morocco, are almoſt as variable as
the opinion of the Emperor; yet, notwithſtanding this fluctuation, I have thought
proper to terminate my obſervations, on
what concerns this empire, by giving an
abſtract of their preſent ſtate.

The duties of exportation and importation have been much altered. Thoſe of
importation, which are paid in effects, and
not in money, have riſen from eight to fifteen per cent., iron excepted, which pays
the fourth, or the third, of its value. Thoſe
of exportation, which I have ſeveral times

ſeen

feen raifed, are entirely arbitrary; the articles do not each pay in the fame proportion. The duties on fome amount to as much as the prime-coft.

Merchant fhips are fubjected to an anchorage duty, which has alfo undergone many variations; neither is this duty the fame in all the ports of the coaft, which ports do not all equally enjoy the freedom of trade and navigation.

The coins, which are current over the coaft of Morocco, are thofe of the Emperor, and thofe of Spain. The coins of the Emperor are in gold, filver, and copper. Their feveral values are not fixed, but the variations, to which they are fubject, do not there influence the price of provifions and goods, as they would in Europe, where money is properly confidered only as the fymbol of wealth.

The gold ducat, which is very fcarce, and therefore little in circulation, is worth fifteen ounces, which correfponds to ten . French

French livres, or eight and four pence English.

The silver money is the current ducat, the ounce, and the blanquil. The current ducat is worth ten ounces, the ounce four blanquils, and the blanquil twenty-four flus. The flus is the only current copper coin. The value of the blanquil is three sous four deniers of France, or nearly seven farthings English ; consequently the ounce is worth thirteen sous four deniers, or six pence three farthings, and the ducat six livres thirteen sous four deniers, or five shillings and six pence three farthings *. The Spanish piastre is current in trade, and in general its value is fixed ; it may, however, vary according to the convenience of the Emperor, and the interest he may have to render piastres scarce or common.

The weights, by which they buy and sell in Morocco, are equivalent to the weights

* The English is the third part of a farthing above the exact estimate in all these three cases. T.

of

of Paris; that is to fay, to the *Poids de marc*, or pound of fixteen ounces; the fubdivifions of which are, at both places, the fame. Merchandize is in general fold by the quintal of one hundred pounds; but fome commodities are fold by the great quintal, or one hundred and fifty pounds.

Corn is meafured, after different manners, along the coaft of Morocco. In the fouthern provinces, known by the name of the kingdom of Morocco, wheat is fold by the Garara and the Mood, which is the modus of the ancients, whence the French have derived their Muid. The garara contains forty mood, and the mood weighs from eighteen to twenty pounds; hence the garara muft be nearly eight hundred weight. In the kingdom of Fez, from Sallee to the north, corn is fold by the Saffa, the Sahah, and the Mood. Four mood make one fahah, and fixty mood one faffa; hence, the mood weighing from eighteen to twenty pounds, the weight of the faffa muft be twelve quintals. Three fahah, or twelve mood, are nearly equivalent to the meafure of Marfeilles, called the

charge,

charge, which alſo nearly correſponds to the Setier of Paris. It is neceſſary to obſerve that the corn meaſures are liable to be varied, according to the will of the Emperor.

The meaſure by which cloths, linen, and woollen, are ſold, is called coode, which is the cubit of the ancients. The coode, which is in uſe throughout all the empire, and which never varies, contains nineteen inches four lines. There are forty-four inches in a French ell, conſequently two coodes and a quarter are equal to an ell, the fraction of half an inch excepted.

THE END.

I N D E X.

A.

ABDA, province of, I. 9.
Abdalharaman, revolt of, II. 45.
Abdallah, first of the Benimerins, II. 36.
——— son of Abu Said, reign of, II. 49.
——— assassinated, II. 50.
Abdallah, Muley, son of Muley Ishmael, generosity of, II. 242.
——— ——— persuaded not to destroy Fez, II. 243.
——— ——— defeated by the Brebes, II. 244.
——— ——— barbarous maxim of, Ibid.
——— ——— cruelty of, II. 245.
——— ——— money promised by, to the Negroes, II. 246.
——— ——— insurgents quelled by, Ibid.
——— ——— clothes the naked, II. 247.
——— ——— general, basely put to death by, Ibid.
——— ——— performs the office of executioner, Ibid.
——— ——— obliges people of all ranks to build the walls of Mequinez, II. 248.
——— ——— project of, to subject the Negroes, II. 250.
——— ——— deposed, II. 251.
——— ——— flight of, Ibid.
——— ——— first restoration of, II. 255.
——— ——— hatred of, to Selim Docquelli, Ibid.
——— ——— deposed the day of his election, II. 257.

Abdallah,

Abdallah, Muley, frantic cruelty of, II. 258.

———— ———— artifice of, to amuse the Negroes, II. 259

———— ———— obliged to sell his horses, arms, and jewels, II. 260.

———— ———— second flight of, II. 262.

———— ———— a fourth time proclaimed, II. 265.

———— ———— projects of, against the Negroes, *Ibid.*

———— ———— recalled by the Negroes, II. 267.

———— ———— a sixth time Emperor, II. 270.

———— ———— anecdote of the justice of, II. 273.

———— ———— not inimical to Christians. II. 274.

———— ———— allows the redemption of slaves, *Ibid.*

———— ———— few children of, II. 278.

———— ———— character of, II. 286.

———— ———— anecdotes of the cruelty of, II. 287.

———— ———— Saints despised by, II. 288.

Abdelmeleck, son of Ishmael, made a governor, II. 224.

———— —— artful behaviour of, II. 225.

———— —— a strict observer of the Koran, II. 232.

———— —— impolitic declaration of, II. 234.

———— —— defeated by the Negroes, II. 235.

———— —— again proclaimed Emperor, II. 237.

———— —— religious barbarity and character of, II. 238.

———— —— flight of, from Mequinez, II. 239.

———— —— besieged in Fez. *Ibid.*

———— —— strangled, II. 240.

Abdelmeleck, Muley, first Emperor, II. 103.

———— ———— character of, *Ibid.*

———— ———— assassinated when drunk, II. 104.

Abdulmomen, acts of, II. 31 to 35.

Abdulmomen, Muley, assassinated, II. 96.

Abu-Artab, II. 41.

Abu-Hennon, rebellion and reign of, II. 44.

Abul-Haffes, II. 41.

———— —— subjects Tremecen, Sugulmessa, Algiers, and Tunis, II. 42.

                                                          Abul-

Abul-Haffen, defeated near Rio Salado, II. 44.
———— — fleet of, defeated, II. 45.
Abu-Said, reign of, II. 40.
———— fucceffor of Abu-Hennon, II. 47.
———— affaffinated, II. 49.
Abu-Teffin, II. 11.
Achica, intoxicating properties of, II. 155.
Acorns, remarkable, L. 104.
Adlon, Chevalier, remarkable action of, L. 318.
Africa, interior, and Morocco ancient trade between, L.
    108, 114.
Agmet, city of, L. 55, 64.
Aguadir, or cape Aguer, L. 47.
———— Toma, city of, L. 54.
Alcaid, foot of an, cut off by Muley Arfhid, II. 146.
Alcaffar, battle of, II. 99.
Alcaffer-Quiber, city of, L. 83.
———— remarkable flory of its foundation, I. 84.
Alcaffar-Seguar, built by Almonfor, II. 29.
Algerines defeat Muley Ifhmael, II. 211.
Algefira, rebuilt by Ben-Jofeph, II. 40.
———— taken by Abdelmeleck, II. 42.
———— retaken, II. 45.
Algiers and Morocco jealous of each other, L. 304.
———— letter of the Divan of, to Muley Ifhmael, II. 195.
Albabid, El-Monfor, II. 10.
Ali, fon of Jofeph Teffin, II. 19.
Ali, Soliman, II. 114.
Almedina, ruins of, I. 37.
Almond harveft, L. 103.
Almonfor, acts of, II. 28 to 33.
———— cities founded by, II. 29.
———— faying of, II. 32.
———— ftrange difappearance of, II. 33.
Alms, giving, I. 198, 199.
Alphonfo III. vanquifhed, II. 31.

Alphonfo X.—II. 30.

Ambaffador bare-footed, anecdote of, I. 349.

Ambaffadors fent from Morocco to France, II. 200.

Amulets, I. 200.

Anafa, or Dar Beyda, town of, I. 36.

Anchorage, the beft, in the road of Sallee, I. 34.

Anecdote, *vide* Abdallah Muley, Alcaid, Alcaffar, Ambaf-
      fador, Affaffin, Avarice, Bofville, Butcher, Can-
      non, Captive, Chriftian, Coofcoofoo, Cruelty,
      Fifh, Gallant, Governor, Ifhmael, Lela, Liar,
      Lion, Marabout, Mazagan, Meffiah, Moors,
      Mofque, Muley Arfhid, Muley Daiby, Negro
      Slave, Prayer, Pudding, Renegado, Saint, Storks,
      Spaniard, Thieves, Teeth, Walnuts.

Antelope, I. 170.

Appeals to the Emperor, I. 216.

Apples, enchanted, I. 370.

Aqueducts, rude, at Morocco, I. 63.

Arabic, the language of Morocco, I. 241.

———— the moft extenfive of living languages, I. 242.

Arbiba, palace of, built by Muley Abdallah, II. 273.

Arga tree, and its almond, I. 102.

———— oil of, I. 103.

———— fruit of, how eaten by goats, *Ibid.*

Armament, French, fent againft Morocco, II. 375.

Arzilla, town of, I. 22.

———— taken by Don Alphonfo of Portugal, II. 51.

Afs, eaten raw by Saints, I. 183.

Affaffin, juft reward of an, II. 97.

Aftrology ftudied by the Talbes, I. 239.

Atlas, mount, fcite of, I. 12, 62.

———— —— riches of, I. 14, 106.

Audience given to all ranks, good effects of, II. 202.

Augury from the heart of a Sheep, I. 197.

Avarice, allegory concerning, I. 250.

———— of the Moors, *Ibid.*

Avarice, anecdotes of, I. 251. Note, and 252.
Azamore, town of, I. 36.

B.

Barbary fig, I. 101.
Barbers shops, the rendezvous of newsmongers, I. 264.
Bashaw, what, I. 262.
Bastinado, guilty and innocent equally liable to, I. 217.
Battle, Moorish, order of, I. 308. II. 76.
——— of the Seven Counts, II. 18.
——— of Alarcos, II. 31.
——— lost by Muley Oaras, II. 77.
Beard, ceremony of swearing by, II. 69.
Beating the high road to preferment, I. 268.
Beef salted by the Moors, I. 164, 271.
Bees wax, I. 104.
Bellote, or Acorns, I. Ibid.
Beni-Hassen, or Habat, I. 7.
Beni-Oaras, II. 53.
Ben-Joseph, reign and acts of, II. 36 to 40.
Beth, river of, I. 26.
Betting, forbidden the Mahometans, I. 258.
Black, peculiarities of the colour of, I. 281.
Boar hunting, I. 342.
Boccari, al, or el, troops, consecrated to, I. 306. II. 191.
Bones liable to be mistaken at the day of judgement, I. 351.
Bonfires of Saint John, I. 292.
——————————— conjectures concerning, I. 293.
Booffer Muley, rival of Muley Abdallah, II. 241, 242.
Booffega, river of, I. 18.
Bosville, Mr., anecdote of, I. 217.
Bougie, derivation of, I. 272.
Brahem, last of the dynasty of Morabethoon, II. 19.
——— throws himself headlong from a rock, II. 21.
Brambles, camp of Abdallah fired by, II. 245.

Brandy

Brandy made from dates, I. 91.

Bread of Morocco, excellent, I. 346.

Brebes, I. 117.

——— dislike, and are more independent than, the Moors, I. 116.

——— have a language of their own, I. 119.

——— vigorous, have fine teeth, *Ibid.*

——— hunt the lion and tiger, I. 120.

——— valour of, II. 182, 185.

——— strange notions of, concerning Christians, II. 185.

Bridges, Moorish, I. 90.

Bodobur, defeat of, II. 37.

Buhason, valour of, II. 77.

——— active conduct of, in Fez, II. 79.

——— league of, with Salah Reis, II. 85.

——— Fez, taken by, II. 88.

——— victory of, over Muley Abdallah, II. 90.

——— killed in battle, II. 91.

Bulahuan, tremendous castle of, I. 87.

——— said to have been built by Ahdulmoumen, II. 25.

Burial service, Moors, sing at, I. 192.

——— opinion of the Moors, concerning, II. 31.

Butcher, a merciful, II. 116.

Butter, how made, I. 346.

Buttons cut from the clothes of an ambassador, I. 348.

C.

Cafiles, what, I. 110.

Caliphs, causes of the decay of the power of the, II. 2.

Camel, I. 165.

——— engendering of the, *Ibid.*

——— flesh of, eaten, I. 166.

——— milk of wholesome, *Ibid.*

——— stomach of, I. 167.

——— hardiness of, I. 194.

Camel, dead, given to poor pilgrims, I. 195.
———— facrifice of, II. 183.
Camp, Moorifh, before Ceuta, II. 205.
———— fired by brambles, II. 245.
Camps, how chofen by the Moors, I. 308.
Cannon founderies, I. 309.
———— anecdote of a, II. 181.
Cape Spartel, I. 22.
Captive and Lion, anecdote concerning, I. 340.
Captives, French, ranfomed, II. 105.
Carra, Alcaid, killed by Muley Ifhmael, II. 151.
Carubin, mofque of, II. 7.
Caftles, walled, but without artillery, in moft of the pro-
          vinces, for the Bafhaws, I. 86.
Cats, forty, of Muley Ifhmael, I. 339.
Cavalry, Moorifh, I. 307.
Ceuta, town and harbour of, I. 19.
———— taken by Don John of Portugal, II. 47.
———— fiege of, II. 203.
Chabanets, vide Shabanets.
Chefs and Hazard, Moorifh games, I. 258.
Children, how taught to read, I. 131.
———————— run naked to the age of nine or ten, Ibid.
Chriftian and Saint, ftory of, I. 357.
Chriftians, hatred of the Moors to, I. 352.
———————— degeneracy of, in Morocco, I. 353.
Circulation, exceedingly flow, I. 331.
Cities, little need of, in Morocco, II. 297.
Climate of Morocco, I. 93, 96.
Climi, city of, I. 54.
Clubs, fanatic prediction concerning, II. 317.
Coffee-houfes of Conftantinople, I. 264.
Coin debafed, I. 331.
Coins of Morocco, II. 386.
Cold, degree of, I. 96, 344.
———— and heat, remark concerning, I. 344.

Coffee,

Cooks, European, at Morocco, II. 309.
Coofcoofoo, preparation of, I. 123.
———— nutritive and agreeable, Ibid.
———— how eaten, I. 271.
———— bloody head in a dish of, II. 289.
———— dreffed in vaft quantities, II. 310.
Corn, manner of grinding, I. 123.
——— preferved, I. 285.
——— exportation of, allowed under Sidi Mahomet, II. 299.
——— quality of, Ibid.
——— exchanged for artillery, II. 300.
——— price of, during the famine, II. 337.
Corfairs purfued by a Dutch frigate and wrecked, II. 358.
Corvée, vide Jew-tailors, II. 310.
Court of Morocco, fimplicity of, II. 308.
Courtfhip, how performed, I. 275.
Cowdung, burnt, I. 132.
———— ufed medicinally, Ibid.
Crefcent, form of the, for the order of battle, I. 306. II. 76.
Crom el Hadgy, character of, II. 107.
———— maffacred by his bride, II. 108.
Cruelty, remarkable anecdotes of, I. 263. II. 121, 134,
    146, 178, 214, 216, 224, 258, 287, 288, 289.
Cuftom-houfe duties paid in kind, I. 333. II. 385.
Cuftom-houfe duties of Morocco, II. 385.

D.

Dates plentiful in Tafilet, I. 91.
Day of judgement, odd opinion concerning, I. 351.
Days, length of, I. 96.
Dead, the, not buried in mofques, I. 291.
——— when interred, I. 291.
——— wept over on Friday, Ibid.
——— queftioned by the Moors, I. 351.
——— fuppofed capable of pain, Ibid.

Death at Tafilet, II. 115, *vide* famine.
Death counterfeited by Abdelmeleck, II. 43.
Denmark, court of, deceived by a Jew, II. 359.
———— ambassador of, seized, II. 360.
———— royal African company of, *Ibid.*
———— tribute paid by, to Morocco, II. 363.
Dervises, I. 179.
Desert, danger of crossing, II. 197.
Despotism, effects of, I. 247.
Dews, corrosive, will rust metal worn in the pocket, I. 57.
Discipline, ill state of, I. 306, 307.
Dogs, numerous, in Morocco, I. 339.
Don Ferdinand, II. 30.
———— king of Castile, II. 38.
Don Sancho III.—II. 26, 40.
Douhars, what, and how regulated, I. 111.
Doum, or wild palm, made into hats, baskets, &c. I. 105.
———— fruit of, *Ibid.*
Dra, province of, I. 11.
Dris, Muley, the friend of Sidi Mahomet, II. 180.
———— power and abilities of, II. 303.
———— cunning of, II. 304.
———— death and character of, II. 305.
Dromedary, swiftness of the, II. 148.
———— white, I. 119.
Dubudu, town of, I. 86.
Ducat, current value of, I. 135.
Duquella, province of, I. 9.
———— inhabitants of, large, robust, and mercantile, *Ibid.*
Dynasty of Morabethoon, II. 13.
———— of the Moahedlins, or Almohades, II. 23.
———— of the Benimerins, II. 36.
———— of Fileli, II. 112.

E.

Eating, Moorish, mode of, I. 271, 347.

Eclipses, terrible, to the Moors, I. 237, 238.

———— strange notion concerning, I. 239.

Edris, adventures of, II. 5.

———— expulsion of, II. 8, 9.

———— veneration of the Moors for, II. 112.

Edrissues, who, II. 2.

Education, I. 237.

———— of the sons of Muley Ishmael, I. 371.

Eels, manner of catching, in the lakes of Mamora, I. 25.

Elcaisseria, what, I. 58.

El-Edrissi the geographer, II. 9.

El-Hadgy, Mahomet, subdued by Muley Ishmael, II. 177.

El-Mobadi, revolt of, II. 9, 10.

El-Valid, Muley, character and reign of, II. 104.

———— suffers French captives to be ransomed, II. 105.

Emperor, despotic power of, I. 203, 204.

———— has no first minister, I. 206.

———— gives audience to people of all ranks, I. 213.

———— title of, first assumed in Morocco, II. 103.

Emperors hold it derogatory to keep their word, I. 208.

Empire of Morocco, ancient wealth of, I. 314.

———— extent and boundaries of, I. 1.

England, ambassador of, to Muley Ishmael, II. 159.

———— first made peace with Morocco, II. 953.

English merchant, suicide of, II. 284.

Enigmas, a Moorish diversion, I. 229.

Escura, or Ascora, province of, I. 12.

Eunuch, behaviour of a, I. 360.

F.

Famine, dreadful, in Morocco, II. 335.

———— effects of, II. 339.

Fatimites,

Fatimites, II. 2.

Fedala, road and town of, I. 35.

Fenis, Bashaw, befriends Muley Muftadi, II. 170.

—— gives up Sallee to Sidi Mahomet, II. 283.

—— is ftoned to death, *Ibid.*

Fertility of Morocco, I. 98, 343, 344.

Feftivals of the Moors and Mahometans, I. 196.

Fevers, common, I. 232.

—— hot and cold fits of, occafioned by a fiend, *Ibid.*

Fez, province of, I. 18.

Fez, city of, I. 70.

—— when founded, *Ibid.*

—— formerly held holy, I. 71.

—— learning of, I. 72, 228.

—— profligacy of, I. 72.

—— manufactures of, I. 73.

—— florid, but falfe defcription of, by Leo Africanus, I. 76.

—— cannot be entered without an order from the Emperor, I. 78.

—— romantic fituation of, *Ibid.*

—— fickleneſs of its inhabitants, I. 79.

—— founded by Edriſs, II. 6.

—— taken by Muley-Mahomet, II. 82.

—— privilege of, II. 86.

—— taken by Muley Buhaſon, II. 88.

—— cruel treatment of, by Muley Mahomet, II. 92.

—— revolt of, under Muley Daiby, II. 133.

—— makes peace with Muley Daiby, II. 135.

—— intended deftruction of, by Muley Abdallah, II. 243.

—— citizens of, repulfe Muley Abdallah, II. 261.

—— fpirited anfwers of the citizens of, II. 331.

Fez, New, when and by whom built, I. 80.

Fight between lions, wolves, and dogs, I. 340.

Figs foon worm-eaten, I. 100.

Fileli, dynafty of, II. 117.

Fiſh, ftrange reafon for prohibiting the eating of, I. 352.

Fleet, French, under Renaud, II. 193, 200.
Fort Charles abandoned, II. 193.
Foxes, I. 170.
Fruits, early, I. 94.
———— what native in Morocco, I. 100.

G.

Gallant, story and punishment of a, I. 268.
Ganger, what, I. 145.
Garb, or El-Garb, province of, I. 6.
Gardens of the Moors, I. 263.
Garet, province of, I. 5.
Gayland, Alcaid, II. 118.
———— bravery and death of, II. 154.
Gayroan, I. 119.
Gazia, II. 18, 30.
General, a treacherous, put to death, II. 164.
Genoa, treaty of, with Morocco, II. 369.
Genoese company, failure of, II. 370.
Geography of Morocco, inaccurate, I. 4.
Georgian, beauteous, strangled, II. 208.
Gesula, province of, I. 11.
Gibraltar taken by the Moors II. 42.
———— victualling of, II. 355, 365.
Gold dust taken at Tagaret, II. 197.
Golius, in Morocco, II. 103.
Government of Morocco, what, I. 202, 359.
———— feudal, I. 298, 300, 301.
Governor put to death by Sidi Mahomet, I. 211.
———— of Fez, anecdotes of, I. 111.
———— condemned to sweep the town he had governed, I. 262.
Governors stripped by the Emperor, I. 213.
Grandees, reason of, convoking in Morocco, II. 187.
Grapes, large and delicious, I. 100.
Guadel- brief and remarkable history of, II. 327.

Gum-

Gum-Sandarac, I. 103.

—— transparent, *Ibid.*

Gunpowder, game of, L. 265, 341.

——————— of Morocco, bad, I. 310.

H.

Hadgy, what, L. 191.

Haicks, how made and worn, I. 125.

Hameda, flory of, L. 374.

Harami, what, L. 275.

Hares, good, L. 170.

Harrifh, office of, II. 311.

Harveft, early, I. 94.

Haffen, tower of, I. 31.

Hats firft worn in Africa, L. 153.

Hazar, a kind of Cedar, L. 8.

Hea, province of, I. 9.

—— inhabitants of, reftlefs, uncivilized, and factious, I. 10.

Head ferved up in a difh of Coofcoofoo, II. 289.

Heads cut off without the owners' knowledge, L. 348.

Hiftorians, itinerant, L. 264.

Holland and Morocco, war between, II. 332.

—————— quarrel of Sidi Mahomet with, II. 357.

Horfemen, Moors excellent, L. 337, 341.

Horfes, numerous and good, L. 167.

——— fluds of, kept by the Emperor and Grandees, *Ibid.*

——— Moors imagine the Chriftians have no, L. 338.

——— revered as Saints, *Ibid.*

Houfes feldom more than one ftory high, I. 141.

——— mode of building, *Ibid.*

——— road over the tops of, L. 364.

Hunting the boar, I. 341.

I.

Infantry, weak state of, I. 307.

Inheritance, laws of, I. 275.

Inoculation practised, I. 233.

Insurrections, frequent, I. 301.

————— how promoted and punished by Sidi Mahomet, II. 316, 318.

Interregnum of the kingdom of Fez. II. 49.

Isac, son of Brahem, strangled, II. 24.

Ishmael, Muley, accession of, II. 148.

————— ————— avarice of, I. 369, 370.

————— ————— hypocrisy of, I. 369.

————— ————— cruelty of, I. 372.

————— ————— guilty conscience of, I. 373.

————— ————— mean appearance of, I. 374.

————— ————— caprice of, I. 375.

————— ————— opposed by his nephew, Muley Achmet, II. 150.

————— ————— victories of, over Muley Achmet, II. 151, 157.

————— ————— conquers Fez, II. 155.

————— ————— cruelty of, I. 340, 358, 362, 363, 366, 368. II. 152, 158, 179, 216, 274, Passim.

————— ————— avarice of, II. 158, 173.

————— ————— anecdotes of the deceit of, II. 160, 171, 220.

————— ————— attempted to be assassinated, II. 164.

————— ————— repulsed at Santa Cruz, II. 165.

————— ————— perfidy of, II. 168.

————— ————— rage of, at entering Morocco, II. 175.

————— ————— revolt quelled by, II. 177.

————— ————— sends ten thousand heads to Fez and Morocco, II. 178.

————— ————— concubines of, II. 179.

————— ————— repulsed by the Brebes, II. 183, 185.

Ishmael,

Ishmael, Muley, passion of, for building, II. 191.
———— Christian captives, how punished by, II. 192.
———— remarkable saying of, II. 195.
———— rebellious sons of, II. 306.
———— defeated by the Algerines, II. 211.
———— anecdotes of the caprice of, I. 338, 339, 365, 367, 368. II. 218.
———— pretended illness of, II. 220.
———— murders his son, II. 222.
———— character of, II. 226.
———— numerous descendants of, Ibid.
———— anecdote of, vide Messiah.
———— and Spaniard, anecdote of, I. 367.

J.

Jacob Almonfor, palace of, at Rabat, I. 29.
———— and fisherman, story of, I. 84.
Jew of the mountain massacred by Muley Arshid, II. 123.
——— tailors, how treated, II. 310.
Jewels, uncommon, I. 145.
Jews in Morocco, formerly much more numerous, I. 157.
——— ill treated and despised, Ibid. 157, 353.
——— understand trade better than the Moors, I. 158.
——— employed by the Emperor, Ibid.
——— of Morocco, superstitious, I. 159.
——— of Morocco, all know Hebrew, I. 160.
——— Shrieks and lamentations of hired women at the funerals of the, I. 161.
——— the tax-gatherers, I. 326.
——— taxation of the, I. 327.
——— strange reason why their prayers are granted, I. 346.
——— two rival, anecdote of, I. 358.
——— generously protected by Muley Ali, II. 341.
——— wives of the, handsome and gallant, I. 143, 159.

D d 3

John,

John, Saint, conjectures concerning the festival of, I. 193.
Joseph, Ben Jacob, II. 41.
Joseph Teffifin, II. 15.
———— ——— conquers the kingdom of Fez, II. 16.
———— ——— alliance of, fought by the Mahometans of Spain, II. 17.
———— ——— gains the battle of the seven Counts, II. 18.
Joseph, son of Abdulmomen, acts of, II. 16.
Judges follow the letter of the law, I. 110.
Justice, ridiculous parade of, I. 339.

K.

Knight of the Ass, a usurper, called the, II. 11.
Knowledge, state of, among the Moors, I. 226.

L.

Lances darted into the air and caught, I. 341, 368.
Language of the Brebes, Shellu, and Moors, compared, I. 244.
Laracha, town of, I. 23.
———— river of, I. 24.
———— taken by Muley Ishmael, II. 203.
Law, men of the, powerless, I. 339.
——— for the safety of travellers, I. 133. II. 140.
Laws, code of religious, I. 315.
Leather, the table and table cloth of the Moors, I. 347.
Legs thought handsome when thick, I. 151.
Lela, what, II. 207.
Lela, Zidana, character of, II. 208.
———— wicked intrigues of, Ibid. 209.
———— inhuman cruelty of, II. 214.
———— daring ambition of, II. 221.
———— anecdotes of the cruelty of, II. 234.

Lena,

Lena, Coneta, mother of Muley Abdallah, prudence of, II. 242.

———————— mercy and wifdom of, II. 244, 245, 250.

———————— pilgrimage of, II. 249.

———————— female flave affaffinated in the arms of, II. 252.

———————— money promifed by, to the Negroes, II. 254.

Liar, anecdote concerning, I. 349.

Limbs amputated, how dreffed, I. 269.

Lions not uncommon, I. 170.

——— feed on young boars, I. 171.

——— manner of hunting, *Ibid.*

——— one-and-twenty killed by one Moor, *Ibid.*

——— taken alive, I. 172, .

——— and Brebe, ftory of, *Ibid.*

——— kept for ftate by the Emperor, I. 174.

——— flow to attack man, *Ibid.*

——— mode of entrapping the young boar, I. 175.

——— flefh of, eaten by the Moors, I. 176.

——— fighting of, I. 340.

Locufh, I. 95.

——— eat by the Moors like red herrings, *Ibid.*

——— dreadful ravages of, II. 333.

Loueti, the Alcaid, influence of, II. 127, 133.

Loyalty of Muley Ali, II. 319.

Lucas, Alcaid, punifhed, II. 286.

Lucas, river of, the Lixos of the Greeks, I. 23, 83, 84.

Ludays, what, II. 191.

Lumthunes, II. 13.

Lunar years, I. 273.

M.

Magafin, what, I. 108.

Mahomet, Abdallah, and Abdulmomen, II. 21.

Mahomet,

Mahomet, Ben Achmet, a Sharif, and his three fons, II. 54.

———————— and his three fons, hypocrify and ambition of, II. 54, Paffim.

———————— and his three fons, fufpected by Muley Naffer, II. 57.

———————— and his three fons, progrefs of, II. 58.

Mahomet, Ben Naffer, defeated, II. 34.

————————— death of, II. 35.

Mahometanifm, by character defpotic, II. 113.

Mamora, river of, I. 6, 7.

——— fort of, I. 26.

———— taken by Muley Ifhmael, II. 199.

Manfooria, caftle of, I. 34.—built by Almonfor, II. 39.

Manufcripts, Arabic, in Spain, I. 231.

Marabout put to death by Sidi Mahomet, II. 317.

——— fent by Mahomet, II. 160.

——— beheaded by Muley Abdallah, II. 243.

Marakefch, II. 15.

Mares, fuppofed error concerning, I. 168, 338.

——— and their colts houfed in their tents, I. 169.

Markets, daily, I. 134.

——— buffoons, fingers, dancers, barbers, and furgeons, at, Ibid.

Marriage ceremonies of the Moors, I. 130, 275.

——— licentious fongs at, I. 277.

——— feftivals, expenfive, I. 276.

Matamores to preferve corn, I. 55, 185.

Maufoleum, in memory of Muley Mahomet, II. 218.

——— in memory of Muley Zidan, II. 223.

Mazagan, city of, I. 37.

——— magnificent ciftern at, I. 38.

——— fanatic anecdote concerning, I. 39.

——— taken by Sidi Mahomet, II. 326.

Meafures of Morocco, II. 368.

Mechanic arts, rude ftate of, I. 259.

Medions, castle of, L. 87.

Melek Alcaid, cruel death of, II. 114.

Melilla, city of, L. 17.

————— siege of, II. 328.

Mequinez, city of, L. 65.

————— Jews quarter at, I. 66.

————— Emperor's palace, L. 67.

————— inhabitants affable, L. 69.

————— women of, handsome, shew themselves to Europeans, Ibid.

————— Spanish convent at, L. 70.

————— by whom founded, II. 8.

————— abandoned by Muley Mahomet, II. 89.

Methooar, what, L. 62, 109, 110.

Messiah, coming of the, anecdote concerning, L. 354.

Milood, a festival, L. 198.

Mines of iron. L. 106.

————— of copper, Ibid.

Mishboya, L. 119.

Mogodore, town of, L. 43.

————— begun in 1760, L. 44.

————— port of, L. 46.

————— built by Sidi Mahomet, II. 295.

Money buried, I. 151, 387.

Monopolies, remark concerning, II. 381.

Moors, indolent, L. 99, 349.

————— ancient commerce of the, conjectures on, L. 108.

————— plead by attorney, L. 116.

————— seldom strike, L. 119.

————— disposed to slavery, L. 348.

————— naturally meager. L. 349.

————— form and features of, Ibid.

————— mournful looks of, Ibid.

————— violence of their passions, L. 351.

————— less sensible of pain than Europeans, L. 367, 369.

————— little dainty, L. 370.

Moors,

Moors chief meal after sun-set, I. 270.
———— imagine themselves free, I. 280.
———— treat their slaves better than Europeans, Ibid.
———— avidity and meanness of the, I. 347.
———— jealousy of the, I. 356.
———— fanaticism of, II. 112.
———— resignation of the, II. 337.
Moors of the cities affirm themselves to be Arabs, I. 140.
——————————— seldom have more than one wife, I. 143.
——————————— have little variety of dress, I. 144.
Moors of the country, manners of, I. 121,
———————————— form of their tents, Ibid.
———————————— simplicity of the, in their camps, I. 122.
———————————— hospitality of, I. 124.
———————————— dress of, I. 126.
———————————— wear no linen, Ibid.
———————————— marriages of, I. 130.
———————————— quarrelsome, Ibid.
———————————— different tribes of, seldom inter-marry, Ibid.
———————————— antediluvian, I. 126, 136.
———————————— anecdotes of the ignorance of, I. 136.
———————————— have no glass, I. 137.
———————————— receive no ideas from pictures, I. 138.
Morabethoon, or Morabites, II. 14.
———————— all put to death, II. 24.
Morbeya, river of, true name of, I. 37, 87.
———————— passage of, I. 89, 90.
Morocco, city of, I. 54.
———————— founded by Abu Teffifin, I. 55.
———————— pleasant plain of, I. 56.
———————— quarter of the Jews, I. 59.
———————— Emperor's palace, Ibid.
———————— passed through a fieve, II. 23, 24.
———————— stormed by Almonfor, II. 32.

Morocco,

Morocco, taken by Muley Mohamet, II. 71.
——— taken and plundered by the Negroes, II. 153.
Morocco, empire of, origin of the inhabitants of, I. 115.
——— women, how employed, I. 122, 125.
——— no inns in the provinces, I. 132.
——— not fortified, I. 304.
——— founded in blood, II. 114.
——— depopulation accounted for, II. 180.
——— state of, under Muley Abdallah, II. 293.
Mosque pulled down because defiled, I. 350.
Mosques, water in all, Ibid.
——— Jew or Christian must not enter the, I. 352.
Mozard, Captain, bravery of, I. 317.
Mules, the breeding of, encouraged, I. 169.
——— used for travelling, I. 82.
——— trade of the English in, II. 356.
Muley, and Sidi, meaning of, I. 319.
Muley Abdallah, reign of, II. 93.
——— cruelty of, II. 94.
——— unsuccessful attack on Mazagan, II. 96.
——— character of, II. 97.
Muley Abdallah, vide Abdallah.
Muley Abdelmeleck, death of, in the moment of victory, II. 99
Muley Achmet, brother of Abdelmeleck, reign of, II. 99.
Muley Achmet, nephew of Ishmael, partisans of, in the city of Morocco, II. 150.
——— defeated by Muley Ishmael, II. 151.
——— saved by the hospitality of a Shaik, II. 152.
——— again defeated, II. 157.
——— recovers the city of Morocco, II. 162.
——— defeats Gerari, Ibid.
——— treachery of a general of, II. 163.
——— more beloved than Muley Ishmael, II. 164.
——— surprized by Muley Ishmael, II. 166.
——— defeated after victory, II. 167.
——— besieged in Morocco, II. 168.

Muley Achmet, danger of, II. 173.

————————— flight of, from Morocco, II. 174.

————————— expedition of, into Sudan, II. 196.

————————— Tagaret, taken by, II. 197.

Muley Achmet, Sharif, reign of, II. 61.

————————— treachery of, II. 68, 71.

————————— taken by his brother, II. 70.

————————— misfortunes of, II. 71. Paſſim.

————————— murdered in priſon, II. 93.

Muley Achmet Sheik, reign, character, and death of, II. 106.

Muley Ali, or Muley Sharif, reign of, piety and character,
    II, 115. Paſſim,

Muley Ali, ſon of Sidi Mahomet, loyalty of, II. 319.

————————— death and excellent character of, II. 340.

————————— brother of Muley Abdallah, elected emperor by
    the Negroes, II. 351.

————————— ferocity and avarice of, II. 352.

————————— money promiſed to the Negroes by, II. 353.

————————— depoſed, II. 354.

Muley Arſhid, rebellion of, II. 120.

————————— ingratitude of, to a faithful ſlave, II. 121.

————————— ſtratagems and cunning of, II. 121, 123,
    124.

————————— abilities and diſſimulation of, II. 123.

————————— enterprizes of, II. 125.

————————— acceſſion of, II. 126.

————————— cruelty of, II. 121, 123, 124, 126, 129,
    130, 133, 139, 142, 146.

————————— conqueſts of, II. 121, 124, 126, 128, 129,
    136.

————————— repulſed by the king of Sudan, II. 137.

————————— buildings of, II. 141.

————————— death of, II. 145.

Muley Daiby, ſize and perſon of, I. 375.

————————— drunkenneſs of, Ibid.

————————— and a Jew, anecdote of, I. 376.

                                              Muley,

Muley Daiby, and a monkey, anecdote of, L 376.
————— named succeffor by Muley Ifhmael, II. 225.
————— feceffion of, II. 229.
————— largefs of, to the Negro troops, II. 230.
————— fubdues the infurgents of Duquella, Ibid.
————— avarice of, II. 231.
————— drunkennefs of, II. 233, 236.
————— cruelty of, II. 233.
————— teeth drawn by command of, L 363.
————— reftoration of, II. 239.
————— death of, II. 240.
Muley Dris, vide Dris.
Muley Haran, king of Tafilet, II. 149.
————— reconciles his brother and nephew, II. 171.
————— dethroned, II. 175.
Muley Ifhmael, vide Ifhmael.
Muley Mahomet, fuperior qualities of, II. 207, 211.
————— made governor of Suz, II. 209.
————— rebellion of, II. 210.
————— takes Morocco, II. 212.
————— defeated by Muley Zidan, II. 214.
————— taken prifoner, II. 215.
————— punifhment of, II. 216.
Muley Mahomet Ool Del Ariba made Emperor, II. 256.
————— again proclaimed, II. 262.
————— ineffectual expedition of, II. 263.
————— depofed, II. 264.
————— amiable character of, Ibid.
Muley Meheris, rebellion of, II. 142.
Muley Mohamet, king of Tarudant, II. 63.
————— defeats the king of Fez, II. 64.
————— and his brother, enterprizes of, II. 66.
————— kingdom of Tafilet feized by, Ibid.
————— and his brother, quarrel between, II. 67.
————— murders his nephews, II. 91.
————— affaffinated by a Turk, II. 93.

Muley

Muley Mohamet, the Negro, cruelty of, II. 90.
——————— dethroned, Ibid.
Muley Mohamet, son of Muley Sharif, reign of, II. 112.
——————— defeat and death of, II. 125.
Muley Muftadi, elected by the Negroes, II. 166.
——————— retires to, and trades at Arzilla, II. 267.
——————— takes refuge in Sallee, II. 268.
——————— delivered from imprisonment, II. 269.
——————— again retires to Arzilla, II. 270.
——————— death of, II. 281.
Muley Shaik, first of the Merini, II. 51.
Muley Sidan, son of the second Muley Achmet, II. 68, 70.
——————— reign of, II. 101.
Muley Yezid, vide Yezid.
Mulluvia, river of, I. 5, 17, 86, II. 181.
Music, I. 263.
——— Moorish, I. 342.
Muskets, Moorish, I. 310.
——————— discharged in the face of an ambassador, I. 342.

N.

Naffer, Bushentuf, assassinated, II. 60.
Negro women paint their cheeks, I. 284.
——— soldiers, establishment of, I. 297.
——— ——— reduction of, I. 298, 299.
——— slave, fidelity and tragical death of, II. 121.
——— troops, how consecrated, II. 190.
Negroes foreboded slavery at the sight of Europeans, I. 110.
——— state of, among the Moors, I. 179, 180, 181.
——— remarkably cheerful and talkative, I. 282.
——— marriages of, Ibid.
——— household furniture of, I. 283.
——— effect of the appearance of, on the Arabs, II. 4.
——— brought to Morocco by Muley Arshid, II. 118.
——— increased and settled by Muley Ishmael, II. 188.
——— state of, II. 189.

Negroes and Ludaya, the standing army of Morocco, II. 191.
———— effects of the introduction of the, II. 227.
———— power of the, II. 228.
———— oppose Abdelmeleck, II. 235.
———— hated by Muley Abdallah, II. 250.
———— take and plunder Morocco, II. 253.
———— refuse to deliver up their general, II. 256.
. ———— dissensions among, II. 257.
———— neutrality of, II. 261.
———— covetous avidity of, II. 254, 260, 261, 262, 264.
———— dissatisfied with Muley Abdallah, II. 265.
———— enfeebled by war, II. 270.
———— cut off by Abdallah, II. 271.
———— revolt of, under Sidi Mahomet, II. 318.
———— how disarmed by Sidi Mahomet, II. 323.
———— insolence and power of, I. 359.
Niger and Nile, I. 290.

O.

Oak, forests of, I. 104.
Oatas, Muley, accession of, II. 62.
——————— defeated by the Sharifs, II. 65.
——————— attacked by Muley Mohamet, II. 75.
——————— defeated and taken prisoner, II. 77.
——————— assassinated, II. 83.
Obeidallah, II. 11.
Officers, principal, the domestics of the Emperor, I. 209.
———— of Abdallah dragged at the tails of mules, II. 349.
Olive trees, I. 102.
Olon, M. de Saint, sent ambassador to Mequinez, II. 101.
Oppression, Moorish, I. 343.
Ornaments, marks of slavery, originally, I. 152.
Oxen plentiful, but small, I. 164, 343.

P.

Pain, Moors less sensible of, than Europeans, I. 267, 269.

Paint and washes of the Moorish women, I. 127, 129, 153.

Painters sent to Morocco by Philip II.—II. 101.

Palace built by Muley Ishmael, I. 364. II. 178.

Palm tree, I. 104.

Partridges, insipid, I. 170.

Patriotism of a citizen of Rabat, II. 284.

Peas and beans sold by tale during the famine, II. 337.

Persian general, valour of, II. 78.

Physic, state of, I. 132.

Physicians, whom, Ibid.

Pigeons, large and excellent, I. 170.

———— stolen, anecdote of, II. 214.

Pilgrimage, veneration for those who have made a, I. 191,
          193.

———————— renders the beast of burthen holy, I. 192.

———————— time of making, I. 193.

———————— route of the caravan of, I. 194.

Pirates of Barbary, II. 351.

Plague in Morocco, dreadful, II. 160.

———— in 1752, II. 275.

———— foretold in Turkey, Ibid.

Population of Morocco, I. 303.

Portugal and Morocco, treaty between, II. 368.

Portuguese in Morocco, II. 51, 57, 67.

Poultry abundant, not good, I. 170.

Power, maritime, of Morocco, I. 312, 316, 319.

———— military, of Morocco, I. 295, 303, 306.

———————————— how established, I. 296.

Prayer, opinion of the Moors concerning, I. 345.

Prayers, Moorish, I. 350.

———— the Moors, how called to, Ibid.

Preachers put to death, II. 16.

Predestination, I. 300, 366. II. 114, 338.

Presents, or bibery, at court, I. 212.

Prickly pear, I. 101.

Progress, slow, of the Moors towards refinement, I. 364.

Prophecy, Moorish, I. 351.

Proverb, Moorish, I. 272, 278.

Provinces of Morocco, I. 1, 2.

Rudding, anecdote of, I. 347.

Punishments, chiefly pecuniary, I. 218.

Purchasing of men, barbarous custom of, I. 358.

Purse, story of a, I. 357.

Q.

Quintal of silver, what, II. 159.

R.

Rabat, town of, I. 28.

—— batteries of, rebuilt by an English renegado, I. 29.

—— walls of, and delightful gardens, I. 30.

—— built by Almonsor, II. 29.

Rabat and Sallee besieged by Sidi Mahomet, II. 281.

—— severe treatment of, II. 327.

—— how preserved from locusts, II. 314.

Rabits found only in the north of the empire, I. 170.

Ragusa, ship of, condemned, II. 371.

Rain, Moors sit naked in, I. 346.

—— how prayed for, I. 345.

Rains, regular and abundant, I. 94.

—— heavy, I. 344.

Rank, little distinction of, I. 260, 262.

—— instability of, Ibid.

Raquette, I. 101.

Rasalema, remarkable river of, I. 80.

Raw hides, plentiful, I. 164.

Religion of the Moors, I. 177.

——————————— which way, different in practice from that of the Turks, I. 178.

Ramna, province of, I. 12.

Renegado, anecdote of a, II. 142.

Renegadoes despised, I. 155.

——————— intermarry only with each other, *Ibid.*

——————— repent, and wish to escape, I. 156.

Reply of Muley Oaras to Muley Mahamet, II. 78.

Revenues of Morocco, I. 322.

Revolt of Muley Messaoor, II. 64.

Rhyming not uncommon among the Moors, I. 139.

Rif, province of, I. 6.

Riperda, the Duke de, anecdotes of, II. 276.

Rio Salado, battle of, II. 44.

River of Negroes, battle of the, II. 67.

Roebuck, I. 170.

Rosaries played with like fans, I. 146.

S.

Sabbath, Moorish, I. 273, 351.

————— derivation of, I. 273.

Sabo, what, I. 209.

Sabres, manufactur.d, I. 310.

Sacrifices, remark concerning, II. 183.

Saddles, form of, I. 337.

Saffi, town of, I. 41.

———— tombs and sanctuaries of, I. 42.

Said, Barrax, short reign and death of, II. 35.

Said, II. 41.

Said, brother of Abu-Said, valour of, II. 48.

Sailors, Moorish, I. 320.

Saint, criminal, and emperor, story of, I. 131.

———— character and cunning of one, I. 186.

Saint, carnal knowledge of one, with a woman, in the open
  street, I. 187, 356.

—— female, prostituted herself for the service of passen-
  gers, I. 188.

—— made humane by a bribe, I. 190.

—— a man made a, for being a rascal, I. 356.

Saints, or Santons, by trade, I. 180.

—————— fools, madmen, and ideots, acknowledged to be,
  Ibid. with Horses.

—————— invoked by the women to make them fertile, I. 182.

—————— eat scorpions, *Ibid.*

—————— how venerated, I. 180, 183.

—————— numerous, I. 184.

—————— put to death by Muley Abdallah, II. 288.

Salah Reis, in league with Muley Buhafon, II. 65.

—————— defeats Muley Abdallah, II. 86.

—————— victory of, at the paffage of the Seboo, II. 87.

—————— discontented with Buhafon, II. 89.

Sallee, town of, I. 27.

—— river of, *Ibid.*

—— rovers, I. 313.

—————— stones, their chief ammunition, I. 314.

Sallee and Rabat, government of, I. 315.

—————— civil war between, II. 269.

—————— municipal government of, II. 269, 281.

Salt pits, I. 104.

Salutation, manner of, I. 343.

Sanctaren, battle of, II. 37.

Sanctuaries, or hospitiums, where criminals are protected,
  I. 180, 188.

—————— violated by Muley Abdallah, II. 259.

Sands of the defert, moving, I. 194. II. 197.

Santa Cruz, town of, I. 46.

—————— by whom built, I. 47.

—————— ruined by Sidi Mahomet, I. 11, 47.

—————— taken by Muley Mohamet, II. 66.

Santa

Santa Cruz, deserted in terror, II. 319.

Scarifications, mode of making, I. 135.

Scavenger and murdered woman, I. 223.

Sebastian, king of Portugal, defeat of, II. 99.

Seboo, river of, I. 26.

—— passage of, disputed, II. 87.

Selim, Duquelli, hatred of Abdallah to, II. 255.

——————— killed by Abdallah, II. 258.

Seraglios of the Emperor and Grand Signior compared, II. 313.

Servility, Moorish, I. 348.

Setier of Paris, what, I. 328.

Shabanets, whom, II. 131

—————— subjected by Muley Arshid, II. 135.

—————— tortured by Muley Ishmael, II. 158.

Shad fishery, I. 27.

Shaik, generosity of a, II. 152.

—— treacherously murdered by Muley Ishmael, II. 172.

—— put to death by the forgery of Lela Zidana, II. 209.

Sharifs of the Mereni, II. 53.

—————— massacred by Crom El Hadgy, II. 106.

Shaus, or Chaus, province of, I. 13, 86.

Shavoya, or Chavoya, province of, I. 13.

—————— mountaineers of, massacred by Muley Ishmael, II. 158.

Sheep, hairy, and men woolly, I. 112.

—— and wool of Morocco, I. 163.

—— few black, I. 164.

Shella, a holy town, I. 34.

Shellu, less ferocious than the Brebes, I. 120.

Sherlof, general, brave conduct of, II. 259.

Sherma, or Cherma, province of, I. 12.

Shewmen and dancers, I. 264.

Ships of enemies allowed to trade with Morocco, II. 295, 382.

Shirts worn over the dress, I. 155.

Fiji

Sidi Mahomet, agitation of, at putting a governor to death, L. 311.

———————— artillery of, L. 309.

———————— knowledge of, how acquired, II. 279.

———————— power of, while prince, II. 280, 286.

———————— severity of, to Sallee and Rabat, II. 282, 283, 284, 326,

———————— guilty of one act of cruelty, II. 185.

———————— views of, on his succession, II. 293. Passim 303.

———————— buildings of, II. 295, 296, 327.

———————— a merchant, II. 298.

———————— character and manners of, II. 307, 343.

———————— domestics of, new clothed annually, II. 310.

———————— prudence of the first wife of, II. 313.

———————— children of, how provided for, Ibid.

———————— ill education of the sons of, Ibid.

———————— strange equivocation of, II. 329.

———————— failure of, the attempt of, on Melilla, II. 330.

———————— artifice of, to appease his subjects, II. 311.

———————— declares war against Holland, II. 312.

———————— great expences, and little wealth of, II. 345.

———————— public declaration of peace by, II. 370.

Silver paid by weight, II. 159.

Slave trade, L. 111, 113, 281.

Slinging, ancient and modern practice of, L. 314.

Small-pox little mischievous, L. 233.

Snipes numerous, L. 170.

Soe, vide markets.

Soil of Morocco, I. 96.

———————— light is ploughed with wooden plough-shares, L. 97.

Sorcerers, I. 288.

Southern Moors, bigotry and thievery of, L. 50.

———————— make their ablutions with sand, L. 51.

Spain

Spain offended by Sidi Mahomet, II. 329, 332.
—— armament of, against Algiers, II. 331.
Spaniard and Englishman, I. 376.
Spaniard and Muley Ishmael, I. 367.
Spanish convent at Mequinez for the relief of captives, I. 70.
—— fathers of, manners of physicking the Moors, *Ibid.*
Spanish Moors, family names of, preserved in Morocco, I. 141.
Speech of Muley Mohamet to his brother, II. 74.
——————————— to his soldiers and chiefs, II. 69, 76.
Stone, disease of the, cut for by the Moors, I. 136.
Storks, sinful to kill, I. 289.
—— emigration and food of, I. 290.
—— Arabs metamorphosed into, I. 339.
Stratagem of Muley Mohamet, II. 77, 91.
Streets, dirtyness of, I. 364.
Succession of Morocco precarious, II. 278, 348.
Sudan, generosity of the king of, II. 138.
—— invaded by Muley Achmet, II. 196.
Suera, town of, I. 43.
Sugulmessa, city of, I. 15, 92.
——————— derivation of, I. 92.
Sun adored by the Negroes, II. 159.
Surgery, state of, I. 135, 236, 269.
Sus, or Suz, province of, decayed by the destruction of Santa Cruz, I. 11.
Sweden, presents sent by, to Morocco, II. 362.
Swine held unclean, I. 350.

T.

Tafilet, or Sugulmessa, kingdom of, I. 15, 99.
—— dates of *Ibid.*
—— taken by stratagem, II. 91.
—— revolt of, II. 182.

Tafilet

Tafilet punished by Sidi Mahomet, II. 139.

Tagaret, capital of Sudan, taken, II. 197.

Tailors, vide Jews.

Talbes, what, L 215, 227, 246, 289.

Tangiers, town of, L 20.

——— ceded to England in 1662, Ibid.

——— bay of, favourable to piracy, L 22.

——— the English attacked in, II. 180.

——— besieged by Muley Ishmael, II. 191.

——— abandoned by the English, II. 201.

——— taken by Muley Abdallah, II. 268.

——— indulgence granted the Spaniards at, II. 366.

Tangiers and Tetuan, favourable situation of, L 210.

Tansit, river of, L 9, 42, 63.

Tarudant, where, L 48.

——— city of, L 54.

Taxation, state of, L 330.

——— of the Jews, L 327, 331.

——— excessive, L 334.

——— ——— impolicy of, II. 297, 301.

Taxes allowed by the Koran, L 322.

——— casual, what, L 332.

Tea drank by the Moors, L 271.

Tedla, province of, L 13.

Teeth drawn as a punishment, L 363.

Temperance of the Moors, L 270, 347. II. 309.

Temsem, province of, L 8.

——— fertility and salubrity of, Ibid.

Tents of the Moors, L 122.

Terraces on the tops of all houses, L 143.

Tesa, castle and town of, L 86.

Tetuan, city and port of, L 18.

——— revolt of, under Muley Daiby, II. 233.

Theft, manner of preventing, L 133.

Thieves, L 254.

——— anecdotes of, L 254, 256, 258.

Thieves, how punished, L. 258, 268.

Tigers common, L. 170.

—— royal, unknown in Morocco, L. 171.

—— hunted by the Moors, *Ibid.*

—— tamed, L. 175.

Timour, L. 119.

Tiles, coloured, L. 58, 69.

Titus, ruins of, L. 37.

Tombs, Moorish, not pompous, L. 291.

Toornadis, what, L. 156.

Torture of the iron ring, L. 362.

Tossing, punishing of, L. 362.

Towns of Morocco ill fortified, L. 17.

Trade, increase of, in Morocco, II. 297.

—— how injured by Sidi Mahomet, II. 398.

—— of the English to Morocco, II. 355.

—— between Holland and Morocco, II. 358.

—— between Spain and Morocco, casual, II. 366.

—— balance of, in favour of Morocco, II. 367.

—— of France, progress of, II. 373.

—— between France and Morocco, II. 378. Passim.

—— free, of Morocco, remarks on, II. 383.

Trades, no dishonour to Grandees, L. 262.

Tradesmen of Fez massacred by Muley Arshid, II. 133.

—— — obliged to work gratis, LL. 312.

Tradition, Mahometan, II. 11.

Travellers supposed safe, if a Saint be in company, L. 189.

Travelling, expeditious, between Fez and Mequinez, L. 82.

Treaties between Europe and Barbary, motives for the, II. 352.

—— of England and Morocco, II. 354.

—— between Denmark and Morocco, II. 360.

—— between Sweden and Morocco, II. 362.

—— between Venice and Morocco, II. 363.

—— between Spain and Morocco, II. 364, 365.

—— between Portugal and Morocco, II. 368.

Treaties

Treaties between Tuscany, Vienna, and Morocco, II. 359.
——— between the United States and Morocco, II. 372.
——— between France and Morocco, II. 377.
Treasury, impoverished state of, I. 335.
Tremecen taken by the sons of Muley Mohamet, II. 84.
——— recovered by the Algerines, II 85.
——— people of, demand assistance against the Algerines,
    II. 194.
Tythes in kind, I. 323, 330.
——— paid by tradesmen, II. 310.

U.

Umbrella, the distinctive mark of royalty, I. 210. II. 307.
United States of America, treaty of, with Sidi Mahomet,
    II. 371.

V.

Valedia, town of, I. 39.
Velez de Pegnon, or Gomera, fortress of, I. 18.
Venice and Morocco, peace between, II. 363.
——— tribute paid by, Ibid.
Virginity, proofs of, I. 277, 278.
Visits, manner of performing, I. 153.
Vizier, a, sewed up in an ox hide, II. 186.
——— remark concerning the title of, II. 187.
Vled, d'Elgerid, I. 15.
Vled, de Nun, I. 11.
——— province of, I. 48.
——— barbarous inhabitants of, I. 49.
Voltaire, error of, I. 141.
——— wrongly asserts the Turks inoculate, I. 235.
Vow of Abdulmomen, II. 23.

W.

Wages not paid by the Emperor, II. 310.

Walking, anecdote concerning, I. 350.

Wall white washed, anecdote of, I. 144.

Walnuts, anecdote of, II. 146.

Wants of the Moors, few, I. 328.

Wars, civil, probable in Morocco hereafter, II. 347.

Watch dogs of the Douhars, I. 121.

Water melons, common, I. 100.

—— drank out of the stomachs of dead camels, I. 195.

Wax candles, I. 272.

Wealth, ancient of Morocco, I. 324, 325.

——— left by Muley Ishmael, II. 231.

Weaving, manner of, I. 125.

Weights of Morocco, II. 387.

Wild boar, common in Morocco, I. 175.

———— how caught by the Lion, Ibid.

———— sometimes conquers the Lion, Ibid.

Windus, Mr. the pocket of, picked, I. 348.

Wives and concubines of the Moors, I. 122, 128, 143, 274, 279.

——— of Muley Daiby, the revolt of, II. 237.

Woman murdered, story of, I. 221.

Women, ornaments of the, I. 126.

———— mode of painting themselves, I. 127, 129.

———— treated as slaves by the country Moors, and yoked to the plough with mules, &c. I. 128.

———— of the cities always veiled, I. 147.

———— shew their faces to foreigners, Ibid.

———— soon old, I. 148.

———— licentious, Ibid.

———— of the south, handsomest, I. 149.

——— —— presented for the use of travellers as an act of hospitality, Ibid.

Women of the cities more addicted to drefs than thofe of
the country, I. 149.
—— drefs of the, I. 150.
—— faſtened like fowls, I. 151.
—— ornaments of, *Ibid.*
—— obliged to eat their own breaſts, II. 314.
—— treatment of, by Sidi Mahomet, II. 311.
Woodcocks fcarce, I. 170.
Wreſtling, *vide* Spaniard and Englifhman.

Y.

Yezid, revolt of, II. 3.
Yezid, Muley, revolt of, II. 319.
—————— timidity of, II. 320.
—————— fent on pilgrimage, II. 311.

Z.

Zaaron, a holy mountain, I. 83.
Zeneters maffacred, II. 16.
—— rebellion of, II. 27.
Zidan, Muley, fent againſt Muley Mahomet, II. 213.
—————— barbarous character of, II. 218.
—————— fufpected by his father, I. 219.
—————— murdered by his wives, II. 221.
Zin, Muley, elected Emperor, II. 264.

————————————

E R R A T U M.

Vol. I. page 269, line 5, for *tar*, read *pitch*.